D1330992

IZA'S BALLAD

Also by Magda Szabó in English translation

The Door

Magda Szabó

Iza's Ballad

TRANSLATED FROM
THE HUNGARIAN BY
GEORGE SZIRTES

Harvill Secker
LONDON

Published by Harvill Secker 2014

2 4 6 8 10 9 7 5 3 1

Copyright © Magda Szabó, 1963 and Editions Viviane Hamy, Paris
English translation copyright © George Szirtes 2014

First published with the title *Pilátus* in 1963
by Magvető, Budapest

First published in Great Britain in 2014 by
Harvill Secker
Random House
20 Vauxhall Bridge Road
London SW1V 2SA

www.vintage-books.co.uk

Addresses for companies within The Random House Group Limited can be found at:
www.randomhouse.co.uk/offices.htm

The Random House Group Limited Reg. No. 954009

A CIP catalogue record for this book
is available from the British Library

ISBN 9781846552656

This publication was assisted by a grant from the Hungarian Books and
Translations Office at Petőfi Literary Museum

HUNGARIAN BOOKS
AND TRANSLATIONS
OFFICE

The Random House Group Limited supports the Forest Stewardship Council® (FSC®),
the leading international forest-certification organisation. Our books carrying the FSC
label are printed on FSC®-certified paper. FSC is the only forest-certification
scheme supported by the leading environmental organisations, including
Greenpeace. Our paper procurement policy can be found at
www.randomhouse.co.uk/environment

MIX
Paper from
responsible sources
FSC
www.fsc.org   FSC® C016897

Typeset in Fournier MT by Palimpsest Book Production Limited,
Falkirk, Stirlingshire

Printed and bound in Great Britain by
Clays Ltd, St Ives PLC

I

EARTH

I

The news arrived just as she was toasting bread.

Three years earlier Iza had sent them a clever little machine that plugged into the wall and made the bread come out a pale pink; she'd turned the contraption this way and that, examined it for a while, then stowed it on the bottom shelf of the kitchen cupboard, never to use it again. She didn't trust machines, but then she didn't trust things as basic as electricity. If there was a prolonged power cut or if lightning had disabled the circuit, she would take down the branched copper candelabrum from the top of the sideboard where the candles were always ready in case the lights went out, and would carry the delicate flame-tipped ornament through the kitchen and into the hall, raising it high above her head the way a tame old stag carries its tines. She couldn't even get used to the idea of an electric toaster: she would have missed crouching by the fire, the fire itself and the strange noise of the embers so like the panting of a live being. The constantly changing colour of the cinders lent the room a peculiar life; when the fire was lit she didn't feel she was alone, not even when the house was empty.

There she was now, squatting on the stool beside the open stove, and when Antal rang the bell she suddenly didn't know what to do with the miniature toasting fork so she took the thing with her, a piece of toast still stuck on the end of it. Antal stared at her at first, then took her arm and the clumsy gesture told her what he didn't want to say. The old woman immediately welled up, but the tears refused to run and remained stubbornly balanced in the corners of her eyes. Her instinctive reaction was, however, governed by her more properly functioning good manners, which were a mixture of instinct and sound training. They even enabled her to force out a 'Thank you, dear'.

Of the two smaller rooms at her disposal, she only heated the back one. When they entered it and the old woman had lowered herself to the stool again, Antal warmed his hands on the side of the stove. They didn't speak but understood each other perfectly. 'I need to gather my strength,' said the old woman's thoughts. 'I loved him very much.' 'Take your time, we're in no hurry,' Antal replied silently. 'In any case there is no use you coming out, there's no one there now. At least you wouldn't know anyone who arrived after dawn. But I'll take you out there, because you have a right to see them too, those people you wouldn't know.'

When they finally set off the old woman took along her string bag. She always took it to the clinic; it was what she carried Vince's stuff in, what he asked for or what she thought it good for him to have: handkerchiefs, biscuits, the lemons he liked. The yellow globes shone jovially through the mesh of the bag. 'She's trying to work magic,' thought the doctor. 'She wants to work magic with three miserable lemons. She thinks if she shows death she is not frightened of it, it will run away. She thinks if she turns up at the old man's bedside with lemons she will find him still alive.'

4

There had been a light frost overnight and the stairs were slippery because the old woman hadn't salted them since the previous evening. He took her arm and led her down. The door of the outhouse was open, with a layer of muddy snow on the threshold, and behind it, as if ensconced in a fortress, Captain was peeking out. You could tell by the way he was digging in the straw that he had messed up his bed again. The old woman looked away; her arm stiffened and her breath came faster. 'She has noticed Captain,' the doctor thought, 'but she's pretending not to have seen him. Captain is black. One is not supposed to see anything black on a day like this, only white.'

Kolman, the shopkeeper, gazed after them from behind the glass door of the state grocer's as they closed the gate and set off towards the taxi rank. It has only just gone seven, it seems the old man is approaching the end. Shame, he was a quiet little thing, patient, always willing to let people, children or adults, go in front of him as he waited for his can of milk. The girls loved him because he'd always bring them flowers from his garden in the summer, and when it was winter he'd bring them tea and bits of roast marrow. Well, poor old boy, time for him to go now. His daughter will have a good cry. She sent them money each month from Pest, the postman told us. What was Antal thinking of, divorcing her like that, though he's decent enough himself and his patients speak well of him.

The old woman too was thinking of Iza as they got into the taxi in front of the cake shop. Dad has cancer, Iza had said in a strangely cold voice, some three months after she had unexpectedly rung from the capital to arrange an examination for him. Iza was scrubbing her hands in the bathroom with slow deliberate movements the way doctors did, the way she got used to in medical school. The old woman herself sank down on the edge of the tub, grabbing at the bath tap because everything had gone dark, then sprang to her feet again and rushed into the hall because she had heard Vince's voice. 'What are you doing, hiding in there?' asked Vince in ill temper, but she just stared at him in repulsion and terror as one might look at an already decomposing body. She couldn't answer, couldn't think of anything to say.

Iza saved her, having stepped out of the bathroom behind her, raising her strong white fingers. 'Not everyone is as dirty as you, old man,' she said and Vince's thin face began to glow. 'Old man' was what Iza used to call him; a younger, loud, shiny-nosed Iza. 'Other people wash their hands several times a day, like me,' said the girl. 'Now get back into the room before you catch a cold. If I had as little salt in my stomach as you do, I'd not be rushing about so much. I'd take some pepsin.'

The old woman knew Vince suspected something. Ever since the uncontrollable agonising pains began and he started losing weight, he had become suspicious and was constantly listening out in case he caught a snippet of some conversation that might tell him why he was growing ever weaker, something that might explain the burning pain that he felt ever more frequently. 'I couldn't possibly shout at him like that,' the old woman thought, and even in her current state of distress was bursting with pride that Iza *could*.

'Come along, mama, let's go down to the Presso for a coffee. Are you coming too?'

Vince smiled at that, proudly surveying his spindly legs: they must still look strong enough to make it down to the Presso. He wagged his head to say no and Iza shrugged, saying she didn't care since he'd only be eyeing the women there. She grabbed her coat and gently bumped her forehead against his own beautifully shaped brow on her way out as she had done since she was a child. 'Now be sure not to cheat on mama while we're out!' Vince just kept wagging his head with a sly look on his face, and his eyes, that for weeks now had looked unfamiliar, so unfamiliar that she found herself gazing at them, puzzling why they should seem both smaller and, at the same time, wider and duller than before, suddenly flickered and came to life. His conversations with Iza always had an element of flirtation, not at all like the ones you usually hear between father and daughter. They were more like friends, or accomplices – heaven knows in what!

Neither of them touched their coffees in the Presso, they just stared at them, turning the small glasses in their hands. Iza looked pale. 'He has about three months,' she said. 'Antal will bring him medication. I'll leave you some money. Buy him anything he wants, however foolish. Don't spare the cash.'

Music was playing and the old woman suddenly felt that she and Iza were like two executioners, planning something terrible right here, in the shade of the red curtain. Knowing that Vince would be gone in three months' time, and being aware that she knew *now* that he would no longer be *then*, had such a powerful effect on her that she imagined Vince a prisoner, one of the condemned, and that she had just been informed of the moment of his execution. She did not dare ask if Dekker's diagnosis was reliable: she knew from both Iza and Antal that Dekker was never wrong. The music grew louder, lovers were gazing at each other, the waitress was asking if she would like some cream in her coffee. Iza answered for her, saying yes.

The cream was stiff and too sweet. She dropped it while she was putting it in the coffee and scraped it off the table in confusion, feeling guilty. 'Try to pull yourself together,' said her daughter. 'Let me tell you what you can expect.' She had to force herself to listen at first as she was again informed that Vince had at most ninety days to live but suddenly she wasn't understanding anything, her tears blurring the great red curtain before her. 'Listen,' said Iza, 'we have very little time and we have to discuss things!'

Iza always spoke in this serious, calm manner when there was something important to settle. She felt like screaming and knocking away the cream but she didn't, of course; she hadn't the strength and wouldn't have dared in any case, it was just for a moment that she wanted to: an old woman does not indulge in hysterics or make scenes. She simply asked, 'Are you coming home?' It was as much a plea as a question; inside she was praying, beseeching God in inchoate, ungrammatical sentences, insisting that she should come home, that her daughter should be with them and not leave her alone to cope with the dying. Iza was a doctor, Iza was her child and had always helped them through. The younger woman took a deep, violent gulp as if the coffee she was raising to her lips at last were solid rather than liquid, and said, 'I can't.'

She comprehended the thought behind it and supposed it to be right. If the girl took a vacation that would mean only that she might visit a little more often than usual and then Vince would guess something was up, would look for the reason and discover it, and that simply must not happen. Iza always came at the regular prearranged time, once a month, and on occasions like birthdays, name days and wedding anniversaries. She couldn't come this time, well of course she couldn't, so the old woman would have to deal with Vince by herself as well as with the terrible secret that Vince was going to die. Iza's promise that Antal would be with them to help was of little consolation. Antal wasn't Iza.

Her tears began to flow and she felt rather than saw that the people at the next table were watching her. Iza didn't try to calm her but simply held her hand. She hung on to the girl's cold, ringless fingers.

The taxi was taking them past bare plane trees down Sándor Street, where a huge, billowing advertisement invited people to a night of dancing. Antal heard a great sigh and looked back from the front passenger seat. The old woman did not respond to his gaze, but coughed and turned aside, watching the street and the swirl of rooks past the wayside trees. Antal was good to her, just as he had been good to Vince, and once upon a time they had loved Antal very much. But Antal had left Iza and that could be neither forgotten nor forgiven.

The radiators down the corridor were pouring out heat. The air was dry and smelled of dishcloths. The porter opened the lift door for them but even at this dreadful time she was cheered because the porter's smile seemed like a form of defence. She sat down in the small waiting room at the turn of the corridor and while Antal went to fetch the professor – it was Dekker's last year at the clinic – she took the handkerchiefs and lemons out of her string bag and put them back in again. She was terrified of the thought of talking things over with a stranger but took strength in recalling that the meeting was not about her but about Vince. The politeness with which she was greeted at the clinic was a mark of respect for Iza.

9

She didn't really believe Antal when he said it was the end. But when Dekker appeared in the corridor and walked towards her, the string bag in her hand felt much heavier. It was as if she were carrying lead rather than lemons. Dekker was a *professor* and she could tell by his face that her poor tremulous questions would be answered directly.

Later Iza asked her what she and the professor had said to each other. She tried to put it together in her mind but she couldn't. She could only remember Dekker touching her on the shoulder because she had shaken off the well-intentioned fingers, as if a sudden fierce bitterness had taken possession of her, more an irritation, a deep antipathy, so she felt that Dekker, who had spent three months moving heaven and earth to help Vince and would have given his soul to save him, was a murderer and, what was more, a murderer of the same age as her husband. What right had he to be so *healthy*?

She stopped in the doorway.

Antal said Vince had been unconscious since sunrise and would probably not recover consciousness but slip into death as he slept. Yes, but if she walked in he might wake; it couldn't be that forty-nine years of physical and spiritual union should prove weaker than death. But what would happen if he should sense her closeness and start speaking in that gentle, childish voice of his, and ask her to account for all that was happening, for his pain and for his ebbing life? What would happen if today, on this his last day, he were suddenly to became aware of the threshold on which he was standing and burst into help-less tears again, sobbing as he did when he lost his job back in the Twenties when he stood beside her bed in his nightshirt, dropping tears, begging, 'Help me, Ettie!' What if he asked her to help him now when he already knew there was no hope yet still begged for his life, for what was impossible. Vince loved life; never mind being a pauper, unemployed, or sick, he still thought merely being alive, simply being on earth, the fact that he could wake up in the morning and go to bed at night, that he could be in a place where the wind blew, where the sun shone and where the rain pattered quietly or poured down, was wonderful. She would have to lie to him as she had been lying continuously for months now. She was afraid that Vince would leave her without a word, that he might cast his terrified conscious eyes on her one last time and, after having dozed off with pain or with the assistance of drugs, his thoughts might turn to silent accusation or complaint.

Antal threw his coat on a chair as he entered. It was only now the old woman noticed he was not wearing a white surgical gown. He didn't look like a doctor without it, just a member of the family, something he hadn't been for a good few years now.

The first person she spotted in the room was Lidia. The nurse turned her way when the door opened and stood up from the chair by the bed, smoothing her apron. She didn't greet the old woman in words, just nodded, the only natural thing to do in these unnatural circumstances. She adjusted Vince's blanket a little, then went straight out, not even casting a glance back at the bed. 'How strange,' the old woman thought. 'She has been at his bedside for weeks and she leaves like that, her eyes quite dry, without any sense that she was part of this. Can people get used to death?'

Vince wasn't conscious but he didn't look detached from the world either, more as though he were simply asleep, the skin on his brow tight and silvery. His nose had grown since yesterday and there was no trace of the little red moon on its bridge where his glasses used to sit. She looked again and realised it was not a matter of his nose growing but of his face falling back. 'He has left me,' thought the old woman. 'He didn't wait for me. For forty-nine years I have known his every thought. Now I don't know what he has taken with him. He has left me behind.'

She sank down on the bed and gazed at him.

She had been nursing him for months, day and night, to the point of exhaustion, but now she didn't feel the least bit tired and could start the whole process afresh if only she could take him home, even as he was, in his sad open nightshirt from which his ribcage emerged, higher up than she expected. Seeing what had become of his body she might even be able to hold him in her lap. She should never have let him out of her sight. Iza meant well in bringing him out here, meant well for them both, but she still shouldn't have allowed it. Perhaps if it were she herself who had been beside him these last few weeks he might have lived a little longer, but it was Lidia who had nursed him, Lidia who changed his bed every day, Lidia who did everything. Lidia was precise, patient and kind, but could she tease him and get some more food into him; could she mock him the way Iza did, telling him there was nothing wrong with him, that he was simply old? Could Lidia hush his choked words of complaint? 'I shouldn't have let him enter the clinic,' thought the old woman. 'Because he has left me like this now, unaware of my presence, without a word of goodbye!' She bent down and kissed him. Vince's brow was dry and smelled of medication. She sat down beside him and held his hand.

About noon Dekker looked in and Lidia returned. Antal was no longer in the room; she hadn't even noticed him going. Dekker was there only for a moment and she thought Lidia had gone with him but the girl hadn't moved. She was by the window, level with the bed, watching them from there. It bothered her having a strange pair of eyes on her so she turned her back, but then, not seeing her any more, she immediately forgot there was someone else there. By that time only Vince's hair was still alive, a few stubborn locks of his white mane. She felt neither tired nor hungry and was unaware of the passage of time. She straightened her back. It hurt having constantly to be leaning over.

In the afternoon Vince spoke.

She thought her heart had stopped. It had been so silent till then, so infinitely silent it seemed she was surrounded by a solemn impregnable wall of silence that would permit no voice. His body trembled as he spoke, even his eyelashes trembled. She leaned to his mouth to catch whatever he was whispering. Lidia was there, also listening, and on seeing the face of the younger woman beside her she suddenly felt angry and downright hostile. She hated Lidia now, felt she was pushing in, that she was soulless. You see, Antal has gone and Dekker too. They are sensitive people. What do you think you are gawping it? Are you deaf? Can't you hear the sick man is calling for water? Why don't you move? She just stands there gawping at Vince without moving at all. She should be leaping up, getting a glass of water from the bedside table that had been totally cleared by someone; Vince's glasses were gone as well as his cup and his little pencil stub. But somewhere inside she was rejoicing because the nurse didn't know what to do and it was only she who could hear Vince's words, she who knew what he wanted, she who could get him something to drink – even now, she could still do something for him. She poured water into the glass and raised Vince's head, putting the glass to his lips.

The mouth wouldn't open and a look of something like disgust, something distinctly unpleasant, flickered across his face. Vince did not drink.

'He's not thirsty,' whispered Lidia. 'Don't try making him drink.'

She could have hit the nurse for saying that. Who was she to look down on her like some kind of god, to be giving her instructions and taking the glass from her hand? And in the meantime that voice again, that strange hoarse breathing. But why won't he drink if it's water he wants?

'I'm here,' said Lidia aloud.

At first she thought the nurse was addressing her and that made her even angrier. But then she saw that Lidia was looking at Vince, not her, and that Vincent's mouth was trembling again in a way that reminded her of how he used to smile, and how it lit up his face for a moment before immediately fading again. Lidia crouched down by the bed and held Vince's hand.

The old woman felt she no longer existed, that she had been ignored, cut out, cheated. She glared at Lidia. Lidia was a complete stranger, someone she'd never met before, whose face was packed with a meaning she didn't recognise, and she felt a peculiarly fierce hatred for her; it was as if, for the first time in her life, her eyes had finally been opened and she could see. Thief, cheat; she was stealing the last moments of her husband's life. It was Antal who had chosen this nurse! Antal had selected her to attend on the sick man. Iza wouldn't have done that. Now there she is, crouching by the bed, holding Vince's hand. A nobody. A stranger.

'Go on, sleep,' said Lidia. 'I'm here.'

The old woman sank back on to the bed. She was so angry that she felt no pain at all. She snatched at Vince's other hand, the tender body lying held up by the pair of them. Vince didn't speak again, his breathing was barely audible. Lidia was still crouching beside him. Her face was no longer visible as she had bent her brow over Vince's hand.

Outside, the March light had frozen between the trees. The old woman closed her eyes and stiffened at the waist. When she looked again, Lidia was standing. Vince lay precisely as before but was quieter still.

'He's gone,' said Lidia. 'It wasn't water he wanted, it was his daughter, Iza. I'll get Dr Antal.'

2

A car stood waiting outside the door. Antal led her to it. It took her some time to understand that Dekker had arranged to have her taken home in his car. She shook her head in terror, no, certainly not, out of the question. It was incomprehensible to her that she should get into a car now and be driven home as if it were a wedding. She'd cut across the small copse of trees in the park to where the rails ran and get a tram home. Or better still, she'd go on foot. She wanted to walk, to move. Antal took a long look back at the porter's cabin where the porter's cape was hanging on a hook. It was as though he wanted to put it on while seeing her home. Don't follow, leave me alone! She just wanted to be left alone. She wouldn't feel ill, why should she, it's fine, just let her go. And she was very grateful for everything, grateful to him and to Dekker.

'At least leave your baggage behind,' Antal begged her.

'Why leave it, it isn't heavy.' The doctor still did not want to let her go so she just set off without saying goodbye. She knew it was churlish and rude but she also knew that if she didn't start she'd have no strength left. Antal shouted something after her, something about telephoning, but she didn't catch it. Couldn't he just leave her alone for God's sake!

The park looked exposed, almost angry, as if it were being

dragooned into spring against its will; a few mounds of snow remained dotted about the grass. Birches had been planted. The trees bent their thin pale bodies with the wind. The grass at the lake's edge had begun to sprout but this was no sweet March, it was severe, the sky clouded over, edgy and dark, with something of Easter about it, the buds on the twigs not dreamy but threatening, a kind of purplish green, like rotting flesh. At the top of the hill stood three threadbare old firs, their flaking trunks so thick only the branches registered the movement of the air; some of last year's cones were still nestling in the boughs. A thin membrane of ice lay over the water, washing away footprints along the path.

There was a bridge to the island in the middle of the artificial lake and she hesitated a moment when she reached it, but she walked across anyway. From here the chimneys of the clinic were clearly visible, smoke billowing from them, blinding, supernaturally white and fat against the steely sky. The triangular roof was also clear in view and she could see the pigeons roosting between the strangely bent mythological figures that served as statuary. She sat down on a bench and gazed at the water.

The fringes of the lake were still iced up but the water was alive now. She couldn't see the fish and could only trace their movements as they suddenly formed rings in one or other part of the lake and broke the surface. The lake was full of brown, ever-hungry carp. A long time ago, when Iza was still a little girl, they'd come down here in summer and feed them, entertained by the way they fought over scraps. You couldn't see the bottom of the lake and the banks were bare, last year's grass blown tensely down the gentle slope. The fern was restless, continually moving. 'What will I do all by myself?' the old woman wondered.

Children clattered along the bridge, playing there for a while, yelling, throwing stones, then clattered off again, running towards the open-air theatre on the far shore. The amphitheatre seats were still in storage and the concrete blocks that in summer were topped by red wooden benches poked stiff thumbs into the afternoon; they looked like a set of clumsy hand-hewn gravestones. As soon as she noticed this she rose and turned her back on the hill with the amphitheatre. Her string bag seemed heavier now, unbearably, comically heavy. She reached into it for a handkerchief, wiped her eyes with one and stuffed it in her pocket. The full-bellied lemons were swelling out the bag: she took out all three, gazed at them, turned them in her hands, then threw them into the lake.

If you set out into town on foot the shortest way was through the new estate.

Last year, when building started and they knocked down the old sty-like wooden shacks and bitumen-roofed buildings of Salétrom Square and those around Balzsamárok, she wept over the loss of the old quarter. She and Vince had even gone for a walk to bid farewell to the streets where they had seen out their youth, their shoes sinking into the soil of the loose sandy lane that people in the area, for some incomprehensible reason, referred to as the *Gázló*, the ford. Iza happened to be home then and she didn't want to tell her where they'd been, but Vince could never keep a secret and as soon as they were back in the hall he told her. Iza gave a wave, stretching her lovely long waist as she leaned backwards. 'So there you go, turning back the wheel of time,' she said, 'two old sentimentalists.'

There was no severity in her voice, but the words were not a kind of joke: Iza always said exactly what she really thought. Vince felt ashamed and muttered something about Balzsamárok and the artesian well there. 'Balzsamárok,' scoffed Iza as though the very word was repugnant. 'Balzsamárok! What about the chemists, why not mention that? Balzsamárok! Look at the statistics, nearly everyone suffered from tuberculosis there.'

She was in the kitchen buttering bread for the sandwiches and she too felt ashamed for having mourned Balzsamárok. Vince came out to join her and mumbled a few words. They avoided each other's eyes. He started singing a tune; his sweet, mellifluous voice had lost nothing of its old quality. It was some chorus of his long-gone school days. *'Her cheeks and breast / Like hills under a shroud . . .'* They burst into laughter because Iza had always taken song lyrics seriously as a child: you couldn't sing anything sad to her and certainly not this, as she would tearfully beg that the maiden should not die but be restored to health. Vince kissed her face as she bent over the sandwiches. A long time ago, when they first got engaged, it was to Balzsamárok they went courting and kissing. They'd never meet anyone they knew there. Iza opened the kitchen door and they sprang apart. 'Well, well,' cried Iza and laughed. 'I'll knock before I enter next time.'

This time, when she reached the corner of what had been Salétrom Square, she felt a great wave of gratitude. It was six months since the old woman had last been there and she had to find a track across the freshly dug soil where the new buildings were to be constructed. The place looked so different from what it had been and, without the huts, it looked even more like a lowland estate than it had before. Only the well remained but there were trucks labouring around it and some long-necked machine was hissing away in the background. The labourers were just finishing for the day, a bell was ringing and someone shouted. She stumbled between the mounds of earth. Someone took her arm and helped her across an unsteady plank. 'Why didn't you go round?' asked a young man. 'Didn't you see the notice, "Building in Progress"?' She mumbled something to the effect that she didn't see it. She started walking faster.

At the next turning her eyes were struck by the plump green ivy bubbling through the fence of her home.

When Vince was rehabilitated and received the twenty-three years' worth of wages he was owed, they didn't speak about it, but both of them knew that it was the end of their life at Darabont Street. The money came in winter, the winter of 1946, and Iza had gone off to university so there were just the two of them at home when the letter informing them arrived. Vince didn't say anything, just offered the postman a cigarette, then went out into the yard in his jacket, without even a scarf or hat. She took his cap out to him but she didn't dare go up to him and stopped at the top of the steps because Vince had ambled over to the neighbour's pigsty, leaned on the fence and looked in as if there were something to see in the trough or the pans full of water. She could guess what he was feeling and didn't want to disturb him, so continued watching from the threshold as he bent awkwardly over the wooden fence and it occurred to her that Vince had grown a stoop in recent years, that he was more hunched than he should be at his age. It started snowing, the flakes settling in Vince's great mane of hair. The first tenant trundled across the yard with the rubbish, quite ready to offer a greeting now. Vince turned round, took a glance across the bare yard, past the neighbour's sties, past the chicken run, past their own solitary patch of ground where no flower ever grew because the first tenant's chickens kept scratching the soil away and, as he looked up, his glance showed that he had the *house* in mind.

He saw that she was standing on the steps, gazing at him, so he blew on his hands to show that he had just realised he was cold, then hurried to her side where they embraced. When she had disentangled herself she saw Vince's innocent eyes were filled with tears.

Iza was late coming home that evening and Vince didn't mention it to her, though Iza was thinking of the rehabilitation and it was Iza who had put in the request for it. They put the letter granting it under her plate. Iza read it through twice, nodded, smiled, then said to her father, 'There you are!' and Vince repeated, 'There you are!' while she just looked at them there-you-are-ing at each other, because under the silly words there lay twenty-three years of humiliation, of acquaintances turning away on meeting, pawnbrokers, a wardrobe made up of flea-market bargains, the flat on Darabont Street.

'They are building a big block on the Nyíres,' said Iza, swallowing her roast potato. 'Centrally heated, permanent lease.'

Vince smiled, shook his head, remained silent for a while, then declared, 'I want to go home.'

'Fine,' said Iza, putting down her fork, 'buy yourselves a little cave and furnish it with bearskin. God, what a hopeless old fool you are!'

Home, in Vince's language, meant his own home, a house where there was space to grow some flowers and a garden

with trees where you could keep an animal, somewhere the attic would belong exclusively to them. Vince was born in a village and, having only moved to town to attend the *gimná-ʒium*, or grammar school, he declared that water from the village well tasted better than from a tap. For three weeks they walked round town until they finally found such a house. They were stood outside his old home looking at the windows and its high fence when Vince squeezed her arm and said, 'This is the one.' It happened to be the time of thaw, everything dripping, the gutter by the brown gate pouring with melted snow. The gutter had a broad dragon-shaped spout at the top and it was from here the water crashed down. There were three small rooms in the house, one bigger than the other two, while outside there was a red-brick-paved path with plane trees either side that led through the yard to the woodshed, the passage vaulted, closed on three sides like a room with an open fourth wall. When the house was requisitioned by the government in 1923 Vince had gone out into the woodshed to weep so no one should have to comfort him. How good now, after all this time, to have reached the age when it could be his again, though he was no longer in the best of health. 'You old capitalist.' Iza laughed. 'Never satisfied till your name is on the deeds.' But that was then. Iza didn't like the house now because she had spent the four years of her marriage in the big room with Antal. She had never stayed over on a visit since the divorce. She gave no reason, but they knew that, for Iza, the big room would always be associated with the memory of Antal and that Iza didn't like remembering.

How could this be 'home' now?

The house was so much associated with Vince that she had

never really regarded it as a joint property though it was registered in both their names. But they had bought it with Vince's
rehabilitation money, at the price of Vince's humiliation over
several terrible years. It was Vince who had really suffered for
it and it meant everything to him: the house justified his whole
life and was his greatest source of pride, apart from Iza. Really,
that is where Vince should be buried: in the garden. What would
she do with this house all by herself? She couldn't go on living
here with just Captain for company. Iza would make fewer visits
home now, there would be no reason to come down for her
father's birthday or name day or for wedding anniversaries.
Should she take a lodger? What would it be like having a lodger?
Would they be like that first tenant in Darabont Street? Or
would it be some old woman, as simple and dull as she was?
But it would be just as much of a burden if she tried to be
friendly. What to do?

None of this had been discussed with Iza.

It was three weeks ago that she had arrived unannounced
and asked Antal to take her father down to the clinic; Iza had
wanted to talk it over with her but she ran away into the pantry,
locking the door after her, because she was superstitious that
way. She had learned in Auntie Emma's house that one shouldn't
say any bad thing out loud, or indeed name anything at all that
threatened one's well-being because there were angels behind
one, listening, two white ones and one black, and the one in
black wasn't well disposed. Should that one hear what people
were most frightened of, should it suspect what caused the fear,
it would bring on precisely that which they had put so carelessly into words. 'I've never come across anything as malicious
as Christian mythology,' said Iza once when her mother had

warned her not to talk about failing her exams. Iza never failed, she just liked giving herself a fright.

But there must have been something to that story of the angel, the bad angel. Because she had also heard Vince, when he first fell ill, at a moment of respite between the pains, cracking his bones and starting to laugh. 'I've got cancer,' he said and she put her hand to her mouth in horror, but Vince just laughed so she didn't think he had stumbled on the truth. 'My stomach feels too full,' he said later. 'Give me a laxative.'

She had shut herself away in the kitchen for the last three weeks and wouldn't let Iza say anything about Vince's impending death. Iza didn't force the issue; she heard the old woman moving about, listened for a while, then went out and left her alone. The old woman knew she meant well, that she wanted to sort out the future so there would be no terrible surprises if what was forecast to happen should happen; she wanted to discuss with her what was to be done about the house and about her life. But it isn't proper to speak about what should happen after someone's death while he's still alive. Until Antal arrived, until Lidia finally rose from her position beside the bed, however unconscious Vince was, there was still hope.

Offices were just closing for the night and the street filled up. She walked a little faster because she didn't want to meet anyone. She gazed at passers-by as they headed home. There was something determined about their expressions, a kind of frozen gaiety. No one ambled or meandered, all were rushing to get home. The shops were full, children were crying, the traffic was heavier. Car indicators were flashing. She envied them their hurry in some way; she had never consciously thought about how someone was *waiting* for them. No one was waiting for her, only the dog, Captain.

She pulled up her collar to cover her face and looked at the ground so if someone greeted her she might not be obliged to notice them. It started raining: a sharp, slow rain, not even quite rain yet, just a spray, and the pavement suddenly flashing light and the windows misting up. Her face, her brow and skin registered the dampness though not a drop had fallen at her feet. Invisible rain was what Vince had called it. The dragon spout stood empty, open-mouthed, as if it were gasping for air. Kolman wasn't around: she didn't have to talk to anybody.

The first thing she saw at the gate was Captain. She turned her gaze from him and leaned against the table that stood under the entrance arch from autumn through to spring. The caution was unnecessary. Captain took no notice of her and was not looking for tenderness. She didn't know whether she welcomed this or felt worse for the animal's indifference. Iza was right: Captain was stupid.

Now she was alone for the first time since the morning, utterly alone.

She could let herself go, allow herself to rest on the arm of the wickerwork chair and wonder what life would be like once all sense of responsibility had been removed. She didn't want to be at home, she feared the evenings, feared the two beds, one of which had finally become redundant. She couldn't sit here for ever, of course; she had to go in. Go in now, or half an hour later – what did it matter? She set off towards the yard, then stopped again. A light had gone on inside, in the bedroom.

It wasn't terror she felt but something else. She sank back

into the chair, put her string bag down on the ground, and stared at the lit window. The light inside seemed much more real than Vince's face with its mysterious expression had been just now. Perhaps this is what reality was, that burning lamp inside; that none of the events of the last few months had actually happened, that Vince was still alive, the afternoon had been no more than a dream, that the eleven weeks that had just passed, and that the sight of Vince's wasted body that had grown so terribly hollow as if it had been preparing for ages to become a vehicle of mortality, were all just dreams and reality was the small, comical, slightly plump figure of Vince as he once was, who was waiting for her at home and who was not really ill.

She felt weaker than she had done at any moment that afternoon. She shut her eyes and rested her head against the back of the chair. The garden, the still bare garden, was rustling around her. Blackbirds, she thought. Then again they might not be blackbirds. The light is on. Anything at all might be making that rustling sound. It might be angels. Or clouds. Anything.

By the time she looked up, the window was dark again.

The disappointment was so profound that she hadn't even the strength to shed tears. She leaned on her thighs and covered her face with her hands. The rustling faded away and there was no more noise at all: it was as if some deaf creature were living nearby. Then the front door creaked open and there was Iza standing in the doorway.

3

She had come. Her daughter was standing next to her. She wasn't alone.

Iza was wearing a black jumper and you could see from the state of her eyes that she had been crying. The old woman felt ambivalent about this; she resisted the implied call for help – it would have meant running over to her, stroking her as she used to when she was little, calming and consoling her, saying there was nothing to cry for. She was too much aware of her own need to lay her head on Iza's shoulders and let it all out. It was a strange moment: they hadn't experienced one like it before. Iza had never needed anyone's help: if something went wrong she took it on the chin with no complaints, and when it came to decisions she didn't ask for advice, she simply announced what she was going to do. There was the time after matriculation when she suddenly declared she was going to apply to medical school, another time when she announced she had found a job, that she was about to marry and, later, the time she told them she was about to be divorced and had found new employment in Budapest. It was the first time in her adulthood that Iza showed she was capable of suffering like everyone else. The old woman was relieved. It was as if her daughter had escaped some terrible danger. At the same time she was in a panic on account of her own suffering; it upset her deeply to see Iza crying and she was desperately wondering how to help her.

Iza didn't kiss her, didn't even touch her. The old woman realised what her daughter was thinking: she was thinking this was a bad time to touch or hug each other because then they'd have no strength left to cope with everything that had happened.

'Come along,' said Iza. 'You'd better get an early night. Come along.'

Iza picked up the string bag, put her arm through it and set off indoors. The old woman stumbled after her. There was a fire lit in both rooms now and all trace of the unwashed break-fast things had vanished. It was tidy, that particular Iza form of tidiness so characteristic of the girl. It was as if she'd been doing nothing but tidying for hours.

Antal must have been shouting that he had rung Iza in Pest and that she had got tickets for the afternoon flight. Her heart gave a great lurch and she closed her eyes. She was terrified of flying, wouldn't get on a plane, not for all the money in the world, and she hated it when Iza wrote to say she was coming by plane rather than rail. Every flight was a form of blasphemy, unnatural, terrifying, especially this swoop over the clouds, racing against that certain *something*, to get to where Vince was.

Iza took her hand.

Now she had her right hand too, in the same way she tried to deceive Vince all those months, her fingers open as though in affectionate play but really to check her pulse. Her heart rate was all over the place. How odd that Iza could tell all that just by feeling with her fingertips.

'I'll make you some tea,' said Iza. 'Your hands are cold as ice.'

She went out to the kitchen. The big room immediately seemed unbearable, almost frightening. Iza had put on the main light as soon as they came in, the light they only used when there were guests. It was unusual, this light, somehow harsh, improper. She turned it off and turned on the small one instead, then she stopped the wall clock and covered the big mirror with the knitted berliner shawl. By the time Iza returned with the tea she sat hunched on the sofa beside the fire. Iza froze on the threshold, the steaming mug in her hand. The clock had stopped, showing a quarter to four: the whole aspect of the room was peculiarly changed now that the mirror was blind.

'She knows,' thought the old woman. 'I told her back *then*.'

Iza's mouth twitched but she didn't say anything. She waited for the old woman to drink her tea, then snatched the shawl from the mirror and put it round her mother instead. She opened the cover of the clock face, moved the hands to the right time and set the thing going.

The old woman shuddered when the mirror glistened behind her once more. She felt something had been taken from Vince, the last thing that belonged to him, and she didn't even dare glance at it. The silvery surface was so alive, so much like a lake; she was afraid he might appear and start swimming, that something, or someone, would shimmer out of it. Even the sound of the clock hurt her; it meant the wheels were moving round though Vince was beyond time. Might it be easier coping with the world like this? Iza didn't believe in anything that old people believed in.

Iza took the mug from her but stayed close, next to her legs.

She was always beside her at every moment of crisis, ever since she was born, not like a child at all, more like a sister. When the first lodger at the old house in Darabont Street made a remark about Vince, Iza answered for him. Iza was just a baby when Vince lost his job and would have known nothing of the circumstances at the time. There she was, defending her father, her face chalk-white with indignation, and the lodger just stared at her: she so small, not quite eight years old, as if her little body were entirely compounded of some dry, defiant passion. When she went to the dentist Iza usually accompanied her and they had their teeth done together, Iza always first in the chair, and she couldn't be a coward afterwards because Iza would not utter a cry when the dentist was drilling or removing a tooth, the only evidence of her pain being a faint fluttering of her eyelids. Iza helped manage her money, helped her cook and even with her spring cleaning when there was no other help; she would help without being asked, of her own free will, as if it were the natural thing to do. Now here she was again, sitting at the end of the divan, clutching her hands. How they adored her, she and Vince, from the day she was born. A tear crept into her eye as she thought of how Vince would never see his daughter again.

'We are not to weep for him,' said Iza.

The old woman looked up at her through her tears because she had heard this from her before. It wasn't a matter of medical concern; the cook had said the same thing when her first child died and she was choking with tears mourning for her little boy. They were still in the nice flat then, the old flat, her cook a gaunt old woman who never went anywhere – summer or winter – without her umbrella, to which she had fixed a porcelain button with a picture of the Empress Elisabeth on it. 'You mustn't shed tears for him,' the cook said, when they took baby Endrus away. 'He won't get any sleep on the other side if you do. You mustn't weep for him.'

'You'll not be alone,' she heard the girl saying. 'You'll sell the house and stay with me in Pest.'

Now she really started crying: the relief, the sense of being saved and liberated, suddenly burst in on her. All those terrors, everything she was afraid of – empty evenings, pointless days, lodgers, long days with nothing to do – all these had come to nothing. By the time Iza came home from the surgery she would have everything prepared for her and they would spend all their free time together, as they did in her childhood. She knew she would not be left to fend for herself but this was more than she had dared hope. She had never even thought of it. No, Vince should not be buried in the garden, no, he should be buried in Pest so that they could both visit his grave.

Iza kissed her and now at last she felt secure under the shawl; they could relax. The girl's mouth was cold as if every part of her felt the cold separately, her lips most of all. She was thirty-nine years old when Iza was born and didn't think she'd ever hold a child in her arms again, and that they'd remain for ever as they were, with just the memory of the dead little boy. Then one day she was there, she had arrived, quicker to speak than to walk, a serious, wise, grown-up sort of child. She had never known anyone like Iza and there was much she couldn't under-stand about her: she could only grasp a fraction of her life, of her books and the world she moved in. She didn't know Iza's new flat, the place she'd moved to somewhere on the Ring. Vince was already ill by then and they couldn't take the trip to the capital to visit her there. How comfortable to live in a new flat! How astonished Captain would be to find himself on an upper floor.

She only realised she had dropped off to sleep when she woke with a start to the sound of the doorbell.

At first she thought she was alone and threw off the shawl in panic, but then she saw that Iza was standing in the room, her forehead propped against the window, examining the dark yard outside. The clock had hardly advanced from the point when she fell asleep; a dream was about to overtake her when the bell rang and dispelled it. Who could it be? Their old circle of friends had dispersed after 1923. Until Vince's rehabilitation they lived like hermits. Those of their old acquaintance who would have returned to them after the war, when Vince's reputation was spotless once again, were dismissed by both Vince and Iza – she herself would have let bygones be bygones, but not those two. At home – their *home*! – they entertained only the most select company: Kolman the grocer, their neighbour Gica who stitched cloaks, the newsagent, the tobacconist, a retired postman, a female teacher with whom they spent the evenings on the bench in front of the museum, Dekker, Antal and a few students with catapults and grazed knees from the school on the corner, invited into the garden by Vince who taught them how to make arrows and hooks for fishing. Everyone knew that guests were not welcome after six in the evening because they'd be drinking their last coffee of the day, and once Vince was approaching eighty he tended to go to bed at seven. 'It must be Kolman,' thought the old woman and hastily warned Iza. Kolman knew nothing as yet and would keep them talking for ages. He was always interested in what was going on and there wasn't a day when he didn't drop in if he failed to see her in the shop.

'I won't let him in,' replied Iza perfectly calmly. 'Go and lie down, I'll send Kolman away.'

How good she was here, she couldn't send him away by herself. She had never been able to turn anyone away. She heard the hall door open and was sure she'd been right because she heard Captain's happy snuffling. Captain was scared of strangers but not of Kolman because he always brought some leftovers from the shop, some cabbages or carrots. She couldn't hear anything else, only the animal snuffling and the patter of his nails as he entered the house. Kolman made no noise of greeting, neither did Iza. Why the silence? Kolman was a loud man usually. It must be that he had heard all about it, that's why he was so quiet. She sat up and straightened her skirt. There was something strangely unsettling about the silence.

It was Antal.

She didn't recognise him at first, seeing only that he was a man to judge by his outline, but Iza turned on the light again, which frightened her so much she leapt off the sofa and looked to escape into her bedroom.

'Where are you going?' asked Iza. 'You see, it wasn't Kolman.'

She felt ashamed and sank back on to the sofa, throwing the shawl across her knees. She understood from Iza's tone that she didn't want to be left alone with him, that she shouldn't leave them, so she remained where she was despite all her instincts to the contrary. It was silly, of course, because they always behaved as though nothing had happened between them and she wouldn't have to witness any embarrassing scenes.

33

While the marriage lasted – that tense, nervous love – they were always disciplined in company, almost unnaturally so, and now they would continue to be courteous. They had been like this ever since they parted seven years ago, ever courteous.

But she still didn't like seeing them together. Iza had loved Antal, not that she ever spoke about her feelings, but you could hear it in her voice and see it in her eyes, the way they followed him, even though she didn't know why he had left her. Something terrible must have occured, which was all the more terrifying since they had lived here together with them, under one roof, with only a wall to separate their bedrooms, and they had never been heard to quarrel or to raise their voices, no, there was never a cross word between them. Then one day they simply announced it: they were separating and Iza gave no reason for it. It was not as if Vince would have asked; his face simply clouded over, he shook his head, kissed first Iza, then Antal, then went out into the kitchen.

'Mama is very tired,' said Iza. 'Don't stay too long, please.'

She spoke gently as if sister to brother. Antal was carrying a suitcase, their suitcase, and she immediately recognised it. Guessing what would be in it, she took a great gulp and turned away. She felt that if Antal opened it and she had to set eyes on Vince's grey housecoat and the mug with the forget-me-not pattern that Lidia had already hidden away that morning, she'd have to leave the room.

Antal shoved the case under the table as if he shared her feelings: let it be hidden.

'I'm not even going to sit down,' he said, bending to Captain, who had pushed his way through the half-open door into the room, and starting to stroke the dog's ears. 'I just wanted to see if mama needed anything. You weren't sure this morning whether you could get here today. When did you arrive?'

'At twelve.'

They both looked at her. The old woman's head suddenly cleared: she had not felt so awake since the morning. She must have misunderstood something, or Iza had misread the clock. Her father had died at a quarter to four. It was impossible.

The silence in the room seemed to have thickened. The old woman stared at her daughter. Iza's face was flushed, even her brow. Antal looked away and stared at the carpet.

'Last time I saw him we were playing cards,' said Iza, the most frightening thing about her voice being that it was calm, not angry, not defensive, not offering any explanation. 'He'd had a really good day, he was fully conscious and laughing. I've seen enough people die to last me a lifetime, I want to remember my father's living face.'

Iza was always right. That was the strange thing about her: she had been right about everything, ever since she was born. When she was told off or accused of something as a child, it always turned out, sooner or later, that no one had any reason to be cross with her: Iza simply knew something that they, the adults, did not and when they apologised to her they did not even have the satisfaction of seeing her sulk or pull faces or so much as complain. Iza simply looked at them in a matter-of-fact way and declared in her thin little voice, 'You see!' And she was right now, too, to preserve the memory of her father's laughing face from that previous day rather than the one with the silvery glaze this afternoon.

Antal lit a cigarette and played with the match a while. His expression was blank, empty of everything including understanding. When he looked up again it was at the old woman, not at Iza.

'Mama,' he said, 'you are likely to be very much alone from now. If you like I can move back in.'

'That's very kind of you,' answered Iza, her voice not mocking but full of gratitude. 'You really are very kind, but we've already found a solution. Mama will come to Pest with me.'

It was the first time they had looked each other in the eye. Antal's look was enquiring, Iza gazed back. The old woman understood neither the question nor the answer. When she was a child and her parents were alive, it was her mother and father who ruled; it was as if she were a child among adults again – hopeful yet afraid.

'That would work too,' Antal answered. He tapped the ash off the cigarette.

The old woman mumbled something, clambered to her feet and took a step towards Antal, feeling that she should understand, embrace him, or at least say something to him – it was a big thing, his offer. But she couldn't say anything because Iza gripped her arm and the movement confused her, prevented her from speaking. She didn't understand what they wanted of her, what she should do, and was afraid that if she became too emotional, too nice, Iza might get cross.

Antal did not repeat the invitation. He smiled, bade her goodbye and was already heading for the door. Iza reached for the shawl and wrapped it about herself to see him out and close the gate after him.

Antal was halfway through it when he stopped again. 'Give me the picture of the mill, mama. Papa said that if he died Lidia should have it. I'll take it to her.'

Iza opened her mouth to say something but shrugged and went to the bedroom. The old woman took hold of the chair back because once again she felt her legs giving way. If he died . . . What did he mean, 'if he died'? Vince's understanding was that he had a bad heart and that he should build himself up, that's why he went to the clinic, the injections were there to give him strength as he slept. Vince had no idea he was dying. How could he think such a thing? And why should he give Lidia the picture of the mill, that bad photograph of the village he was born in, with the river, the Karikás, running through it, the riverbank with some old mill in the background. That picture had always hung above Vince's bed, next to the picture of the angel that watched over his dreams. Why did he give it to Lidia? When?

Iza fetched the black-framed picture and now that she was under the light she took a last look at it, as if it were the first time. The photograph was of a river with something like a lock, a tiny waterfall with a wooden building crouched over it. In the foreground there were bushes and a few barefoot children. Unidentifiable faces, a faded early century photograph. The river was the colour of coffee. She wrapped it in newspaper and handed it to Antal.

The old woman started weeping. She felt this new weight was heavier than the rest of the day put together. She stood helpless, pulling at the bottom of her cardigan. It was the second time that day Lidia had crossed her path, this meeting more mysterious, more bitter than the last. Feeling this helped decide whether to kiss Antal or not: she didn't have the strength. Captain was sniffing around the top of the table, standing on two legs as if he understood what was happening.

She heard the door open and close, looked at the carpet and wiped her eyes. Iza returned quickly and that too seemed somehow unnatural because before Antal married her he could barely leave the house: sometimes they'd have to wait for as long as half an hour for Iza to come back in. Now it seemed they had nothing more to say to each other. The girl picked up Captain and put him out in the yard, then turned the key in the hall door and came over to her. As if aware that she needed consolation, she put her hand on her head in the way priests did, as a form of blessing. Then she went over to the window and drew the curtains as had been her habit all those years when she was still living at home, and closed the shutters. The rain was pouring now, they could hear it loud against the glass. She didn't go over to the old woman again but stopped at the big chair. Her mother could see she was weeping, her expression tender, childish and angry under the flowing tears.

4

Iza left the light burning that night.

The objects in the room, those beyond the circle of yellow light, were just about glimmering and she couldn't see the picture above the bed, only the gilded underside of its frame. But she could see it with her inner eye, in her thoughts and memories. The picture, lacking its companion, was merely a remnant. The mill was missing.

Iza fell asleep before she did. The old woman had cheated her.

They had gone to bed at the same time and she had not been answering Iza's questions for a while, breathing regularly so her daughter would think she was drowsing. The girl kept tossing and turning for a long time, it wouldn't have been an easy night for her even if her father had not died that day. She hadn't slept here ever since she had moved to Pest. The bed she was sleeping in was her father's, not the old sofa of her married years. Once she had left the house it had returned to much as it was before. The second-hand office came for their joint furniture and she bought whatever she needed new in Budapest. Nobody finds it easy sleeping in their childhood home, of course.

Iza didn't want to leave her mother alone on this night,

which was why she didn't check into a hotel as she had always done to avoid staying with her parents. It must have been the supreme sacrifice for her. The girl took a long time getting to sleep and kept turning and sighing, looking over at the old woman, then suddenly got up and took something, which was also unusual as she never took sleeping pills and looked down on people who reached for drugs at the least excuse. But this time, just this once, she did take one and it succeeded in putting her to sleep. The old woman lay there with her daughter next to her, so close she could feel her breath on her face as she had done when the girl was a child. She had never seen anyone sleep as beautifully as Iza did, her head laid on her elbow, with that black arc of her eyelashes. She didn't dare kiss her and kissed the hem of the pillow instead as she slipped out of bed and through the door.

The sitting room was the same as it had been in the afternoon, the morning, or any other day, and yet, somehow, it was different. It was as if it had grown and the walls were higher and wider too. Iza's note remained on the table and she scanned it again. Ever since she was a child Iza had written down things to do the next day and couldn't go to sleep unless she'd done so. 'Estate agent,' she read. 'Clinic, undertakers, medical panel, packing.'

The last word on the list: that's why she'd got up. Tomorrow would be the reading through of documents and Iza would decide what they should take back to Pest, and tomorrow they'd have to open the drawers of Vince's little writing desk.

No one else had ever looked inside it and even after forty-nine years of marriage she had no idea what he kept in there bar official papers about the family and so forth. The house rule was that no one would disturb anyone else's things. Aunt Emma, in whose house she grew up, would always be waiting for the postman outside the house and she didn't baulk at tearing up letters to other members of the family right there in the street. She didn't want to be like Aunt Emma.

If Antal hadn't turned up with that strange request she'd be lying next to Iza, allowing herself to fall asleep. But her son-in-law had disturbed her, much as the nurse had disturbed her at the clinic and, for the first time, she was beginning to wonder whether she knew everything about Vince. This bad feeling led her to think about the writing desk and what would happen if Iza should stumble across something she wasn't supposed to see, some secret of Vince's that was his alone and which he should have taken with him because it was nothing to do with those still living. He was thirty-one when he married, which is not that young after all, and why should Iza go through the God-knows-what souvenirs of his youth? She herself couldn't say what exactly these might be or what she was afraid of, but it was a panicky feeling: Vince had given a present to Lidia but she – his wife – had no idea of how that came about or what it meant, since she had always believed that Vince kept the picture of the mill above his bed out of habit, nothing else, and if this wasn't the case there was something she didn't know about Vince and she should be the one to discover it.

It wasn't an easy task she had given herself and she didn't feel free to cry. Iza must have suspected something in her sleep: she could hear her through the open door, moving, sighing and turning from one side to the other. She pulled the first drawer open but she didn't touch anything for a while, she simply closed her eyes so she couldn't see, all her deepest, most commanding instincts being against what she was about to do, which was a breach of trust, as if she were robbing and humiliating Vince who was lying helpless in the clinic and could no longer stop her. At the same time she felt closer to him than ever these last few afternoons; the drawers brought to mind a living Vince, it was the real Vince who was looking back at her, everything she came across, alive, speaking, full of energy.

The contents of the writing desk were in perfect order, as Vince's things always were. Order was as characteristic of her husband as it was of Iza, just as relative, unfeminine mess was characteristic of her. In the topmost drawer were tins and all kinds of official papers tied round with ribbons in the red-white-and-green national colours. The tins ranged from the tiny to a normal size, like treasures on a child's toy shelf.

In the first she opened there was a lock of Endrus's hair. She hadn't realised that he too had cut off a lock: there were two strands of hair either side of his medal, under glass, one from each child. Endrus's was soft and dark. How clearly it brought him back, this soft little snippet, that small cheerful face so like his mother's you could see it at a glance, so early lost that they had not so much as a photograph of him. Had he lived he would be forty-eight years old now. Oh, God, dear God!

She twisted the shiny lock of dark hair this way and that. Now he'd be together with his father. Endrus would have made a clumsy angel since he was a clumsy toddler too, dropping things all the time, his arm so weak.

What could it be like in heaven?

Certificates. Vince had shown her these once. The stream
of distinctions from the village school in Karikásgyüd and the
local *gimnázium*. Student name: Vince Szőcs; religion: protestant; born: 11 January 1880; birthplace: Karikásgyüd; father's
name: Máté Szőcs; occupation: dike-keeper.

How furious Aunt Emma was, slamming down her coffee
cup so hard it cracked. Dike-keeper! What's a dike-keeper?
She was not easily calmed down, to be told it didn't matter, he
had been dead a very long time and that it was Gergely Dávid
who had brought Vince up. 'The teacher in Karikásgyüd?'
asked Aunt Emma. 'Wonderful! Does he think a law degree
makes him one of the gentry now? Dike-keeper! And they sent
him to school, on public taxes, because he was so clever. Typical
of this ridiculously liberal country!'

She was sipping her coffee in the arbour, the lilac bent
towards her greying blonde hair, so she looked like a faded
bridesmaid with her dry, painted face and all those heavy slack
rings on her fingers. She thought how Aunt Emma went around
telling everyone, 'She is my goddaughter,' while she was
working in the kitchen and that she'd only be allowed into
the parlour when there were guests. 'She's the orphan of my
poor departed Margit.' To them she was a servant one moment
and a member of the family the next. Of course, if she married
Vince, who would read to Aunt Emma in the evenings, and
who would get up and keep her company when she had a fit
of asthma? She didn't allow servants in her room: their place
was in the cellar because all kinds of criminal acts are
committed at night and a servant might steal or even murder
a person.

She took the empty cup but she didn't run off into the kitchen with it, she ran to the gate instead. Vince was waiting for her on the small bench outside, his hat in his hands turning it over and round, and he laughed when he saw how she was out of breath from running, and there in her hand was Aunt Emma's coffee cup. 'Are you bringing that to me?' he asked and she just stood there not knowing whether to laugh or to cry because she had a fancy to do both. She answered, 'Ask her!'

The university handbook: *Vol. 1 of the Gaius Institution. One hour per week. Hungarian History and Constitution. Two hours a week*. Two picture postcards from Szentmáté that she sent to him when Aunt Emma took her there as a companion. Bills. Ilona Dávid's Certificate of Merit from the Girls' Finishing School, academic year 1904–5. Gergely Dávid, teacher's nursing expenses at the hospital in Békéscsaba 4–27 November 1907. Receipt for the payment of costs of gravestone for Gergely Dávid, teacher, erected Karikásgyüd, 22 April 1909.

Gergely Dávid.

'You don't know what he was like,' said Vince. 'Six foot six, thin as a rake, always smiling, though he was so poor he could hardly feed his children. When the river burst its banks everyone headed for cemetery hill, which was the highest point in the village. It was night and they were ringing bells. Two of my aunts ran after my mother towards the dike and I followed them but I fell and the people running behind me trampled over me. The two biggest terrors of our lives were Karikás, the river, and the dike. It was the teacher who found me, picked me up and carried me up the hill. I clung on to his neck and cried. I never saw any members of my family after that, my father's body was never even found. I'm really scared of water, Ettie.'

Two pebbles, clearly from Endrus's grave or from the teacher's, two smooth snow-white pebbles. One broken ivory paperknife, one unaddressed plain envelope, green, with a wax-paper patch in the middle, an ivory cigarette holder, also broken.

This ribbon was the one she wore in her hair. She never sat down in the Lion Ballroom, not for a moment, but kept spinning and twirling while the chandeliers danced in the mirror. It was a night to make her forget poor Aunt Emma and that she'd been an orphan since she was eight. She was waltzing with Ernő Szekeres, with Aunt Emma looking on, her knot of hair full of sparkling flame-like feathers, like an ageing parrot. Her gaze was disapproving because Ernő Szekeres was not *one of us*, with nothing to his name except a few more names. 'There's a lad there who never dances.' She pricked up her ears when they had completed God-knows-how-many circles of the hall. 'Vince Szőcs,' said Szekeres. 'A court clerk. He can't dance.' She almost missed her step, astonished that a young man should not know how to dance and simply stand there under the mirror watching other people dancing. She stared at Vince Szőcs in an insensitive, unbecoming manner. He in the meantime had just waved at Szekeres and made eye contact with him.

Here was Aunt Emma's obituary notice in which her name did not appear. Klári, the next poor relation in the line, whom Aunt Emma took in after Aranka, had sent it to them. And there was some earth in a box, and an empty piggy bank. Press cuttings dating to back to 1907. *South Hungary News*, 18 March. 'It's twenty years today since the Karikás flooded and burst the dike at Karikásrév, destroying five villages overnight, killing almost 200 people. The worst affected were Karikásrév and Karikásgyüd.'

A. P. Weisz's letter from America.

Good heavens, Weisz the chemist! How deathly cold he was in the attic: they brought him an eiderdown but he was still shivering under it, his hands and feet frozen as he sat on a mattress in the corner, weeping over his family. Vince had snatched him from the crowd in the air-raid darkness as he was standing in the queue in front of their house in Darabont Street. Vince just took a step out, the sky being pitch black, and tugged the nearest figure through the gap in the fence. The sirens were sounding by then and the guards were watching the sky, not those about to be marched off to forced labour. Weisz, the first tenant of the cellar, was in a panic, reciting psalms in an obsessive accusing voice. Haven't they had enough? Can't people respect his need for silence? Are those people still dropping bombs? Is God deaf? Can't people hear that he is praying? He had no great regard for Szőcs's family. The first time a respectful look flickered across his face was later, in the thick of the bombing, when at last they too took shelter in the cellar. You might very well be a scoundrel who was sacked from his job all those years ago – and what kind of people are you if the university rejects your daughter when you're not even Jewish? – but credit where it's due, you're not cowards. It wasn't that Vince wasn't frightened: his feet and hands were trembling with worry about Weisz, and the bombs.

No, she must stop, it was too painful. Suddenly it all seemed so recent, the voices, the very words, Iza whispering: 'Why hide him?' 'Because I had the chance to,' her father whispering back. Iza falling silent, folding her hands, clearly thinking it over. 'You're always doing good, but not in the best way,' she had said when she looked up. 'You're too naive.' 'I may be naive but I do know some things,' Vince had answered, his face twitching because a bomb had just fallen and he was terrified.

There were some photographs in the lower drawer, pictures of himself and Iza. Iza looked grumpy in her degree-award photo, her hair cropped, her eyes sullen, like a boy. Here were Vince's slides too. There was a time he was keen on photography, then in 1923 he sold the camera. She held the slides up to the light and tried to guess the subjects. There were shadows, black and white, unknown faces, men with moustaches and bowler hats, women with feathered hats and skirts that reached the ground. Who were they? Why did he take the pictures? There was a wood of some kind too, if that's what it was, and some rural buildings. She recognised the last: it was a negative of the picture he had given to Lidia. She put the box down as though she had burned herself.

Her own letters. Prospectuses, brochures advertising foreign towns, package holidays. A run of magazines: *Popular Physics*. Picture postcards from foreign places. He collected them though he never travelled anywhere; by the time he was ready to do so he wasn't well enough. Family documents, Iza's papers, baptismal certificates.

Here's the notice sacking him and here, on top of it, his rehabilitation document. Regarding *the terms of article 9590/1945 M.E.* . . .

'If you leave that man you can come back and all will be forgotten,' said Aunt Emma. 'What a disaster he is! But I warned you. What kind of man is it that can be brushed aside like that, as if he were a thieving servant? And him a county judge! Come home, I'm very lonely and you are familiar with my needs.' (Aranka, who succeeded her at Aunt Emma's, had just run off with Pista Vitáry.)

Aunt Emma sipped at her coffee and explained. 'I mean he wasn't mad, he knew very well what verdict he was supposed to bring in. He gets a cushy job, him, a boy raised on beggar's alms by that teacher who kept him financially, year by year, and then he does this. He knew he should have found them guilty, everybody knew that, but there he goes, letting off those four worthless peasants, excusing them in the name of the Sacred Crown of Hungary, the idiot. And when his colleagues try to repair the damage and offer him an opportunity to put things right, or at least retire quietly, he carries on bleating about justice – and refuses. Now he can see what justice means: it's been served on him. Your poor mother would turn in her grave if I deserted you now, so you can come back, dear, and live with me just as before, even though you left me in such an ungrateful way. I am willing to take you back if you like, but not with him. And you'll get no money, you needn't ask for that, I have no money myself and even if I had I wouldn't let your husband have it. Extraordinary! I hope he moves out of town. He can't stay here, that's impossible.'

After that she didn't go straight home but took a walk to the cemetery. It was summer, early summer, the roses were blooming on Endrus's grave. He'd been dead precisely eight years. She sat on a bench and gazed at his gravestone, overrun by roses, at the lush grass and the slow dense clouds. Nature was so calm, not *indifferent*, just calm. Bees were flitting around the graves. She felt deeply disappointed, gazing at the red roses and the blue sky. Why should a cemetery be so beautiful and so peaceful, so full of birdsong and scuffling in the branches when it wasn't reality? Reality was mortality and the sense of dread waiting for her at home.

She sat and sat. Then a pebble squeaked behind her. Startled, she turned round. It was Vince. He sat down beside her on the bench and stroked Endrus's grave as he did each time he came. 'I guessed you'd come here,' said Vince. She bent her head, ashamed that her first act had been to run to Aunt Emma for money and to complain, and how could she have spent a minute with Aunt Emma when she knew that she never liked Vince, that she was secretly glad how things turned out because she remembered the dike-keeper, their first conversations and was proud that her instincts had been proved correct when she disapproved of the marriage twelve years before.

It was so strange during the night to think that though Vince was always beside her while he lived, and healthy too, there was something that could have so embittered her. How she cried, how heart-rendingly when, after having been sacked, Vince explained that he was right, not the people who had sacked him, and of course she believed her husband but was unhappy because of money, because of all kinds of silly things, unhappy because acquaintances deserted them, because the family avoided them, because she was no longer greeted with as deep a bow as before. She felt ashamed now to recall what hurt her then, how cowardly she was, how humiliating her cowardice, how some of Aunt Emma's warnings took root in her. One night she tried to persuade Vince that they should move elsewhere. Anywhere, to Gyüd if he liked. Vince loved Gyüd. Each summer he would return there to stay with the teacher and his family and go on about what a lovely village it was, how the herbs were so fragrant by the river, how deep the whirlpools of the Karikás were and how the islands were a primeval forest of reeds. But Vince didn't want to move, which would be another reason to cry, because she thought moving was a wonderful idea, because they wouldn't be bumping into their town acquaintances, and because life was cheaper in villages and they could live on her widow's pension (Vince received nothing, but the generosity of the Ministry of Justice allowed her to draw such a pension, it being deemed possible to be the widow of a living man). No, said Vince, his face clouding over, he wouldn't go, he wasn't guilty, and there was no need for him to hide from people. Then he turned away and didn't want to talk about it any more.

Before his rehabilitation she could never persuade him to visit Gyüd and in November 1946, when the letter arrived, trembling, lips twitching, he took his small suitcase from the top of the wardrobe and started packing. She didn't need to ask him where he was going, she could see it from his face, the way he was shaking. She asked Iza to see him down there but she shook her head, pointed to her books and was interested in nothing but her approaching university exams. She wanted to talk her father out of the trip too, and spent the evening explaining to him that there were no hotels in Gyüd, that he had practically no living acquaintances there, that the teacher was long dead and that the Dávid children were all gone, working in one place or another. Those who were still there would stare at him as if he were some kind of curiosity. 'What do you want to see in Gyüd?' she asked her father. Vince stubbornly continued to pack his bag and answered, 'The dike!'

'Excuse me but I have not the least interest in the dike,' said Iza, lovingly stroking her father's arm. 'I'm afraid you can't pass on memories as if they were a kind of inheritance.' Vince just looked at her, his hand still above the suitcase, his face suddenly thinner, thinner and sadder. In the end he didn't go, since that was the time she got that awful flu and he didn't want to leave her while she was ill, and, besides, the weather was worse than usual, nor did he ever make the journey. He never saw his birthplace again, didn't even mention it much; he grew older and weaker, and rarely left the house. He was past sixty-six when they rehabilitated him, his movement was limited on account of rheumatism and his stomach was already troubling him; it was just that no one suspected what it would turn out to be.

She pushed the drawers shut. There was nothing unexpected here, which is to say no more than everything associated with fifty years of shared life. But there were no secrets among these common things, no photographs of women, no pressed flowers, no secret letters, nothing that did not pertain to Vince's childhood or family life. She felt ashamed of herself for ever having doubted him, even for a moment – she should have known Vince better. It was the effect of Antal and Lidia. By the time they got there, Dekker told them Vince was no longer conscious and he remained unconscious when she sat down beside him. Maybe he never told Antal to give the picture to Lidia but simply happened to whisper something and Antal misunderstood him. He was constantly whispering, poor thing, whispering time after time when he got the injections. And why would he have talked about dying? Vince knew nothing of that, never suspected.

She went into the hall, opened the door and looked out at the yard. The rain was still pouring down but it felt milder than in the afternoon. Captain spotted her and leapt up the steps. Ten years before he had done just the same, just as cheekily, when he skipped through their open door for the first time. It was 1 May and they were standing on the threshold, watching the flowers strewn from aeroplanes and the flight of doves that signalled the end of the day's festivities in the main square, as promised by the papers. Suddenly there was a knocking sound at the gate and a creature rather like a black rabbit, no bigger than someone's fist, slipped in. 'Here's the dove,' said Vince, laughing, 'strutting like a captain. It's just that it's black.'

The memory was so fresh, so hauntingly alive that she couldn't bear to bend down to the animal but turned round into the hall. The neighbour's cockerel crowed and slowly people woke. The sky was black, a single dark mass. 'Dawn,' thought the old woman. 'I wonder if he can see it?'

It was warm in the bedroom, too warm after the damp dawn breeze on the doorstep. She threw off the dressing gown and prepared to lie down next to Iza again. The girl turned but didn't wake: fast asleep and dreaming, her very breath a form of sadness. Now that she was facing the wall she could clearly see the picture, the painting above her bed that watched over her dreams. There goes the little girl, her basket on her arm, treading a rickety old footbridge, under the bridge a foaming mountain stream, her basket full of strawberries. You could practically hear the water beating at the rocks below, almost sucking her in, sweeping away the little aproned figure, and yet you wouldn't worry for her, because an angel was hovering over her, its sandal-shod feet steady in the air above the loose planks, its two arms extended in protection round the child who is carefree, chasing a butterfly over the rocky depths and the small, severe river.

The order of the next few days was determined by rural funeral customs. The mourners who came home with her were not too fussed about proprieties and stayed longer than the generally approved fifteen minutes though the old woman didn't mind: she liked talking about Vince. She served liqueur to her guests because the weather was unusually cold again, as if March were at war with itself, bringing hard winter days to frustrate the promise of spring. Iza said it was a barbaric custom having crowds round before a burial. She hated guests and was never at home. But there was no alternative and there was so much to do. Iza spent one morning at the clinic with Dekker, arranging things with the trade union social services, organised the funeral and was constantly negotiating at the estate office since it was no simple matter selling the house.

Apart from one unexpected local council member and a young clerk of court who was a total stranger, there was no one who failed to speak of Iza as well as Vince. Iza's reputation, her important job and the money she sent monthly, the regular supply of fuel she ordered for her parents, how she took them to the shoe shop, to the tailor's and to the doctor, was a matter of constant street gossip. The idea that she was moving her mother to Budapest was no surprise to anyone. Iza couldn't have done anything else; that was just the way she was. She was not only a brilliant doctor, a properly grateful child, but a good person. Mrs Szőcs must be so pleased with her. Old Vince had gone, of course, poor thing, but here was his daughter to take his place as protector. What delight it must be to move to Budapest, to leave sad memories behind and to enjoy a happy old age in new circumstances: it was not just to be free of cares and worries but to avoid loneliness at seventy-five and to give oneself over to peaceful reflection! Iza would look after her, she'd have nothing to worry about for the rest of her life.

Iza really did do everything for her mother, even tiny, insignificant-looking things. She cooked for her, made sure she ate, and when the doorbell rang and she happened to be at home she ran to answer it to make sure her mother didn't have to rush. Her great head of hair floated after her as she made speed. Vince hadn't been the same for ages and had to be excused various duties so all the responsibility was on the old woman's shoulders, right down to apparently small and insignificant tasks like opening the gate, which could be a serious problem when it rained in the winter because of the mud. Now it was Iza who would run to answer in the heavy downpour in her black skirt and pullover, looking as young as she had when she lived in the house as a girl, or as a bride of two days.

There was plenty for her to do and not much time for crying or thinking.

Before she left Pest she had taken a few days out of those due for her summer vacation and wanted to settle everything in that time – the funeral, discussions about the inheritance, the sale of now useless possessions, the moving and even the matter of the house. 'I don't want you to be involved in the removals,' she told her mother, 'you wouldn't be able to stop helping me and you won't be in top condition after the funeral. You're going to take a couple of days off in Dorozs, mama, I'll phone the sanatorium this evening. There you can relax, have a lie-in, look at the trees, read, sleep and buy a couple of sessions at the baths because it looks as though your bones need it. Once I've arranged everything I'll come to fetch you. Dekker is going to Pest on the eleventh and can give us both a lift in his car.'

Dorozs was a nearby town some fifteen kilometres away and had a sulphur-iodine spa whose hot waters had been described three hundred years ago, though the spa-sanatorium in the park was only six years old. It was a place they had longed to go to and had several times decided to take a trip there but, though there was an hourly bus, something always got in the way so they never went, just as they had never made it to the seaside, or to a good many other places in the world that they had talked about and prepared for. The old woman looked down into her lap as she listened to Iza's offer, then felt around for her handkerchief. It made her so happy to think how much Iza loved her and took care of her, but she had never been so sad in her life as when she finally went to Dorozs.

It was an enormous relief to her that she wouldn't have to live by herself in a house bereft of Vince, but it was terrifying not to be present while Iza packed up ready for the removal men. 'You'd only torture yourself,' retorted Iza, 'you have spent enough time crying. I know my flat, know where I am taking you, I know where things will fit and what will look best. I want you to be happy from now on.'

The thought that she would be looked after, that someone else would do her thinking for her, moved her again: her eyes filled with tears of gratitude. Iza was right, of course, she always was, it really would be awful if she herself had to pack Vince's belongings, it might be quite beyond her to fold away his familiar old-fashioned clothes and his brightly coloured caps. Ever since he got older, Vince had refused to wear proper hats and always wore caps with visors. Let Iza get on with packing those, once they are up in Pest and she feels better, she can put them into some order and stow them in the wardrobe. It will be as though both of them had moved up to live with Iza and maybe she would even talk to Vince's walking stick sometimes, or his heavy glass, his tin can, the one he used to warm shaving water in on the stove when the winter was extra cold. She secretly hoped that they could take everything to the city with them. Iza hadn't received a proper trousseau when she got married and Vince in particular felt very ashamed that it was only their own belongings they could share. Now she could happily make a gift of the lot, let it all go to Pest. She watched the girl's face in hope that she might like the idea of the gift but Iza shook her head and told her not to worry about things like that but to leave the job of moving to her. She calmly accepted: Iza always knew everything better than she did and no doubt she knew better now. Pity it seemed she couldn't take everything. Well, no doubt the girl would choose what she thought they would need in the big city, and as for the rest . . .

It does no good to think about that, she thought, so she turned her mind elsewhere.

She had spent a lifetime with this furniture that had grown

57

old and tired along with her, every piece with a history of its own. It hurt that she couldn't take it all. It hurt that she couldn't take the entire house and carry it with her to Budapest, because the house was only frightening if she had to be alone in it; if her daughter could be with her it would the most desirable of residences. But Iza had a freehold flat, why should they continue to pay tax on the house – if she wants to sell it, that's what she should do. And who would buy it? Anyone – she wished them well of it. But it was a shame about the little things that would have to be left behind. Never mind, there was no way round it. When Vince was alive he arranged everything for her, now it would be Iza. Wasn't it great that she wouldn't have to negotiate with the property office!

The night before the funeral, on that wholly unexpected evening, just as Iza was struggling to prepare a fish in the unheated kitchen, Antal appeared again. It was she, for once, who let him in. Iza was frying fish in breadcrumbs and she shouted to her to open the gate as she had to attend to the meal. It was raining, as it had done constantly for days. Antal was bareheaded, and his hair and brow were dripping. She couldn't remember ever seeing him in a hat; in winter his head was always covered in snow. Hearing his steps, Iza looked out of the kitchen. Seeing it was him, her face immediately froze into a polite smile. She excused herself, said she was cooking and asked if he fancied supper with them because there was enough. Antal thanked her and said he had already eaten. That clearly wasn't true but it wasn't something you could argue with.

Antal didn't beat about the bush. He asked how much it was for the house. Last time Iza was at the clinic she mentioned it was for sale. He himself was looking to move and would be pleased to buy it if they could agree a price.

She stared at Antal in astonishment. She hadn't thought of him as someone who would ever buy a house.

'If you cared to leave some furniture behind, mama,' said Antal, 'I would be happy to take that off your hands too.'

She looked so delighted, she hadn't felt as happy since just before Dekker's diagnosis three months before. She still didn't know what Iza wanted to keep or sell, but she was already sorry for such items as fell into other hands; it was as if they were endowed with life, with voices and feelings, that they were beings who, having enjoyed long-term security, were now obliged to go into exile and spend the night in strange people's houses, sighing for home. Antal, it is true, had abandoned them, but in some ways he did belong here.

But, having heard this, she had to call in Iza now.

Iza smelled of fish and oil, and this made her unrecognisable in some way. Iza was always so clean, so cool, it was as if she wanted to distance her body from the grime and grease of house-keeping, so she was quite shocked to see her flushed with cooking. There was something in Iza that didn't resist this time: she was about more important business so she let the kitchen get the better of her. 'It's a matter of care and necessity,' the girl had explained once. 'A person can be in possession of herself, even in a kitchen.' She was not in possession now: cooking and its ingredients had overcome her composure. Iza was less bothered with herself this evening. What was she bothered with?

She stood and listened to the reason for his visit. Later the old woman would be puzzled to explain the peculiar look on her face. For some reason she did not seem to welcome

Antal's offer. She was inwardly praying that her daughter, whatever her reasons, would not reject it. If they couldn't be here at least let Antal remain. She didn't dare say anything since all her life it was someone else who arranged things, but deep inside her she would have been willing to let the house go at any price Antal offered, provided the dragon spout was looked after and Antal was conscientious about watering Vince's flowers. Antal had always helped Vince chop wood and knew that the trunk they used to cut on had its own pet name, Dagi.

'Do you really want to settle here?' asked Iza.

Her voice was calm and so controlled that even the old woman noticed it was costing her a great deal of effort to hold something back, that there was an unspoken question lurking somewhere in the background. Antal didn't answer but looked for his cigarettes while Iza just stood there. The old woman muttered something, feeling Iza wouldn't mind if on this one occasion she broke the agreement not to leave them together by themselves. Yesterday, or the day before yesterday, they had after all been obliged to speak to each other when Iza was at the clinic thanking Dekker and that nurse for their kindness. She whispered something about supper and sneaked out. The oil was simmering on the cooker though Iza had taken the pan off the flame. Suddenly she felt she couldn't eat a mouthful: the oily half of the fish was glimmering as if it were alive.

She sat out there a good while till eventually Iza raised her voice to tell her Antal was leaving.

'Have you agreed?' she asked in hope.

He was setting off but the old woman didn't want to let him go out unescorted so she saw him out. Antal hesitated in the doorway for a moment, as though he wanted to say something conciliatory or reassuring but said nothing in the end, simply kissed her, turned up his collar and went off into the rain. She gazed after him until he was gone, though it wasn't Antal she wanted to see but the image, to hold on to it as long as possible, the gentle curve of the street, the lights in the windows, Kolman's crude but proudly lit shop display. People squelched their way through the water, the tops of their umbrellas flashing in the light. The wind was southerly again, the clouds, the moonless sky, squatting on the low roofs. It was the first time in her life she felt the earth was round, not flat; that it was slowly but unmistakably turning under her feet. How could Vince's tiny and ever more wasted body represent such security for her? She stood there, leaning against the gatepost that hadn't seemed quite real to her for days, as if Vince had taken the reality of the stones and planks away with him and left only a ball of white noise, a mere fog behind. Under the teeming March evening and the cloudburst sky she felt once more, as for the last time, the close physical presence of Vince, his grey hair floating around the street lamp at the bend of the road. Fog was settling, a spring mist, and in the distance she could hear the swish of wheels cutting through standing water in the rain-drenched main road.

They were driven to the funeral in Dekker's car. The professor was sensitive and ordered a taxi for himself so as to leave Iza and the old woman alone. Mrs Szőcs had wanted to set out long before the ceremony started but Iza wouldn't let her, which seriously upset her; she wanted a few minutes alone with the coffin before it was surrounded by strangers. 'You are my only relative,' said Iza, keeping her lovely, serious eyes on her. 'I am both your daughter and your doctor, mum.

It's not just the dead that need to rest, the living do too. I don't want you to have cried your eyes out: your heart is old, you are no longer young. I have to take care of you.'

She didn't cry at first, not because of the medicine Iza made her take, but because her grief was tinged with a kind of awkward joy: it was days since she had seen Vince and now that she knew she would see him one more time she would be free to kiss him and adjust his tie. She did not look out from the car window but kept her eyes fixed on her lap, thinking of what she would say to him when she saw him. He must know that Iza had decided to take her back to Pest but he might not have caught up with Antal's offer yet. She would promise him to eat more from now on, and apologise to him for not giving him enough painkillers but she had very much wanted him to live, to live at least as long as possible. She was preparing to talk to him as though he were alive, the only problem being that time was limited.

All the same, she was trembling before they arrived at the mortuary. The velvet-covered doors and the bare ornamental trees in their plant stands frightened her. The first person she saw on opening the door was Kolman, who was wearing a black tie – she liked that – and then the bier. She stopped on the threshhold and burst into tears. The coffin lid was closed.

That hurt her more than the last four days with all their sorrows had. Iza took her arm and led her to the bench. She sat down, the tears escaping through her gloved hands. Iza said nothing, just sat beside her, her back straight, absolutely still. She knew Iza was acting for the best, that it was wiser to behave like this, that Iza was protecting her, that she was acting as a barrier between her and death, but still it hurt that she could not see his face which even four days ago had begun to look like that of a stranger. She listened to the service, weeping throughout, feeling it was not addressed to her or anything to do with her; she couldn't follow the prayer either and felt further from the peace of the grave and the thought of resurrection than she had ever done. She sobbed stubbornly like a child, and was not in the least comforted by the promise that the grave represented calm after a life of tribulation and that it would be followed by eternal light. She clung to Vince's body as she had done in the first terrifying, passionate months of their marriage. Heaven was a long way off and offered no recompense.

When the funeral procession set off she followed the coffin, leaning on Iza's arm, not seeing who came after them, feeling simply that there were more people than she expected. The carriage left deep tracks in the mud, the dripping damp soaked into their coats. No one put up an umbrella: no one felt it was appropriate. Vince had never ridden in such a vehicle before, such a dignified, black, glazed car, and no one had ever paid as much respect to him as these people from the undertaker's. Everything she was going to say remained unsaid and she couldn't even string sentences together as they trooped along. There was nothing of Vince on show, just the lid of the coffin that covered him. The priest looked a little offended at the graveside, possibly annoyed at having wasted his time promising eternal joy to people who didn't appreciate it, but she carried on sobbing as the earth was shovelled in. Vince's grave was small, somehow much smaller than she had imagined it would be. She didn't care how many people were looking; she knelt down and kissed the wooden headpost.

As she was bending down, wiping away the tears, she spotted Lidia. She was in a black coat that she must have borrowed because it didn't fit her, with black gloves and hat. She had never liked this girl, and was pained by the sad look in her eyes and the movement with which she laid a small bouquet on the mound.

When they reached town the car stopped in the central square without turning down their street. She stared ahead. There was the yellowish glow of the hotel where they had sat just three months before in the café with the red curtains discussing Vince's impending death, and next to it, in the downpour, the travel and airline offices, with a bus, and in the yard next to it a long-distance coach, its heavy blue bulk washed with rain.

Iza got out; they were looking for something at the back of the car and emerged with a suitcase. It was Iza's brown travelling case, the light luggage she had arrived with. Iza shook the driver's hand and the car drove off.

'Now you are to drink some coffee and then you're off.'

She didn't understand at first and simply stared.

'You need coffee because you're frozen through, then you are getting on the bus. It leaves in ten minutes for Dorozs. Here's your case.'

'Now?'

'Now,' Iza answered. 'You've shed enough tears. If you went back to the house now you'd only go round and round the rooms and get yourself worked up again. I'll arrange everything here and once I've finished I'll follow you. There are books and medicine in the case, and I have asked the hotel to get the desk clerk to help you fill in the official papers relating to your arrival.'

She followed her obediently, in silence. There were just three people in there. They immediately brought the coffee. She stared at the brown surface of the liquid, stirring it. It was very dreamlike. Here she was, a small child again with a bag on her arm, led by her mother, an adult Iza — Iza in black, looking pale. Iza's hand was strong, as was her voice telling her, 'No crying!'

Would she never see this town again, nor the house where she had lived with Vince?

Iza rose and paid.

The bus smelled of petrol. There were hardly any passengers on board: a woman with a stick was clambering on before them. Iza put the case on the luggage rack. She must have packed it at night, while she was asleep, and when would she have had time to talk to the hotel?

The bus set off so soon they didn't even have time for a proper goodbye. Iza simply took a step back and the conductor slammed the door. The rain was so dense it was almost impossible to see through it and she could only guess at her daughter's shape as she stood in the hotel entrance. 'To Dorozs?' asked the conductor. The word suggested summer, the scent of flowers, and Vince was present, somewhere behind the words, but suddenly it was as if a force had seized him: he was sliding away, vanishing. The bus was passing through the railway workers' quarter, over the big bridge. She could see the white board of the railway station, trains were puffing under the bridge. The rain fell in sheets.

'To Dorozs,' the old woman confirmed.

The windscreen wiper was moving up and down the windscreen.

II

FIRE

I

Though she had seen more than one photograph of the town, Dorozs didn't look as she had imagined it.

Once, as a young girl, she had escorted Aunt Emma to the spa at Szentmáté and it was the picture of the town that remained with her: the sound of bells in the main square, musicians in the open air at lunchtime, drinking fountains in the shade of the plane trees, an awkward-looking restaurant with shutters and a large coach entrance at the foot of rolling hills, the lake shore, the lido, the violet-coloured, grass-green, steel-grey, sometimes dark-red waves, the juddering white teeth of the foam when the wind blew. The village of Szentmáté was high up the hill, the streets climbing the slope as if the whole settlement were on a race to the top. When they went for a walk in the village they would be greeted by thin grumpy men drying nets rather than by mugs and tankards on racks, long-eyed, dark-skinned women, and barefoot children scampering after chickens or watching the guests at the spa. The houses were thatched, on the thatch there were storks and above the village the hard, cold sky, with tiny tree-capped peaks of volcanoes in the far distance; the window of the village store displayed flypaper and yellow sugar for sale.

There was no post office in the village, just the one at the spa. It was the same with the chemists and the surgery, though the funeral parlour was in the main street of the village, its light-blue and dark coffee-coloured coffins on show next to the shoe shop. Kammerman's coffins would have been out of place at the spa.

Dorozs was a lowland village, built on sand surrounded by a dark ring of forests and was nothing like Szentmáté; in fact it was like no village she remembered from her childhood. Looking through the bus window she saw a pastry shop, a cinema, a sports pitch, the doctor's surgery, and they passed a big building where a programme was posted on the gate as on a theatre entrance. The goods in the butcher's tiled shop were glowing pink with an extensive choice of pork chops and she turned her head away because the sight of fresh meat upset her though she couldn't have said why. There were large greenhouses dense with early peppers and lettuce. Antennae – some of them TV antennae – had replaced the storks on top of the roofs and in the general store there were plastic tablecloths, various kinds of spray, nylon stockings, washing machines and buckets. The little yard in front of the school was loud with children, the girls in neat shiny aprons with embroidered pockets over blue tracksuits, their ponytails tied round with wide silk ribbons. Somehow she imagined children wearing everyday boots but most of the little boys had ski boots or cross-laced maroon hiking shoes. The children were chubby, clean and well behaved, chattering away, waiting for noon when they could go home. A mother was pushing a pram, a deep, rose-coloured, streamlined pram. None of the younger people looked like a peasant, thought the old woman, and this very much surprised her.

As if ashamed of themselves, the clouds broke and bare trees began to tremble in the intensely bright unexpected sunlight: they looked as though they were gasping for air or exhausted after a furious dash. The sun rested on the water gathered in the ditch, now dipping, now rising. Cars were battling through the mud and commercial vehicles were chugging towards approach roads. The sky was still grey on either side but blue in the middle, and the individual colours above the village were constantly changing, as though searchlights were sweeping the sky above the street and between the houses, now faintly smoke-coloured, now a kind of yellow. The road turned off into the forest and, a stone's throw from the last house in the main street, the spa hotel rose like a tower before her. It was Iza's tower.

It was the first time she had actually seen it.

Ever since childhood Iza had been interested in the wagons arriving from Dorozs, and was particularly fascinated by Dániel Bérczes's scruffy little horses, so much so she couldn't be drawn away until she had watched them taking thermal water to whichever house had ordered it, her little face transformed in the steam, mysterious, almost expressionless. Her father had explained to her why local people ordered the waters from Dorozs and told how, when he was a child, the peasants would sit round the spring with their trousers rolled up, soaking their feet in the clay basins at the spring edge, drawing in their breath on account of the heat. The last two years of Iza's and Antal's engagement were dedicated to the fight for the spa, their ideas for the hotel, the chemical analyses of the waters, the conferences and the discussions. By the time the spa opened, Iza and Antal had separated, Vince's health had begun to decline and it was only in the press that they read of the ceremony whereby the building was handed over to the village. The girl should have been there at the opening but she just sent a telegram and didn't go; Antal went by himself.

Iza's involvement with the spa was so close it was almost as if she were part of the brickwork, said Dekker on one occasion.

Now there it stood in front of her, the five-storey concrete-and-glass hotel-sanatorium, a monument to her daughter's will and care, in the middle of enormous grounds that looked like nothing she had ever seen, that didn't even remind her of the drinking fountain and shuttered hotel at Szentmáté. Iza had shown her architect's drawings and photographs of the whole site on completion, but she was no good at visualising plans and the press photo didn't really give an idea of scale. Now she stood in awe, swallowing deeply and staring at the façade with its enormous lettering.

The woman with the stick, who had got on the bus before her, now got off. She moved with difficulty and the driver handed down her luggage separately.

A man in a uniform stepped over from the stop, looked through the door and asked if she was Mrs Szőcs because, if she was, he had come to meet her. She babbled something and stretched up to get her case but the uniformed man sprang up and lifted it off for her. He helped her get off too and, taking her arm, escorted her into the entrance hall that smelled of sulphur and was steamy, but somehow quite dry and warm at the same time. There were palms in maiolica pots standing in a circle and, under them, small yellow tables. She had no idea where to go so the uniformed man led her to the carpeted part. The checkered stone floor had been polished to a blinding gloss and was slippery.

The clerks at the reception desk had prepared the necessary papers for her and she just had to sign them. The uniformed man took her to the lift — it was her one anxious moment because she didn't like lifts — and took her up to the fourth floor. The door he opened for her led into a hall, where the uniformed man deposited her luggage in front of the built-in wardrobe and left through the inner door. The old woman looked after him in confusion because she felt she ought to have tipped him, he being so nice, but she calmed down when she remembered hearing or reading somewhere that nowadays people didn't give tips.

She had never stayed in a hotel by herself before and she felt a little frightened.

She'd like to have known whether there were people staying either side of her, and whether she could leave everything safely in the wardrobe when she went out because there might be thieves in such places too. She consoled herself with the thought that, because of Iza, they would take special care of her, so eventually she started looking around. She opened every door, including the cupboard doors, thinking they might lead to a sitting room or a parlour, and she inspected the bathroom and the cupboards inside it. She found it all strange, uncomfortable and cold. She dragged her finger along the arms of the chair and felt confused and disappointed: the furniture was ugly. The colours, the patterns, the vases, the ashtrays — everything — was somehow comical, frightening, almost grotesque. She was sorry that Iza's fine plans had been so much ignored, that they had ruined her dreams. There was a picture on the wall, nothing but a mass of blotches that might perhaps represent a landscape – she had done some drawing in her youth and thought she understood art – and immediately concluded that the thing couldn't be worth much. There wasn't any pattern she could pick out on the carpet either, though later she spotted an image of some kind of bird in the blue material, a bird with broken wings. Poor little creature.

She unpacked and was amazed to see how Iza knew exactly what she needed: all her washing things were there, the medicine to take for her blood pressure and the laxative. She'd even put a book in, one of Vince's books, by someone called Kis, next to her lilac bed jacket and her reading glasses. Iza wouldn't know, of course, that she rarely read now because her eyes were increasingly not up to it. She leafed through the book and started in horror. Under the title page there was money, hundred-forint notes. How lucky she had spotted them and hadn't left it out! Why did the girl give her so much money, after all, she was coming herself and would pay the bill, wouldn't she? How could she walk around with so much money on her? She'd worry about leaving such a sum in the room in case someone stole it, but if she took it with her she'd be in fear of everyone in the street. Five hundred forints! It was a vast amount.

Feeling fed up, she put the money in her cardigan pocket, which she fastened with a safety pin. She pondered what to do. She didn't feel like walking and rather fancied a lie down but was worried in case she fell asleep and missed dinner. That was another thing she'd like to get over and done with: it was frightening to think of going down into the restaurant by herself and ordering food. Iza had packed her crochet work too; however did she find it? She hadn't done any crocheting for years; it was three years since she started on that nice star pattern but then Vince had ever more problems, there was far too much to think about, not to mention her eyes, and she had abandoned it. But how nice it would be to crochet again.

She tried starting on a small star, crocheted for a few minutes, then dropped the yarn because it wasn't going well. What a shame, that was one less harmless pastime. Though she had been given the pattern by Gica and it would have made a beautiful tablecloth, just right for Iza's flat.

Thinking of Gica suddenly terrified her.

Rural customs cast their long shadows over her so she couldn't see anything else. The leafless, agitated trees and the tremulous sunshine disappeared. Dear Lord, she had failed to register who had been at the funeral; Iza had sat her in the car before she could count them and discover who had sent flowers and wreaths, and now she couldn't thank them. Custom demanded that she should stay home for a week after the funeral, then, in the second week, begin to do the rounds of mourners and write the appropriate letters of thanks for flowers and for being there. She was bound to remember the local people but, to her embarrassment, she couldn't remember whose hands she had shaken that morning, nor did she hold out much hope that Iza would remember because she didn't know everyone in town and, if she herself paid insufficient attention, how could she expect the girl to have done so when she was busy looking after her mother too? Apart from a couple of close acquaintances and friends she recalled just one face: Lidia's, with childish tears in the corner of her eyes. There were some unfamiliar people there, who looked like doctors and might have been old colleagues of Iza's. Who else was at the funeral? Whom should she write to?

Iza hadn't put any paper in the suitcase, but maybe she has a calling card somewhere. Aunt Emma had taught her always to have one. Yes, there it was. She found a pencil and listed the names of people who had visited her at home. She felt a little easier now. This was at least one thing she could do, having left town so quickly without thanking anyone. How fortunate that she realised it in time – it would have been a gross insult if she hadn't.

She was startled to hear someone knocking and said nothing, just waited. When they knocked again she went to the door and opened it just a little so she could look out. It was the waiter bringing a menu, who explained that the doctor lady had arranged for her to have her meal in the room.

She was childishly pleased about this. She chose the children's portions because they were cheaper, and once they had removed the dishes from the room she lay down on the sofa with the maddening pattern and immediately fell asleep.

It was the first time since Vince had died that she slept without dreaming. When she woke she felt frightened and upset. Throughout these last days she had somehow felt her husband's presence close to her, had seen him in all her dreams, but now, as never before, she felt he had forsaken her. He wasn't there any more; he had flittered off somewhere. At home she would get such a fright at Vince's returning image that she would wake up, even in the middle of the night, and burst into tears; here she missed the fright those dreams had given her.

At first she thought she might go for a walk, but then decided otherwise. Dorozs – Dorozs the village – seemed too much of an excursion for the first day, it would be better if she sat down and wrote those letters. She made her way down to the check-in desk and asked if they could get her some writing paper suitable for correspondence. They gave her a whole dozen: fine, long, narrow sheets of paper, satin-textured, with a blue stamp in the corner saying Dorozs Sanatorium, showing a fountain spurting a high slender stream of water. Nothing to pay – the clerk just smiled.

She wrote the same letter to everyone. It took her a long time and a lot of care, and she had to keep rubbing her eyes because it was tiring work. She had trouble addressing the envelopes because besides their own, she only knew a few of the more recent street names; they had been changed so often she lost track and it was only the wartime changes of name that she recalled or, sometimes, the original name of her childhood. The letter to the newsagent she addressed to *The House at The Unicorn Pharmacy*, which she knew must be wrong because the name, The Unicorn Pharmacy, had long been changed to some ordinary number and instead of the clumsily drawn, melancholy unicorn's head there was a simple black trade sign over the entrance. Ever since that sign was put up she had hated going to the chemist's. Why couldn't they have a standard red pharmacy sign: red stood for health. Why black? She couldn't remember the name of the street where the teacher lived either so she addressed it to *Franz Joseph Street* and immediately felt ashamed because Vince had no time for Franz Joseph. She put 'ex' in brackets next to it. So many names: *Sóvágó Street, Salétrom, Oldalkosár Road, Gubás Street.*

Everything had a new name, even Balzsamárok Street. The post office would know.

She planned to order some coffee, toast and a boiled egg for supper but however she studied the menu she couldn't find the items on it. Then, of course very shyly, she asked the waiter about them and he, after a moment's hesitation, brought her everything she wanted. Having dozed off in the afternoon she thought she wouldn't be able to sleep, but as soon as she climbed into bed she was gone. Her last thought was that the convertible bed was far too narrow and uncomfortable for the purpose.

She woke in the morning thinking that somehow she was not so fond of Dorozs after all.

It wasn't a simple feeling: there was far too much involved in it. Because she liked Dorozs itself, and that included Dorozs the village too; it was a good place for walking in, gazing at the shops, watching the traffic pass through the narrow streets, the voices of strangers buying souvenirs in the general store, taking pictures of the sanatorium from every possible angle. She liked the baths too and she took pride in the main weights pool, the little booths with their steam-covered walls, the hot springs where the afflicted could splash about inside a glass cage shaped like a cave, under the cooling pipes. She liked the spa quarters of the hotel, but not the hotel itself. She felt it wasn't homely, not even as comfortable as a guesthouse might be, every object in it confusing and as alien to her eyes as the electric toaster back home. She could hardly wait to get to Pest and start building a proper home again, complete with Captain, house plants and old furniture . . .

She had one carefree afternoon when she imagined furnishing their new flat. She felt good about this, cheerful, almost happy.

She had never seen Iza's flat in Pest, had never really seen Pest itself. The only time she had visited it was on her honeymoon; their marriage was preceded by so much trouble, so many arguments and family anxieties, and life seemed so uncertain, that their lives together started on a very tight budget. They had to go somewhere, because every couple they knew went away on honeymoon. Venice was too far away, as was the mountainous Tátra region and Transylvania; Pest looked more likely and it didn't much matter where they went really, the main thing was that they shouldn't become objects of local gossip. When she was a young woman it was improper not to go away after you were married.

Pest had been a special experience, one she wouldn't forget. Even today she treasured its charm, its bohemian quality, its mild frivolity, that certain lightness in the air, the women and men with their quite different looks. Well now, there were real hotels there, with real beds and real wardrobes with mirrored doors. Poor Iza, how excited she was about this building. She must have felt like a mother does about her child – even the ugly looks beautiful.

Antal left Iza in 1952. She changed clinics and moved out in 1953. It took her less than six months to find a suitable flat in Pest. Two rooms, a hall and a servants' room – Iza had written – the furnishing was far from settled. That was no surprise to either Vince or herself; it takes a long time to make a home, a very long time. There was probably about as much space in the flat as there was in the house, though sadly it came without a garden, but then it might be possible to do something with the balcony. How wonderful it would be to furnish Iza's flat, how happy she would be when she first came back to the finished thing and saw everything in its place, just as she remembered it from childhood, and mama's best home cooking.

She made a drawing of the flat using her imagination and planned where she would put everything, finding room for all the furniture. It might be a little crowded but it would all be there apart from the kitchen table and the pantry cupboard, the silly girl having arranged a built-in kitchen, which meant having to sell some of the older items, though it was the best wood and the paintwork was only a little worn, because they took great care of it. She took great delight in the effort, drawing little semicircles for chairs, a square for the table and oblongs for the beds. She carefully put the plan away in her bag so she could produce it when Iza appeared and they could get straight to work. The furniture would have arrived by now, Iza will have sent it up by truck. There'd be plenty to do once they got to Pest. But it would be good work and it made her happy to think about it. Making a home.

It was a week before Iza came for her.

She was already asleep when, on the third day, the phone on her bedside table rang and she felt around for it in a panic. She didn't know how to put on her reading lamp and it was always the ceiling light that came on instead. She picked the phone up clumsily, in the same state of agitation she experienced each time it was Budapest on the other line. In fact, the old woman was as terrified of the phone as she would have been of some tamed but unpredictable wild animal.

It was Iza calling from Pest. She kept gripping the phone. How come Iza was in Pest? Why had she left her here?

'I had to change the plans,' said Iza, 'though it meant

rearranging my timetable. I realised it would be best for me to come here first and attend to things. Can you hear me, darling?'

She had heard.

'Everything will be ready by the time you arrive. Pleased?'

She wasn't pleased, but she didn't say so. She was happy that, once again, everything had been done for her, but she thought of the slip of paper in her handbag and tears came to her eyes. She would so have loved arranging the flat herself! It was Iza having to manage everything again. What she and Vince had been hoping for round about Christmas – that once, just this once, she would forget to give them a present and that there would only be presents for Iza under the tree, small, worthless, glittering things they had bought for her – that hope was gone. Iza always arrived with a mass of presents, and it made everything they had bought look so cheap and insignificant that they felt ashamed each time they lit the candles and, furthermore, it sometimes occurred to them that Iza was having to tear herself away from so much work that the festive season and Christmas Eve must be a nuisance to her.

'I'll be with you by Thursday,' Iza promised. 'I'll come by train. You can meet me at the station if you like and we can turn right round after I've had a quick lunch. I'll pick you up and carry you home the way a dog does its puppies. We'll dash off to Pest. I'm so looking forward to seeing you, mama!'

This calmed her somehow and she felt more at peace though Thursday was four days away yet and she still had no idea what to do with the time. She was 'looking forward' to seeing her, said the girl. She played around with the expression and was still thinking about it the next day as she went for a walk to the village and back, gazing at the fields that were being readied for spring, aware of the bitter scent of bark and leaves and snowmelt that promised the onset of milder weather. She ventured into the forest too but stuck to the path parallel with the trunk road because she felt safer there, bending down now and then to pick up a small twig. If they were heating the flat for the first time they could use her twigs to start the fire. She would dry out the twigs in the hotel where it's always far too warm, the heat rising from a sheet of metal punched full of holes under the window. She'd place the twigs in the grate and they'd be dry as bone. Once the fire was lit the twigs would conjure her birthplace, even the old house perhaps, so there'd be no break, life would simply continue, its seam unbroken.

She wanted to pick twigs that were exactly similar, perfect twigs not rotten ones wasted under snow, so it was no easy task. She spent four days walking slowly, delicately along the forest path, four full mornings collecting enough for a bundle. She spent the four afternoons sleeping and dreaming, occasionally weeping, thinking of Vince and the people at home, wondering whether they'd consider her letters boastful or flashy with the glossy print of the sanatorium on the letterhead. Perhaps not. After all, they knew her.

On Thursday a uniformed driver took her to the railway station, explaining on the way that it was the usual practice to fetch the chief medical officer – meaning her daughter – when she arrived. The train was precisely on time. Iza was no longer in black and was calmer, almost cheerful. She didn't complain of tiredness; on the contrary she took delight in explaining that she had done all she had intended to do. Antal had actually gone and bought the house, all the furniture had been moved and the money received for the property and the effects was safely stowed in a savings account. And her mother looked very well, so she was really happy. It hadn't been an easy week, of course. How could it have been?

After the meal, while she was washing her hands and stuffing her overnight things next to the twigs in the suitcase, she caught herself smiling and humming some old tune. Tonight she'd light a fire and she'd have a home again. She blushed in alarm — it was as if she'd committed an act of infidelity. How could she feel so good without Vince?

Iza went to the desk to pay.

She gazed at her daughter, watching her taking her leave and paying the bill, thinking how clever she was, how charming, how polite, how well she knew what to say, when and to whom. She had often thought she should take a husband again because life consisted of such things as well as her medical work, but now she was glad there wouldn't be a stranger waiting for them. The old woman felt light-hearted and strong this afternoon: she thought of the twigs in the suitcase and that Iza would never guess that it was not she taking her mother home, but the other way round because she would light the fire for her, the first real fire in the place.

The uniformed man took her baggage on to the express and put it on the rack but Iza adjusted it a little. She always had to be doing something, it just couldn't be helped.

'Did you buy any salt in Dorozs?' she asked.

She didn't answer but smiled and gazed through the window.

The train both scared and bewitched her. It was a long time since she last travelled by the express, and the worm-like green of the locomotive and its carriages with their strong lights and almost silent running cast a spell on her. They took supper in the dining car and it saddened her a little that she couldn't cut up her meat in the shaking carriage. Iza sliced up the fried ribs and poured a beer for her. It also upset her to think they were going so extraordinarily fast she couldn't see out though it was still light. When Iza told her they were nearing Pest, she smiled and even felt a little moved. When she last came this way forty-nine years ago, Vince was wearing a black cape with a wide collar, a travelling cap, and a wild-pigeon-coloured suit. Behind the newspapers and bags of sweets they kept reaching for each other's hands. Old Pest was like a coloured balloon floating over reality, closer to heaven than to earth.

She saw nothing of the suburbs; the express clattered through Greater Budapest, and once they arrived at the terminal she felt quite lost. Iza was annoyed. There wasn't a porter nearby and she had to carry the luggage herself, constantly stopping and changing hands. The old woman didn't dare ask her if she had remembered to bring the firewood as well as the furniture from home, not wishing to irritate her, though it had just occurred to her how useful it would have been had Iza not forgotten it. The girl was bent over sideways with the weight of the case, running towards a taxi while the old woman was being swept along by the crowd.

She recognised nothing in town even though Iza was constantly keeping her informed as to where they were, but she recalled having once been to the National Theatre to see the classic, *Bánk Bán*. The big ring road was quite different from how she remembered it and she felt ashamed for having imagined it the way she had seen it before, since it was obvious this was just another road full of cars, buses and trams – horses were uncommon even back home by then. But all the same.

The crowds were overwhelming, as were the neon signs flashing on the buildings. Pest was much bigger than she remembered — it was an alarming metropolis.

They stopped in front of a house. She stared at it. Iza paid the driver and by the time she turned round she no longer looked annoyed. She smiled at her, stroked her shoulders and pointed to their new home.

It was a six-storey house, a cube faced in smooth masonry with a balustrade running round the top of it and fully glazed rooms facing the street. There was a mosaic next to the entrance and a young overweight mother was sitting on the steps breast-feeding her baby. The old woman tried to imagine she was arriving home but it was impossible. She just kept staring.

Iza went ahead and rang for the lift. There were a great many names on the board in the hall: vast numbers of people lived here. She pulled herself together so her expression should not give her away. She couldn't help it, the poor girl, that she could only afford something in a house like this. She musn't depress her with her own disappointment. And in any case, once they stepped through the door they'd be back in the old house until they had to go downstairs; they could forget where they were. What wonderful luck that they could bring every-thing they could with them, what wonderful God-given luck!

She felt able to smile again.

The lift stopped on the third floor and not even the door to the flat looked like any other door: it was as though someone had used a plane to cut a narrow channel into a piece of wood. Iza put down the case and the door opened.

'Welcome, dear guest,' said Iza. Her voice was solemn and loving.

She walked into blinding light, with a peculiar-shaped lamp on the ceiling, and nothing on the walls of the hall bar a couple of odd iron hooks for coats. Where did the girl put the old coat stand? There was a parquet floor and Captain knew how to behave, but what would happen if he ever . . . Where was Captain?

The flat was nothing like the one she imagined in Dorozs. There were two big intercommunicating rooms opening on the street side, both full of furniture. Blue, yellow, purple and black chairs were ranged in a row and the walls were coloured too. There were no lace curtains but a kind of thick, green and lilac striped canvas.

Could Iza have put all the home furniture into her room? Might her room be big enough to accommodate it all?

'And where is my room?' she asked. Her tongue felt dry in her mouth, as if she had a fever.

Iza opened the hall door smiling exactly as she had done when she let her into the flat, a smile that seemed even brighter than before, and opened another door, one of two practically identical doors, and reached for the light switch. 'Here, mama.'

Once again light, light, light. It was a small square room with her old bed in the corner, and a strange new lamp by the bedside in the shape of some black bird with a sulphur-yellow umbrella in its mouth. There was a cupboard on the right and a big chair that might have been Vince's but re-covered, her little sewing table in front of it and a tiny writing table by the window with its own chair.

There was a new bookcase and shelves on the wall, the shelves full of all kinds of strange objects. Her bureau. Nothing else. The carpet was new too, the old worn one having vanished: she was standing on a fine, deep-blue Persian carpet.

Her savings book was on the writing desk.

She needed to do something, to gain time, so that she'd know what to say. She made her way over to the writing table, picked up the savings book and leafed through it. Without her glasses she couldn't make out the balance but she looked at it anyway as if she could read it. Her hand was shaking so much that the thin sheets trembled against her fingers.

Iza gave her a hug.

'The other things had to stay behind, darling. What we have here has been repaired by the upholsterer and the furniture man. Isn't it perfect and lovely? What do you think of the lamp? Is it right, do you think? Do you like it? And the carpet? Pretty, isn't it?'

She made no answer.

'You're home. Look at me! Aren't you pleased?'

'Where's Captain?' asked the old woman.

'With Antal. You didn't want to bring the old rabbity dog too?'

She didn't ask about the house plants, about Vince's peaked caps or his cherrywood stick. She undid the top buttons of her coat because she felt she might suffocate. It was hot here, too hot, and she glanced here and there looking for the stove. There was no stove in the room, only a red-coloured radiator, its controls shaped like slices of lemon, like a kind of laughing red mouth.

The telephone rang in the hall. Iza ran out and the old woman sank into the armchair. She used to be able to feel every spring of it – now it was smooth, comfortable, soft. Then she stood up again in alarm and while Iza was on the phone she knelt down on the carpet and opened her suitcase. She pulled out the bottom drawer of the bureau and threw in the dry twigs so the girl shouldn't see what she had brought with her from Dorozs.

2

She felt as if some elemental blow had destroyed everything around her and that only now did she really know what it was to be a widow, someone absolutely abandoned.

She didn't cry while Iza was in the room, just looked pale and was more quiet than usual, but she tried to say something nice, however awkward, about the practicality of the arrangement and Iza's helpfulness and kindness. She opened the bottom of the wardrobe and found some clothes there, mostly linen, but only a fraction of the amount she'd had at the house – all the patched jumpers, all the stitched and tacked remnants, all the thriftily squirrelled-away towels and sheets had vanished. Iza had only saved things that were in perfect order. There were no dishes, no china: Iza said the pots and pans were beyond repair since they had lost some of their enamel and it was a miracle they hadn't all got appendicitis ages ago, besides which she had her dinner set from Jena so why should she bring along damaged stuff with handles missing when they have proper things here. The pastry board? There was the plastic worktop on the kitchen cupboard for that, it's heatproof and doesn't mind water, and as for the mincer, why bring that heavy thing along when there was an electric grinder here. Antal had inherited the dust catcher for the vitrine, the little porcelain shoe and the mouse without a tail, but she had brought the three undamaged Old Vienna pieces, which would look nice on the little shelf. The china shepherd wasn't here — it had a broken neck and was dreadful to look at, so sad that one really shouldn't keep it.

When Iza finally left her alone and wished her great happiness in the flat, the old woman struggled over to Vince's old armchair whose cover she had always taken such care to patch and sat down. It was only the lovely shape of the chair that reminded her of its old condition, rejuvenated as it was in its new blue-and-grey stripes, looking a touch brash. All reminders of an earlier poverty that witnessed to her craft and skill, her inexhaustible invention in so lightly and imaginatively fending off the perils of the times, had vanished. The room was nice and when she thought about it she had to admit she really didn't need any more than it contained, and Iza had replaced whatever she had thrown out: a brand-new set of towels made a multi-coloured pile on the shelf and there was new linen in a nylon bag. It was a terrible experience.

She spent the first night counting the missing items. She had her old bed, it was just not the same forty-nine-year-old pillowslip, carefully patched and worn down to the consistency of a cobweb, over her pillow but a new one — and Iza had changed the eiderdown too. She went to the trouble of finding a pencil so she could make a list of everything that had *not* come to Pest with her. While hunting for a sheet of paper she came across the headed sheet from Dorozs where she had drawn a plan of their new home: she gazed at the clumsy oblongs and semicircles and wept.

Vince's house plants would not have survived here of course.

No flower, except a cactus perhaps, could survive in the murderous heat of the radiator. They should have brought them all the same – it would have been a useful distraction looking after the sickly things, putting them here or there, finding a place for them. And Captain! Captain was the last living breathing creature that could make Vince laugh the day they took him to the clinic. Captain, who for some mysterious reason had stolen one of his handkerchiefs and was playing with it in the yard.

Iza had bought her handkerchiefs too, two dozen of them. The old ones had disappeared – nearly all of them had had some minor blemish.

She sat in the armchair and tried to cry silently, afraid that Iza would hear her through the thin walls and come in and accuse her of being ungrateful. As indeed she was. The girl had told her she would sell the house and anything inessential, and it was her fault for not thinking it through, not including everything that would make a dwelling look harmonious, comfortable and attractive. Iza had always teased them that their house was like a furniture warehouse and why, for example, did they have a tobacco bowl when neither of them smoked a pipe. She was right, she was always right, it was just that old people grow fond of things that mean much more to them than to the young.

She tried to think about how much money she had suddenly come into but instead of joy she felt a flush of shame: this was how Judas must have felt when he received his thirty pieces of silver. It was like selling your dependants, your best friends. What would she do with all that money?

She kept weeping and writing, noting the bill of loss and

what now belonged to someone else. There were one or two things she remembered later and others she thought lost, so she had to remove them from the list; she almost cried out in relief when she saw that the silk-lined box for handkerchiefs was still here and she tapped it to make sure. The alarm clock was here too – henceforth it would tell Budapest time – and there was the picture of the little girl with the basket. Iza had hung it over the bed. Everything required for comfort was present and correct but she still felt as though she had been robbed.

She wept and noted items with sore eyes, half-blind, all the while feeling that Iza had been extraordinarily good to her, and she even experienced a kind of naive piety in remembering that there was an ancient people that buried its dead with grave goods and that the vanished things, those witnesses to their lives together, might, by way of farewell, have accompanied Vince, escorted him and become his. So she stopped weeping because she wouldn't stint Vince anything.

She thought dawn looked different in Pest and that somehow there was no great difference between dawn and night, just that the sky was suddenly brighter again and that the traffic outside, having quietened down a shade for a couple of hours, now sounded louder. It was a while before she realised why dawn was different here. Gica's cockerel would always crow at half past two even when it was dark; Vince would remark how his watch was fast. She wept a little more on account of Gica's cockerel and then again because Vince wasn't here.

She fell asleep just as she heard Iza getting up. Iza started running the bath tap at six and there was something so re-assuring about her presence, her movements, her tiny noises, that the tension inside her finally gave way and she nodded off for a few hours. It was the last day of Iza's vacation and they spent the whole day together. They even went for a walk when the old woman fancied a pretzel and Iza bought her one to munch in front of the National Theatre. They dined at the Corvin store. The town was a little frightening, a strange capital city to find herself in, amazing and worthy of respect, and she wondered why it was so different from the way she remembered it, considering at the same time how to spend her days there and how best to help Iza, who was so nice to her it was as if she were her mother, not her daughter. The old woman was starting to suspect that what she had planned back home might not be so easy to carry out; it was going to be hard to guess how she could make her daughter's life easier, because Iza was clearly thinking the same, her hands posed in a gesture of childhood thoughtfulness.

She knew from Iza that the housekeeping was done by Teréz – she had taken time off today as she was having some teeth extracted – and the girl had put her mind at rest by pointing out what a splendid person Teréz was and that she'd be no bother to her, though she didn't take that seriously, not for a moment. Until he was forced into retirement, Vince had always been the real help to her: the maid stayed in her corner and Aunt Emma had taught her to keep an eye on the cook, in case she was tempted to steal anything. She resolved to be Iza's eyes and ears as far as Teréz was concerned. She'd leave the cleaning to her, if she was properly clean, but she'd do the cooking herself. She had been an outstanding cook as far back as anyone could remember, so Teréz could light the gas or whatever, then go out and do the shopping. On Saturday morning the old woman went out to the nearest stationer's and bought an exercise book that would serve as a kitchen record of expenses. Iza didn't have the time for all this and, as Iza herself said, Teréz never showed her the bill, only told her what it cost. But that was all right because Teréz was absolutely honest and, even if she weren't, whoever had the time to waste precious minutes on paying a penny or two less for a sprig of parsley!

But things would be different now. Teréz shouldn't be going on shopping sprees with Iza's hard-earned money. It wasn't just a question of saving and good housekeeping. Iza looked thin: she needed feeding up. She remembered how fond Iza had been of cabbage as a child. She hadn't been eating properly since she left – what, after all, could you expect of canteen food, or the meal Teréz cooked her? When she thought about it she realised that Iza can't have had proper food for years because she never ate with them but dined at the hotel. Iza had never wanted her to tire herself out by making meals for her.

Teréz arrived at ten so they immediately got off on the wrong foot as the old woman was expecting her at half past nine. The woman introduced herself, shook hands and announced that she'd start with her room so that madam might relax all the sooner, advising her to read or listen to the radio while she worked.

Teréz addressed her as an equal. She had an enormous bun of brown hair, a maroon coat and as soon as she put her things down she took a kind of boiler suit – it turned out to be hers – from the cupboard and got herself into it. She unpacked her string bag, having come straight over from the covered market where she had been shopping.

The old woman informed her that it would be she who would be doing the cooking henceforth.

Teréz stared at her. She had brown eyes, eyes so dark you could hardly see the pupils. The old woman thought she was mocking her. Teréz suggested that she leave it for today because that was what she had agreed with Iza, but she should feel free to cook from the next day on if she liked, so if she'd be so kind as to decide what she needed from the shops now she wouldn't have to go back out tomorrow. She took the broom and turned on the radio. The old woman stood straight up and turned it off again, saying they were in mourning so there couldn't be any radio. Teréz looked at her in amazement, shrugged and said, as you please, and went out. She wasn't a nice servant. Not at all. She didn't even behave like a servant.

Naturally, she didn't sit where Teréz suggested she should sit but followed Teréz around, watching her every move, correcting her if she saw she hadn't done something properly. Teréz's answers became ever more curt and she eventually stopped answering altogether. The old woman was tired but felt she had won a victory and when Teréz eventually left, she felt she had achieved something useful and important, and that it was a good thing she had come to Pest to take over the household. She was no longer concerned about her lost furniture and her scattered belongings. She lunched and felt proud, inwardly contemptuous of Teréz's cooking: the woman was all mouth, there was no real flavour to her food, you'd only upset your stomach if you ate it. And to top it all she even locked the bathroom when she went there! She'd have followed her in if she could but the bolt was shot. Of course, she could tell what she was doing from the running water. She had the nerve to use Iza's bath!

'Look, mother,' said Iza, more severe than usual. 'Please don't annoy Teréz.' Iza's sharpness shocked her. 'Please, I beg you, don't upset her! Of course she takes a bath, thank heavens she does, she is unusually clean. Would you prefer her to be filthy? She takes a bath here because this is where she works. She doesn't like to leave smelling of food.'

The old woman couldn't follow the logic of this but she had to accept it. She hadn't yet revealed that she'd be cooking from now on, thinking that would be a surprise, a kind of experiment to see when the girl would notice that everything was *real* again, proper home cooking. Luckily, the recipe book had not been thrown away, it was only the shelf that was new. The first thing she'd cook would be cabbage: Iza will be so happy.

Iza was not happy. As soon as she stepped through the door she took a sniff and said the whole place smelled of food. What had got into Teréz? She knew she couldn't stand cabbage. The old woman got cross about this. She reminded her daughter how they would laugh when she was little because of the way she'd gobble it up, cooked or raw. They had nicknamed her 'the cabbage girl', in case she had forgotten. 'That was years ago,' Iza gestured, 'a few things have happened since then – a war and a siege, for example. My appetite was different then. The poor little "cabbage girl" is a thing of the past. Please tell Teréz not to cook anything new and to stick to what we arranged.'

It was a week before Iza found out that it was her mother, not Teréz, who was doing the cooking. She discovered this from Teréz herself, who turned up in the clinic one afternoon and announced that if her mother went on pestering her in the kitchen she would be forced to seek employment elsewhere. The old woman kept leaving the electric oven on and she'd find the frying pan on the ring with nothing in it. The old woman didn't trust the refrigerator, complaining that there was no real ice there; she'd gather up the leftovers in a saucepan and put it out on the balcony; she spilled everything, so pans and dishes had to scrubbed all the time. When Teréz told her not to let stuff drip all over the balcony she put the pan on the window ledge and Teréz said she wouldn't be responsible if there was a gust and it all fell on someone's head. And she shouldn't heat up leftovers to eat the next day. Who'd take the blame if one of them suffered from food poisoning?

Iza was worried and tried to make Teréz understand that things couldn't change from one day to the next, and it was no use expecting miracles from an old country woman who was used to living in an old house and couldn't imagine toasting a piece of bread without a fork. Teréz would not be calmed. Teréz had had enough of the old woman and told her something she had been reluctant to reveal, that the old woman would look suspiciously through her shopping basket when she was about to leave, and would suddenly sweep into the kitchen after her as if on a raid and raise the tin lid of the sugar bowl and the box of tea to check she wasn't stealing anything. She was not used to this kind of treatment.

Teréz had been working six months for Iza, was wonderfully quick, completely trustworthy and highly intelligent. Iza had tried various cleaners over several months before she found her. Teréz could follow instructions on the phone and worked because she liked to, not because she had to. Teréz had been widowed relatively young and her pension was sufficient to cover her needs, but thought it ridiculous that she should work only for herself until the day she died. She liked Iza and had known her for years, Iza having cured her of infection of the joints.

In the evening when she got home – she could tell the old woman had been cooking beans because of the heavy sweet smell – she went into her mother's room and asked her to have respect for Teréz's wishes.

The old woman sat in the armchair, her face in shadow with the light to the left of her catching her left hand on which she wore two gold rings, a larger and a smaller, the larger not fitting her: they were Vince's and her own wedding rings.

'Teréz must do the cooking, mama,' said Iza. 'It's part of her contract. Teréz will cook you lunch, then supper for both of us. She'll do the shopping, bring up the milk and boil it. That's what I agreed with her. Teréz is in charge of the house-keeping, she and no one else. Do you think I brought you to Pest to work?'

The old woman listened. She felt silly and unable to mount an argument; she was so cowed by the accusation that she got on Teréz's nerves that she dared not say a word. Should she say that *she'd* like to be the one who looked after her, and that she'd enjoy taking care of things and finding out what she liked? Or that she had worked all her life, that she liked working and would like to find a way of showing how grateful she was for not being left alone? She kept quiet.

'You're old now, darling. You don't have to keep working. You should rest.'

'What am I to do the whole day?' asked the old woman.

'Take walks,' said Iza. 'It's spring. Go down to the ring road, find a park, look around, watch the children playing. It would be good for you to find a green space somewhere not too far before you get to know the area. There is the City Park and Hűvösvölgy, but the air is excellent in Krisztina Square and the Vérmező Green too, and none of these is hard to get to. It would be nice for you to look around and take the sun. You could spend the afternoon at home reading, doing some handiwork, playing patience,' she said, 'and there is a cinema three doors down you could go to if you like.'

The old woman stared at her dress. She couldn't possibly think of the cinema before the year of mourning was done. She would have liked to tell Iza that her eyesight was not what it once was and that in Dorozs she imagined Iza might read old books or the papers to her, as Vince used to do after supper. A week in the new place was enough to persuade her that it was no use asking for such things. Iza was never free; she would come home tired, have a bath, listen to music, eat something, then lie down or rush off again. Iza probably had a boyfriend too because there was a man constantly wanting to speak to her on the phone and it wasn't likely that she'd go out by herself at night.

'As for the leftovers, my dear,' said Iza, 'just throw them away. If something is particularly nice and it hasn't gone off, put it in the fridge but, as for the rest, get rid of it and don't leave it on the balcony.'

She was patient and loving about her request.

'I'd like you to be able to save,' said the old woman.

Iza laughed. 'We don't need to save, dear. I earn enough. And anyway, I hate eating yesterday's leftovers.'

'That's another thing I can't explain,' thought the old woman. She didn't have the words to tell Iza how much she respected her, how much she wanted to try to be a good house-keeper to her, how she would take care of their home, how she was trying to supplement Iza's hard-earned income.

'There's no dog here, mama, nor a pig. Why save the leftovers?'

'Do you get beggars round here?' the old woman asked. Her gaze was innocent, eager to learn, a most gentle blue. It was with those beautiful, clear, honest eyes that Vince fell in love at that county ball.

Iza laughed again. 'No,' she said, 'and if you take a look around the town you'll see there isn't one anywhere. You surely don't think there are people going from block to block begging for soup in 1960?'

From that day on the old woman threw away the leftovers, tried to avoid Teréz and let her do the cooking. Teréz, to her great credit, did not go around with a triumphant look; in fact, she was sweeter to her than she was to Iza. Now that the old woman knew her place it was possible to love her; Teréz did her all kinds of favours, tried to please her and would have spoiled her like a child. But the old woman couldn't stand her, couldn't even bear to look at her when she said goodbye and would always air the room a long time after she had gone. Teréz was a thief – she had stolen her work.

Back home she used to dry the clothes in the attic. She had never seen retractable washing lines before but once she learned to operate the wall-mounted system she was modestly delighted to see how easy it made washing the linen. She continued boiling water on the electric stove as before, being too frightened to turn on the hot tap of the boiler because it hissed and might explode. She rinsed everything for herself once Teréz was out of the house. She found the laundry basket with Iza's things hidden in the bathroom wall, grabbed the fine blouses and nighties and carefully, lovingly, washed those too. Drying was more difficult as she couldn't reach the washing lines. Iza really shouldn't have sold the stool; if she still had it she would have something to stand on without wobbling about on this ridiculous kitchen chair with its steel legs. Normally Teréz would take the washing away in a suitcase because she preferred to wash and iron at home, then bring the fresh things back a week later in the same suitcase. She was paid extra for this. It was another thing they wouldn't have to spend on, thought the old woman.

When Iza arrived home that day she was really annoyed. The clothes had been wrung out but her mother's hands were clearly too weak to do it properly and everything was dripping on the floor. The hopeful look on her mother's face, clearly expecting to be praised, immediately vanished.

'You mustn't do this with your blood pressure, darling!' said Iza. 'In any case, I hate water dripping down my neck. There is a dryer downstairs next to the shelter but as far as I'm concerned it's much simpler if Teréz takes the clothes away. I don't even like hand-washing at home – why should we walk across pools of water on the bathroom floor?'

She kissed her mother's hand and face, and let her finger flutter over her pulse a moment. The pulse was strong and regular. Luckily washing hadn't been too much of a strain. Iza went into the kitchen to heat up supper while the old woman took down the washing line, quickly removing her own things, the warm trousers and the flannel shirts so that they, at least, wouldn't drip on Iza's head. She spread them out to dry on the radiator in her room and turned them over now and then so they wouldn't overheat. Clothes dried surprisingly fast, as if some invisible mouth were breathing hot air on them from below. She smoothed the washing out and put it away in the cupboard, then just stood and stared out on to the ring road. There was a blue glow out there like a blinding electric light, where men in steel masks and huge gloves were bending between the tram rails with sparks raining down beside them. It was like fire, but it wasn't fire. It was something else. A big city fire, a Pest fire, thought the old woman. She felt lost, scared and sad.

She tried one more experiment.

Whether alone or with visitors, Iza drank gallons of coffee. As soon as people arrived she would plug in the coffee machine. How inconvenient, thought the old woman, and how tiring always to be jumping up and checking that the coffee didn't boil over. It was a stupid way of making coffee, another of those machines. They used to drink Turkish coffee at home when they were young and Vince loved it.

The man who rang Iza almost every day had just come up for the third time since she had arrived when she surprised them with coffee. She waited a quarter of an hour after his arrival, remembering from her own time as a maid that it wasn't done to offer things to guests immediately because people like to have a smoke and a chat first. In the morning she had gone down to the ring road and, having slowly familiarised herself with the neighbouring shops, was delighted to find a copper flask and a fast-boiling spirit stove in the second-hand shop next door. If Iza hadn't left their old one behind she wouldn't have had to buy another because the one they had was really good. It was what she used to heat the goffering iron on when flouncing was in fashion, to heat the milk when Iza was a baby and to make camomile tea when one of them had a toothache. This new purchase could do all those clever things, so she bought some paraffin in the household store and was really pleased by the time she got home.

As soon as she heard the guest ring the bell she measured out two spoonfuls of Turkish coffee, careful not to stint, humming to herself, red-faced and hot as she brewed it. She had never actually met any of Iza's guests yet, because people in Pest tended to call at such impossible times, as late as nine or ten at night, and she was awake only when they arrived, not when they left. She carried on humming happily, pleased to have overcome her sleepiness and to have brewed the coffee instead of Iza. She would stay awake every time now. Old people did not need as much sleep as that. This much at least she could do for Iza. And if there were no guests, just Iza herself, she could still make the coffee from now on.

She knew her way around the kitchen cupboard by now and put two funny-shaped small cups on the tray. (But what was wrong with her own china set with its gilded rim and clover pattern? She failed to see that these thick, purple cups were any more beautiful.) She used her elbow to open the door to Iza's room. The coffee was steaming in the middle of the tray. The sugar cubes were on a small plate as there was no sugar bowl.

Iza stood up when she entered. The man too stood up. The old woman stood beaming on the threshold.

'This is Domokos,' said Iza.

She was delighted that the man kissed her hand. It was nice to think that Iza's visitors knew their manners. Iza glanced at the electric socket. Her own coffee-maker wasn't plugged in yet.

'I've brought you a little coffee.'

'That's very kind of you. Thank you.'

The old woman sat down, folded her hands and waited. No one said anything. That was fine, she understood they wanted to be alone, she was only waiting for them to taste the coffee and for Iza's expression to show that she was grateful and pleased to have something made for her.

Iza poured out the coffee, took some sugar, the man drinking it as it was. They quickly gulped it down, then Iza suddenly grabbed everything and dashed into the kitchen with the tray. 'Why doesn't he say anything,' thought the old woman. 'So silent. Not handsome but not ugly either. I wonder what he does for a living?' She was a little disappointed not to get much praise. Iza said nothing at all. The man just glanced at her and said the coffee was very nice.

She said goodnight to them, feeling very satisfied with herself. Back in her room she ground a little more coffee and prepared everything ready for brewing tomorrow. She refilled the paraffin too, then went to bed. The guest didn't stay long since she was still awake when she heard him leaving. As soon as the door in the hall closed, Iza came in to see her.

She'd be coming to thank her. She was always a most grateful child.

Iza didn't sit down for long, just a few minutes, and turned out the light as she left, encouraging her to sleep. But the old woman didn't sleep; she lay in the dark, tearing at the edges of the pillow. The coffee smelled of paraffin. Everything smelled of paraffin and Iza asked her not to bother with it next time. It was nothing brewing coffee, the old woman said, she was pleased to do it. All day long she was trying to move her rheumatic limbs and it was good to be doing little things like this. 'It was a lovely idea and thank you very much,' said Iza, but she really didn't want it. Not any more. 'And please pour the paraffin out,' she added, 'because it's impossible to live with that smell.'

The night was full of flashing lights as it always was on the ring road, the neon advertising signs flickering on and off, the trams rumbling past. She gazed ahead.

Tomorrow she'd pour away the paraffin though it had such a lovely proper flame, like a tiny iron stove. There was no real fire in the flat, it was all electric. Well of course paraffin was smelly. Her own sense of smell might have deteriorated in the past years, because she hadn't noticed it.

There were no experiments after this.

3

She had never had so much time in her life.

Ever since she could remember they had gone through the list of things to do for the day so there would be no worrying about it in the evening. When she was young it was pointless having someone to help her; she'd be out in the kitchen hurrying things up or doing the cooking and cleaning herself. In the old days Aunt Emma was always chivvying her so it was wonderful – she was deliriously happy – when she finally had her own house and she could decide when to do the cleaning and any other number of useful tasks. When Vince lost his job and their own maid was gone, she suddenly bore the responsibility for everything including the troubles of child rearing. By the time she was old she had got used to doing things by herself and even after Vince's rehabilitation she only engaged help for the really heavy work; she no longer carried wood or washed the bedding and tended to oversee spring cleaning rather than do it. While Vince was well he helped her and never made a distinction between man's work and woman's work, and Antal helped too, though he was a doctor, not a pensioner like Vince. Antal said housework relaxed him and he'd even go up to the attic to hang out the washing, his lines tidier, drier and much more evenly spread than Mála, the home help's.

The old woman also enjoyed the daily struggle with housework: a month with some really good meals and a thorough clean always felt like a triumph. It was as though the house were surrounded by invisible demons, wicked little demons that had to be defeated each time because they were always scheming, always looking to burn the food and soak the winter fuel. Whenever something succeeded particularly well she could practically see the demons slinking around the house, their heads hung in shame, retreating to a cave where they could moan to each other. In the meantime everything was going well: Vince had been rehabilitated and the circuit judge had ordered a pension for him; Iza had qualified as a doctor; they had more money than they needed and there was no longer any need to struggle with the demons. But the old woman had got used to living on a shoestring and lived as frugally as before, still watching the pennies as if each penny of housekeeping might make or break their lives. Vince always praised her for this, understanding that he should still congratulate her on her bloodless victory over the demons every month when the old woman closed the squared-up accounts book, her face shining, and slipped a few notes of paper money into the childhood commonplace book she hid under the sheets in the cupboard.

Now there was no housework, no routine, no cares, no chats with old acquaintances, no need to go round the market looking for bargains or to calculate whether she could afford the perfect apple or accept the second-rate one. There was no need to scour the shops for cheap clothes, no need to wrest the bargain item from someone else's grasp and wonder in a careless moment, when she hadn't paid sufficient attention to the condition of her puchase, whether she could stitch a new collar on to an old shirt.

Everything stopped, in fact.

She didn't see Iza from morning through to the late afternoon, and when she did come home it was only to ask her how she was, then to sigh and say how good it was not to be among strange faces but be home at last; then she'd go to her room to read a book, to prepare for guests, to go out, to rush to a theatre, to listen to music, or to sit at her writing desk and consult a textbook in order to write a note or to compose an article.

Iza needed silence to function: she needed it for both work and rest. The old woman had never been a great fan of the radio but, since the six weeks of mourning with its ban on music had passed and she was always alone with nothing to do, she resigned herself to it. She felt a bitter yet consoling satisfaction at not switching on the radio in the evening when the programmes were most interesting, refusing to be entertained so that her daughter should not be disturbed. At least in this respect she could do something for her.

She would have given anything to be able to help her, it was just that there was never any opportunity.

The girl had no need of her cooking nor of her coffee; she didn't even want help when visitors called, though she had offered to make friends with Iza's guests. The girl thanked her but refused, saying her guests always came long after the old woman should be in bed. Sometimes, when the girl was still at the clinic and Teréz had gone, she crept over to her desk, opened her folders and tried to guess what Iza was doing, even sneaking a couple of textbooks back to her room in the innocent hope of learning something of Iza's work, not much, just enough so, should Iza be working on important things and suddenly need something, she could bring her the item without Iza needing to stand up and break her concentration. The trouble was that Iza's books were mostly in French and Russian, so she couldn't make any sense of even their titles and as for reading Iza's notes, however she strained her eyes she couldn't make out the handwriting and abbreviations. She never even mentioned such plans to her.

She no longer dared offer the slightest help, not even the simplest things such as emptying an ashtray, or tidying the room when Iza was suddenly called away somewhere. Once she had thrown out a teaspoon along with the coffee grounds and the dog ends. The janitor brought it back up in the morning and Teréz made such a fuss about it that she was too scared even to throw out dead flowers. Generally, she went in terror of Teréz.

Her window looked out over the József ring road.

She spent most of her time dragging Vince's chair over, gazing at passers-by, at the snub-nosed buses, the changing traffic lights and the billowing canvas of the cinema advertisements stretched on nets between the two sides of the street. She looked at everything as though it had nothing to do with her. She thought of Gica, the cloak-maker, and how little work she had nowadays, though what she did was lovely, a real craft, it being a far from simple matter gathering the pleats round the shoulder so there should be no ugly creases. The streetscape below meant nothing to her however much she gazed. Occasionally Teréz would remark that the weather was lovely and she should get out a little, then she would obediently put on her coat and go down as far as the corner of Ráday Street, to the tiny playground and sit there watching children playing in the sandpit without ever feeling the point of sitting there or walking around — she didn't know why she was doing it. Teréz's good intentions in wanting the best for her health were wasted because the fresh air she managed to breathe under the trees was not enough to compensate her for the anxiety of having to cross a street where there wasn't a policeman guiding the traffic and where she had to wait for the green light in order to get to the playground in the square while trams clattered next to her and cars swept by her.

The square seemed real enough, chiefly because of the pigeons, the flock reminding her of Captain in some way, and after a while she started bringing crumbs and imagined that a particular ruff-necked pigeon with blue eyes had befriended her because it often perched on her bench.

Other old women came to Ráday Square to catch the sun, and some old men too, men who resembled Vince, the skin in soft folds under their chins, often wearing a woollen scarf even in the surprisingly warm spring sunshine. The old men read papers or just sat with closed eyes, their heads turned to the sun, lost in thought, much as she was. Slowly she got used to it and made it her favourite place to go. There was no grass there yet, just the promise of a park; gardeners were working around her, digging flower beds, and a path was being built in the centre; and this too was entertainment of a sort, watching the cauldron, the low fire under the simmering asphalt, the flames that were now yellow, now carmine red.

Back home old people tended to gather round the statue of Kossuth to get the air and everyone knew everybody.

She had never become part of that group of 'pensioners': she would take her place on the bench even on less than fine summer mornings but would never greet those who had looked at Vince in *that* way back *then*, not Bella Tahy, nor Tódorka Kovács, nobody. Actually it would have been easier to take the sun and make friends here with someone as solitary as herself, someone who had never known Vince or hurt him.

For days she kept gazing at the faces.

The old people, the old of the square, would arrive at almost the same time while the sun was at its height at noon and, when possible, would take their usual seats. Slowly she got to recognise them all and could see that some were happy, minding little children, and had friends to play pocket chess with, who ate pretzels and, occasionally, laughed. There was an old man who every lunch hour was sought out by someone from the workshop opposite the park to chat or for advice on drawings and tools. She did not dare approach the men though they were in a majority because even at that age, she thought, it wasn't right. She just sat and dreamt the time away before lunch waiting for someone to speak to her. Teréz was amazed – she was often late.

For a long time nothing happened.

Then one day the hoped-for event did occur. An old, deeply wrinkled woman settled down beside her. Her face made up, her nails painted, she was wearing a fur collar and high heels, and was something of mutton dressed as lamb. She drew away from her and felt sad and inadequate: others could look after themselves. She couldn't even manage this. She had never used nail varnish.

She felt the stranger was sizing her up and was in two minds: should she talk to her? Shouldn't she? She was practically trembling with pleasure at the thought of someone wanting to talk to her. 'Go on,' she said to herself in a two-syllable prayer. 'Go on, say something.' She was almost overcome by happiness when the old woman eventually asked her whether she didn't think that, after all that horrible rain, an unusually nice spring seemed to be on its way.

After half an hour of telling the stranger everything about herself she could still not stop talking. The woman listened, interjecting a word here and there, nodding and smoking, responding with her own sadness or delight as she went on. Having sketched out her life she felt strangely relieved. The other woman was looking at her with such undisguised envy, clearly thinking, here is a woman with nothing to do, that she suddenly felt it was quite nice like this: it was just that she hadn't anticipated it, hadn't thought it through. Well, of course Iza was so busy she didn't have time for anything — she didn't really need her help and everything that happened or didn't happen at home was just Iza looking after her. The old woman beside her was called Hilda, Hilda Virág, and it turned out they lived very close to each other, just three blocks away.

Hilda Virág said she shared a room with her young relatives. Well then, they should meet not at her place but at Iza's. She would be happy to see her this afternoon at four if that's convenient, she told Hilda. On her way home she first thought of baking something, but then she dropped the idea: it was not worth the risk because Teréz was sure to notice. She bought biscuits instead. Once home she ate with a good appetite, prettied her room and felt it looked unusually impressive. All the furniture looked impeccably nice thanks to Iza, so clever to make sure everything in the room was perfect – it was a real pleasure to look at.

Hilda Virág arrived on time and praised the coffee put before her. She didn't want to discuss her family though the old woman would have liked to know more about her, and after a while she stopped questioning her and let her talk about whatever she wanted. Hilda knew all kinds of amusing stories about Pest as it had once been, remembered clearly the details of her honeymoon year, 1911, and rolled out great lists of cabaret and music-hall venues, one of which at least she and Vince had been to but had left, blushing and embarrassed, at the interval. Hilda Virág knew a lot of songs and had a nice voice if a little tremulous. She was orphaned early in her life and all she would say about herself is that she lived independently without any support. Her younger relatives cared only for themselves and expected her to clean and cook for them without anything in return. And she had never won anything on the lottery yet, though she'd love to.

The old woman was ready to offer her money but, just in time, thought better of it. When Hilda Virág talked of her old friends she mentioned such prominent names of the past that the old woman realised there could be no thought of insulting her with a cash gift. If the woman's young relatives neglected her to such a degree, she'd look to help Hilda Virág in this or that way of her own instead. What a good creature she was and what fun it was being with her. She showed her a

photograph of Vince and several of Iza as a child. Her guest
loved it all. She kept tapping the radiator, saying she wished
just once in her life she had a flat like this where you didn't
have to keep feeding the fire and it was so heavenly and warm.
The old woman looked around her with innocent pride, feeling
how beautiful the room was and thought she must have been
blinded by years of unhappiness not to notice it – she had
simply not adjusted to her new life. 'Teréz,' sighed Hilda Virág.
If only she had a Teréz in her life! But it was she who played
the role of Teréz where she lived. How terrible!

Iza was astounded when she returned and heard laughter.
Her mother's voice sounded full of life. She was clearly chatting to someone who was humming in an awful old voice. She
took off her coat and walked in.

'My daughter,' the old woman declared, glowing. 'My little
daughter, the doctor. She has just returned from work and is
tired, the poor thing. Will you sit down, Izzy?'

Iza stood in the doorway and looked at Hilda Virág. The
visitor muttered something and stood up. The old woman felt
bad about this for some reason. Why should the elderly woman
stand up when a younger woman enters the room? Because the
flat belonged to Iza? No, it must be something else. Iza did not
sit down and was remarkably unfriendly, saying simply hello,
then turning on her heel and leaving. The conversation came
to an awkward stop. Hilda Virág stuttered something about
how young and vigorous Iza looked while the old woman was
consumed with shame: she did not think Iza was being energetic
but offensive. Her visitor left, a lot less sparkling than when
she had arrived, without inviting the old woman back to her
place even though she was trembling with excitement at the

prospect – it is what she had been waiting for all afternoon. The young relatives wouldn't have bothered her. She liked young people. She wouldn't even have had to cross the street to get to Hilda Virág's flat. What a convenient friendship it might have been.

She rinsed the cups. Unfortunately Iza had noticed that she hadn't emptied the spirit burner and had made the coffee in the quick boiler, but then it was in her own room and here, she thought, she might be free to do as she liked; after all, she didn't know how to operate Iza's coffee-maker. Iza didn't come to her room till supper.

'Where did you pick up that old baggage?' asked Iza.

She didn't understand the word at first and thought her daughter was talking about clothes. Iza sometimes called patched jumpers and nighties the 'baggage', so she had to ask again and have the answer using a different word before she understood what she was being asked, and then she was so frightened her eyes began to fill with tears.

'I come home to find you having coffee with a prostitute. Have you lost your mind, mother? What were you thinking of? This is Pest, a city of two million people; did you think you were home in the village? Where did you pick her up? In Ráday Square? How do you know who is likely to come and sit down beside you? She started the conversation – that I can well imagine. What if you brought a murderer home one day and he decided to cut your throat, some hooligan who tells you he's a novice monk? Don't get into conversations in the street, mother, and on no account think of bringing anyone home. It was sheer luck that I hadn't planned anything for this afternoon, that I happened to be tired and needed a rest, but I might have come home with a guest or with work to do. I find this woman sitting here, boasting how this or that grand acquaintance of hers is a proper gentleman. Amazing!'

She threw the crumbs she had collected for the ruff-necked pigeons in Ráday Square out of the window and watched anxiously from above in case there was a policeman coming up to punish her for littering the street, but she didn't dare take the bag for the crumbs into the kitchen because she was frightened of being told off, of being asked what was up with her now, with this beggarly mania of hers for sweeping the crumbs on the tablecloth into bags. She no longer visited the square and stuck to wandering the side streets, looking in shop windows, thinking what might be nice to have but she couldn't think of anything. She did see Hilda Virág one more time, leaving the house whose number she had mentioned when talking about her flat. She was carrying a string bag, her face lavishly painted as before, dark circles round her sad eyes. She felt so ashamed she slipped into a doorway so she shouldn't have to greet her.

After the experience with Hilda, any stranger frightened her.

She never opened the door to anyone unless Teréz was in the house, not even the postman. The janitor brought up any letters addressed to Iza in the evening, and he always made some remark to the effect that if the old lady never went out why did she burden someone else with the post? She felt bad about this and afterwards would look through the spyhole in the door and, depending on what the caller wanted, would shout that her daughter wasn't at home and that she wasn't allowed to let anybody in, that the key had been taken away and she didn't want brushes or washing powder or patched rugs because she was a widow with a very small pension which, in any case, she did not keep at home. But she also felt bad if the visitor went away and once, when Iza was spending the weekend elsewhere, she didn't undress but went to bed fully clothed wondering how she would defend herself if she were attacked.

Days floated by in a quite unreal fashion.

In the morning she had to wait until Iza was finished in the bathroom and then she rushed through everything in a panic so that Teréz shouldn't surprise her. While Teréz was there she had to keep out of her way by making herself small in the big armchair or by going out to the street. And then there was Iza to wait for, Iza with her unpredictable moods, having to sit by the window with her eyes on the bus stop, with a heart-breaking anxiety she had never experienced before, wondering if Iza was safe or had been run down, because she had never imagined there could be as much traffic as there was in Pest. When the girl arrived she had to wait for the most unobtrusive moment to go into the kitchen and have some supper, and hope that Iza would eat a little more than usual; you couldn't tell by looking at her how little she ate and how, when tired, she wanted nothing more than a very watery lemonade, a piece of cheese and an apple. After supper she'd wait for that man, Domokos, who was a regular visitor and wonder what the faint noises, those hardly audible noises, meant. What could they be doing in Iza's room and surely it couldn't be what she thought? Once she remembered what Iza had called Hilda Virág and started weeping because if Iza's relationship with Domokos was of the same kind then Iza couldn't be a respectable girl either.

The hours of waiting were filled with memories.

She never thought that remembering could be such an energetic activity.

Little by little the old lady went through the events of her life. She had never had time for it before. Her options, all those possibilities she had thought through and through, had solidified around her: recalling the arrival of Captain, getting him to adapt and become house-trained, always made her think he was actually here, just hiding under the bed, as he used to do sometimes back home when he heard Iza's footsteps. Captain was frightened of Iza. She gave up on Aunt Emma, growing bitter about the wickedness, a wickedness that time somehow refused to heal. Teréz would look at her suspiciously the way she sat in her big chair doing absolutely nothing with just a mysterious smile on her face, or some inexpressible sadness – what on earth was going on in that old woman's mind? The old woman thought and thought about the loss of Endrus and the days she spent with Vince, and it turned out it hardly mattered what oceans of time had passed, she remembered everything, not only things that happened to them personally but events in the life of the town, and above the busy traffic of the ring road she was wondering whether it was in 1903 that they built the pavilion in the copse, the one where the band played every Sunday afternoon. Teréz froze and listened every time she heard a noise from within. She didn't know the tune and the old woman couldn't sing so she couldn't know that she was trying to recall the German song, *Alle miteinander, alle miteinander, grüss euch Gott!* The old woman had even given up on Queen Zita's dress, the bunch of violets in her hands that she was nervously sniffing at and which was almost certainly sprinkled with antiseptic. The king and queen were passing through town just when Spanish flu was raging, when little Dóri Kubek and Aurél Inárcs died of it. She had stood right at the back of the queue of ladies, and she only went to annoy Aunt Emma, despite Vince begging her not to. It was the only time she and Vince had a real row because he stayed right at home, claiming at court that he had been ill with a touch of Spanish flu. In reality he was at home reading Dickens and she even remembered the name of the book, *Dombey and Son*, and that he said he wasn't interested in kings and would rather read.

Sometimes she thought about herself and felt a simple pride in having always done her duty. She saw herself with the washing tub, and at Endrus's grave on 1 November with the All Souls' Eve illuminations; she saw herself baking rolls, at social functions, as a young girl, with Vince by his sickbed, at the county ball, with her first dead mouse that she had excavated from the trap with such dignity when she was still a young woman, just to show that she had her own pantry, and that there was flour in there, as demonstrated by the presence of the mouse.

Most of the time it was Iza she thought about, more often than Vince.

She thought of the Iza that was yet to be born, of the constant feeling of sickness and general illness throughout the pregnancy. She saw Iza as a young child, a serious little girl with big round eyes who was always being punished for things she didn't do, who defended her father against the neighbours and who was like a little wise woman full of wise sayings constantly preaching to them. She recalled the grammar-school girl who never had to be told to work, nor to help out in the house, the matriculation exams and her blazing eyes when she discovered she had been rejected by the university. That war lasted two years. God forgive her but she looked disapprovingly at Vince, because the whole tug-of-war was down to him, he was the reason they rejected the girl, that is until Dekker kicked up a fuss on her behalf.

Iza was a good child, she kept thinking, good, loyal, clever and hard-working. She understood things about the world her mother never could. She had been sickly when young and they had had to spend a lot of time looking after her when she was at primary school. She was slow to start reading for some reason. How many afternoons did they spend practising together until she got into grammar school! The nights she spent stitching her old clothes so they would still fit her and she'd look smart though poor. Once – she was at university by that time – she got her fingers caught in the doors of the tram and she and Vince spent weeks writing up the dissection notes that had to be returned to the person she borrowed them from, horrible notes that frightened her. She recalled Iza who thought of them even when she got married, awkwardly happy, reluctantly radiant, and Iza silent too, when she went up to Pest, and Iza who reclaimed their pension for them, and the considerable sums she sent home even when they didn't need it. She recalled the Iza who visited every fourth Sunday and helped them through every difficulty, right down to the last one, Vince's merciful death.

She thought about Iza every day, Iza who did not abandon her in their last house, who arranged everything for her, who relieved her of work and responsibility, who was looking after her and richly providing for her. And, having thought that, she would feel helpless and break down in tears of shame.

4

Iza tended to stay longer at the clinic now after the day's work was over.

Nobody really wondered at it. Iza liked her work and set about it with greater ambition than any of her colleagues. She listened right through to all her patients and while she was with them made notes not just about the pain in the hands or feet or aching joints, but about the person and their sense of the world. Iza believed it was necessary to know the whole body in order to deal with a problem, and she was equally sure that body and nervous condition worked together to influence the course of a disease. Every patient represented an exciting new potential solution for her and no one left her with the feeling that they were part of a production line or that in two more minutes an invisible force would carry them away with a prescription in their hands for a course of injections, a medicinal bath or to lie under a great electric machine. When people came to Iza they immediately felt this doctor cared for them as much as if they had been a wealthy private patient. The director said she was an outstanding diagnostician, it was just that she dilly-dallied a little, and it was true she saw fewer patients than others in the various wards, but she cured more people too. Patients relaxed in her presence and there were those who poured out their private griefs to her, but Iza sent no one away without hearing them out. The youngest doctor, Bárdi, once made up a teasing song about her for a party, and he drew her too, with ten pairs of ears and a vast number of arms like some white-overalled Buddha. Bárdi liked Iza and only tortured her with his jokes because he was ashamed of respecting her so much.

Iza received more bonuses than the other doctors, which didn't surprise her since, despite the will of some of the authorities, she had been given many scholarships as a student. In view of her success they simply had to agree. She was a natural student who never let people down. She had no off days or wasted afternoons, she prepared systematically for all her examinations, everything about her suggesting a rigorous, precise order. Her mother was often amused when she came home from university exhausted and instead of eating then lying down, she started tidying things. 'Haven't you had enough for today?' asked her mother, laughing. 'I can't lie down, not when you haven't turned off the tap properly and left your shoes in the bathroom,' Iza complained. If she ever promised anything, even as a child, you could be sure she would do it. You couldn't say that about Vince.

Vince had often promised Iza something, then forgotten it or lacked the money to make it happen. At such times the old woman would find Iza in the pantry tucked in by the shelves, having a lonely cry, and each time she had the uncomfortable feeling that what upset her wasn't the loss of the present she might have had but the offence to her moral sense, the fact that someone hadn't kept a promise. Bárdi was always in despair when, having just caught up with something he should have done six months before, he saw Iza's statistics with their beautiful graphs and charts on the director's table and heard that Szőcs's were the first to arrive again.

She was never late but it wasn't like her to stay so long at work. When she finished and she wasn't too tired, she'd have coffee or a beer with her colleagues if someone asked her, or she'd invite someone to go for a walk with her, usually a divorced woman or a young girl. Iza didn't like listening to happy mothers or women with good marriages – the memory of Antal was still too raw.

Latterly, while tidying things, putting her notes into order, making strong coffee, leafing through the papers or just sitting scribbling, she found herself doing what the old woman was doing: in her own way, with due respect to her own circumstances, in the brief moments left to her she thought about her life.

She was thinking particularly hard about the problem of her mother.

Iza loved her parents, not just the way a child might, but in a comradely fashion, as fellow sufferers, quickly understanding why their lives were not like the lives of her acquaintances, and was fully convinced – more fully convinced than her mother – that being Vince's daughter was not a matter of shame but of pride, and that any wife of Vince should be happy to have a husband like him. Material difficulties didn't bother her, it rather pleased her that, though a child, she could help her mother sort out a really knotty problem. Iza was convinced that her whole outlook – including her entirely instinctive political attitudes based on purely human reflexes – was down to the example of Vince and that the fact she got through university and emerged with qualifications was attributable to her mother's practical mind in getting over the complications of poverty. Iza set about her obligations to them whenever and however she could, in the most natural way without ever being asked or called upon.

Each payday Bárdi would complain about the pittance left to him of his half-monthly salary after he had shared it with 'the old woman' back in Szalka but Iza never told anyone she was supporting her parents or that she had a family at all. When it came to the childlessness tax or when paying into the obligatory state bonds she never argued that she was looking after her mother and father. Her rural self was familiar only to the simple, none too clever people of her home town, denizens of the old woman's and Vince's world. When she asked for time off because her father was dying and that after the funeral she'd like her mother to move in with her, Bárdi, who took over her work, felt very bad and didn't go to offer his condolences – what in heaven's name can a man say at such a time? He was thinking that he wouldn't want his old woman to move in with him, he'd rather give her three-quarters of his pay and walk the wards.

Antal's message was shocking precisely because it was no different in lacking any show of emotion.

Lack of emotion characterised their relationship even at its most passionate. One day they were walking through the copse together discussing some film or other when Antal carelessly asked, almost by way of a passing remark, whether she would marry him and she replied, of course. There was a monument to a local poet along the woodland path, a clumsy bronze head on a twisted column, the only poetic thing about it being the eyes that looked as though they might have meant something to someone. They stopped by it, fell silent in the middle of a sentence, and it was there Antal kissed her. It was early afternoon on a bright day and it was only when Dekker, who always walked that way to his villa, approached that they leapt apart. 'Nice to see you,' said Dekker when Antal started to explain and he immediately walked on. He already knew, as Iza didn't, that the matter of the girl's position had been sorted out.

Antal's message was to say that her father was expected to die that day and it would be good if she were there. Looking down from the plane, the clouds looked leaden with an occasional unreal white patch, rising in woollen towers like a flock of dim sheep. It was because of the old woman that she caught the first flight; she already knew she would not see her father alive. Iza didn't want another emotional crisis, there had been one in her life and that was enough, now she needed all her strength. She had already said goodbye to her father once when Dekker first showed her Vince's test results. She had kept staring at his desk, noticing how like a child's desk it was, so unfit for a great scientist, the writing desk of a simpleton, littered with erasers and coloured crayons as if he spent every free minute drawing pictures of houses, hussars and snowmen on his writing pad, and her eyes filled with tears as she bent over the pens and bright little notebooks.

She was never in any doubt that she would have to take the old woman home with her.

When Iza first received the drawings for her flat Vince was still relatively healthy, the only unusual thing about him was that he looked prematurely aged. She took a pencil and redrew the walls, diminishing the size of her own two rooms so that there should be space for a third. One of the old folk was bound to die sooner or later, as she thought at the time, and the other could not live alone down there. It was impossible.

She saves sex for the end of the month, thought Bárdi, noting how every fourth Saturday Iza turned up with a suitcase and ordered a taxi for the station once noon surgery was finished. Later, when it turned out that the girl was visiting her parents, he felt ashamed of himself. Iza, like her father, was instinctively attentive, kept a note of her colleagues' name days and promotions, and it wasn't too difficult to imagine her at the end of each month, appearing somewhere out in the country, laden with presents, chatting and giggling like a girl, stuffing silly little gifts into the pockets of housecoats and dressing gowns.

Iza's sex life was quite different from that imagined by Bárdi or indeed by anyone.

It took years for the memory of Antal to heal but the girl wasn't vain; she didn't feel she needed the attentions of a man – any man – to assure her that her husband was a fool to leave her. In the first few months of moving into the new flat in Pest she took every opportunity to spend time at the clinic; she started no new lasting relationship, she went out with her colleagues but they were all married and those who weren't were all younger than she was. The company she kept at the time was fun but impersonal.

There were occasionally particularly interesting men among her patients, including well-known public figures with a national reputation. Hardly anyone at Iza's clinic had personal patients: in all serious cases the course of treatment involved the whole staff. She would visit her notable patients, form a diagnosis, then forget them. It was impossible to have private feelings about them: they were simply ill. Men hung their heads and sucked in their breath while being examined. Famous artists shyly admitted their real age, trembled at the thought of treatment and lamented – their voices strangely thin, almost feminine – the fact that they were due a course of medical massage or the weight baths. It never occurred to her that one of them might pick up the telephone one day and ask her for a date after surgery hours.

Nevertheless this did happen, just once, with Domokos.

It was the Writers Union that rang to tell her about Domokos and a problem with his elbow. As usual she looked carefully into his eyes in the course of the examination, the condition of the eyes and the hair being as much a sign of sickness as anything to do with the body. In examining him she noticed that Domokos was returning her gaze as a man, as if assuming a different kind of eye contact. It didn't embarrass her, it made her angry. She told Domokos not to stare at her but to submit to the examination and, contrary to her usual practice, she prescribed electric treatment for him before sending him on his way. Electrotherapy was in a new wing of the clinic, an extension of her own department, the first modern department of its kind, and Domokos would have to undergo treatment there. It was where she herself worked, though they entered by different doors. After each appointment he would look in on her to 'report in' as he called it, letting her know how much his condition had improved. She wouldn't look into his eyes now and behaved coldly to him, treating him worse than she did others. This amused Domokos as it was impossible not to notice it, and he sent her a bunch of flowers after each appointment, a gift she didn't know what to do with and which, from the first time on, she regularly handed over to the janitor's wife. She wouldn't mention the flowers to him, never thanked him and hoped that he would simply give up but, when Domokos called in for the fifth time to show her how he could now bend his elbow without pain, she sent her administrator out to fetch some new boxes and told him whatever his purpose in sending her the flowers he should stop sending them.

Domokos answered that he had no purpose. It was simple courtesy. In any case it was not unusual for a man to send flowers to an attractive young woman, especially one to whom he feels some sort of tie, and maybe she should consult someone herself since she seemed unduly agitated. Hearing this she simply opened the door, ushered him out and called in the next patient. That night Domokos rang her for the first time.

Their relationship developed relatively quickly, Iza allowing herself passively, a little suspiciously, to be seduced by Domokos's half-teasing, half-touching ardour. When Vince was in hospital and she met Antal at her father's bedside for the first time, she blushed and felt sick as though she had something to hide, as if she owed him something, a kind of honesty or fidelity – who knows what? Domokos was full of fun, full of ideas, always accommodating. He put up with her earlier moods and helped cheer her when she was tired but Iza never felt – not even in their most passionate moments – quite as certain as she had with Antal while she was still married to him, that Domokos was the man for her. That was partly because of Domokos's profession and partly because of Antal. After all this time, after everything that had happened, Antal was still the measure of things: Antal gave himself over completely to acts of love, his eyes closed, fierce yet tender; with Domokos she always felt he was awake and watching, observing an experience that he would later put into words and look to use somehow. It wasn't a nice thought but life with Domokos was simple and easy. There was something essentially cheerful about him, as there had been about Vince.

Today, as on other days, she stayed behind and sat down to examine a set of files, but she wasn't really reading, she smoked instead and made a call. She tried to ring Domokos but he wasn't there. She didn't mind: the act of dialling and waiting for someone to pick up the phone was just a way of delaying things, a defence against enquiring glances and having to give explanations. It showed that she had an official reason for still being here after others had left, that she had work to do, someone important to speak to. Once everyone had gone and she heard the door at the end of corridor close, she stopped trying the telephone. She leaned back and looked at the sky through the window, the clouds dark and dense, scampering towards the city. 'There'll be a storm,' she thought. 'The first real storm of the year.'

She was deeply concerned that the old woman's constant presence was getting on her nerves.

Iza loved her mother no less than she did her father, but she loved her differently and for different reasons. She hadn't slept at home for seven years, not even as a guest; whenever she visited she booked a room at the clinic or at the hotel. It was only once her mother was up at Pest that she got to know her as she was in old age. Her early memories of her mother were of a jolly, courageous, sensitive, somewhat frightened, bustling, good-hearted figure, someone waving at her from the past, someone who, despite her amusing hare-brained nature, was loved by everyone for her charm and sweetness, and for her gift for making people feel at home. Before she brought her to Pest there was something disarming about the old woman's utter ignorance of all the changes in the country; it was only Vince who used to keep track of them, relying on the evening news bulletin to build up a picture of the present, that was when he didn't feel too tired to listen.

From such a distance it was possible to smile at the old woman's instinctive feudalism, at the naive way she addressed everyone younger than her, or, as she saw it, of the servant class – woodyard workers, charwomen – by the familiar *te* form of 'you', the way she learned from Aunt Emma, but up close it was impossible. Iza had lived alone for years in Pest – the last time she lived with anyone was in the house with the dragon-shaped spout where she and Antal had only to knock at the door on their return from work to sit down to a ready supper, hungry and pleased, eating up everything with great relish, Iza warming her cold hands against the white ceramic stove through whose glazed door the fire her mother had made glowed and danced. Her mother made good fires. She had only to poke it and the flames shot up. This was the home she wanted around her now; she yearned for the harmony of those happy days but knew, just a few weeks after her mother had moved in with her, that there was no point in hoping.

Nor any sense in beating around the bush: the old woman irritated her.

In the first few days it truly astonished her to sense the extraordinary energy in her mother's old body, the never-flagging insistence that she play a part in her daughter's life. Her constant presence, the way she kept opening doors, always wanting something to *happen* at precisely the times Iza was exhausted and wanted rest and quiet, a space where nothing happened, saddened her and forced her to spend ever less time at home, only as much as was absolutely necessary. For a while Teréz was the solution to all her problems, but now she felt Teréz too was under threat, and when she was away she felt such anxiety thinking of the flat, it was as if she had left an unruly child behind, and you never knew when this child would somehow find some matches and set fire to the curtains. Her stomach had by now adapted to big city tastes and she found her mother's cooking too heavy and too greasy. Over the years she had got used to the melancholy freedom of the lonely, to not having to give an account of herself to anyone, to not having to tell people where she was going and when, and when she'd be back. She didn't really understand why it was so irritating to have to tell her mother where she was preparing to go – there was nothing secret about her excursions and, apart from her well-established habits and her need for silence, there was no reason she should not be happy to have someone home waiting for her – or why it so depressed her to hear someone shuffling into the hallway while she was turning the key in the lock, or showering her with questions as she was removing her gloves: where have you been, what did you do, whom did you meet?

Iza didn't feel like entertaining her mother with the thrilling events of her day. She arrived home tired and longed for some quiet. She herself was surprised to discover how much she resisted conversation at such times, or what an irrational temper she'd get into when the old woman shuffled after her just as she was about to go out, suggesting a coat or a mac or a cardigan to wear on top – or under – her clothes, telling her what bad weather it was outside and that she would get soaked or catch a cold, the old woman's face etched with disappointment when she failed to convince her at least to take an umbrella.

She sat looking at the dense dusk, wondering how to occupy her mother. The old woman's selfless, ever-anxious, incomprehensibly youthful energy had been so completely directed towards Vince that she herself had failed to notice it. There could be no question of introducing her mother to her few friends because her political naivety and country manner of asking direct questions would simply frighten them away. She couldn't give her jobs to do because, even if she didn't know how much that ancient body could cope with, her day would be disturbed by the constant bustle. 'How frenetic her love is!' she thought in horror. 'How unrelenting! Does everyone love like she does, demanding every moment of the day?'

The spectre of Antal's disappearing figure rose before her, the way he turned his head against the irreversible tide of time and looked at her. She couldn't think of him with as much indifference as she would have liked to, shrugging her shoulders, dismissing him with a wave of her hand as if to say, 'You were just another thing in my life and now it's over.' She felt humiliated every time she thought of him. No one could have been a better wife than she was, so why did he go? If they hadn't divorced she could have asked him directly what to do about her mother, but the Antal to whom she could have taken her problems and disappointments, especially after he had offered to move back into the old house so the old woman could stay at home, was gone. Perhaps he already suspected something.

She couldn't tell Domokos that she found her own home

stifling and that it was like being a bee on the lip of a jar of honey, her mother's fingers always dipping her into the sticky heavy mass, her mouth and nose blocked by the golden sweetness. She couldn't tell Domokos such things because he'd write them down and make a story of them. Everything was a subject for some story to him. She shocked herself by admitting how repelled she was by Domokos's art.

Out in the corridor an open window slams shut. A gusty shower. Once again she hasn't thought of anything but has simply decided that the way they were going was all but intolerable and precisely the opposite of what she had imagined. At home, with Vince, when Iza was a child, maybe even when she was Antal's wife, the old woman was an angel, a good-natured, sensitive angel, her attention warm and welcome. 'I'm getting older,' thought Iza and shuddered, not because it was true, but because it was her own diagnosis. 'I was still young when I lived with her and in many ways depended on her, even as a woman; she cooked and cleaned for us, she patched Antal's clothes. But now she can't see that I have fully grown up and don't need to be mothered. She has aged and grown weak, she needs support and advice. If I want her to be happy with me I have to pretend to be a child. That way she'd be satisfied nannying me during the day and she'd be tired by the evening. I brought her here. I invited her because I wanted her to live a long time and to be happy. The trouble is that now I have to behave in a way she understands. I don't want displays of feeling, don't need help. When I'm tired I just want to be quiet. Will she be able to cope with that? Will I? How is it going to work?'

A clap of thunder rang out. She thought she should wait

until the storm was over but she didn't dare. She decided to call a taxi and rush home, providing she could get a cab. The old woman was always worrying that she might have had an accident and whenever she was late became quite overwrought with anxiety wondering where she was. Iza hated being worried about. During the war, while still at university, she regularly carried a gun and sheaves of subversive leaflets in Vince's old briefcase, and when any policeman asked for her papers she gave him such a contemptuous look he immediately let her go. If Antal did ever worry about her he didn't show it, however late she arrived at university, though there was plenty to worry about. It was a risky business rushing about under the cover of some air-raid blackout pressing sticky-backed leaflets to walls. And when she did appear at the evening seminar, usually at the last moment, out of breath, Antal would tease her about what a fine doctor she would make being so untidy and so unpunctual. He was particularly cold and rude to her before strangers.

She stepped over to the window and looked down. The traffic was heavy and the city seemed to be cowering before the oncoming storm, the hour offices finished work but before theatres and cinemas opened, the whole city swarming, a rolling mass of people moving towards bus stops and tram stops, so many you could hardly see the road for them. If she didn't get a taxi it would take an hour to get home and she'd be soaked through to the skin by then. The old woman had been pleading with her to take her plastic mac when she set out at noon. But it was sunny then.

She called a taxi and, wonder of wonders, the rank actually had one. She gathered her things together and ran down the stairs so she'd be there when it arrived. She took a look into the street and saw a taxi swing in from the square. Her heart lurched at what she saw.

There was a tram stop opposite the clinic. One had just arrived with the usual rush-hour crowd hanging on to it, dripping from it like a bunch of grapes, the bunch suddenly shaken as if by a supernatural force under the high thong-like lamp posts. The crowd opened up and from their midst lurched a figure in black who, having landed awkwardly on the traffic island, quickly adjusted her crooked hat. Iza trembled as she watched her mother looking around in confusion, the storm lifting her open coat. A stranger took her by the arm and led her across the road, the old woman hardly daring to step in front of braking cars. The man kept explaining something to her until they got to the other side. Iza rushed across, slapping her keys down at the porter's lodge, the porter just gazing after her because she had never passed him without shaking his hand. Her taxi arrived in front of the building just as the old woman walked through the door, her face bright, extending a string bag with Iza's shining purple mac in it.

Suddenly the shower hit them. Iza hesitated for a second in the downpour before pushing her mother into the taxi. The old woman sat stiff-backed, her eyes closed. When she first appeared her face had a glow to it that had disappeared by now.

Iza took the string bag from her and threw it on the taxi floor. 'You do look after me, darling,' she said courteously. 'Don't think I'm not grateful, but you really shouldn't have bothered.'

The old woman didn't reply, just gazed at the driver's back.

The sky was rumbling. 'She travels by taxi,' thought the old woman. 'How simple it all is. When the weather is bad she calls a taxi.' She was aware her heart was beating unusually fast, a little irregularly even, and she felt as though she was drowning. It had been a horrible journey in the crowded tram – she had never been on the street so late, in the terrifying neon-flashing dark. And all the time the fear, the helpless feeling, what if the girl was caught in the storm?

Iza was pale and in a bad mood. 'She travels by taxi,' the old woman thought again and looked at her string bag. It was a very ugly string bag.

5

Without telling each other both Teréz and Iza tried to help the old woman. Teréz, who had taken the job because she felt restless not having enough housework to do, was suspicious at first, feeling the old woman was a hostile new presence in the flat, someone who was always following her around, doubting her honesty. She wanted to put her in her place and show what she thought of her. Iza did that for her: the old woman stopped harassing her. But now that she wasn't always following her, messing up the kitchen, now that she was no longer dripping coffee on the freshly scrubbed floorboards and had retreated to her armchair, simply sitting there, looking out at the ring road which couldn't have been of any interest to her, Teréz took no joy in her victory, in fact it rather worried her. She was an intelligent person and quickly realised that she had failed to do certain things in those first few weeks. She understood how an old woman rapidly heading towards eighty, who had spent all her life on firm ground, coping with straightforward problems, would now feel as though her life were hanging by a thread, and she also understood the bitterness she must be feeling, a bitterness she had never articulated in words that must have been there all the time: she was, after all, an old but still active woman, and she was in mourning. Having established the nature of their relationship, Teréz wanted to show her some tenderness without endangering her own importance and position.

One morning she arrived with an empty shopping bag, clearly not from the market but straight from home. She called in on the old woman, who turned away in terror when she opened the door, muttering something, then immediately stood up thinking that, unusually, Teréz intended to start the cleaning in her room. At such times she would go through to Iza's room and was about to do that.

'I had no time to do the shopping this morning,' said Teréz. 'If you fancy it, why not go down to the covered market and buy the necessaries. I've made a list.'

She was surprised by the enthusiasm with which the offer was accepted. The old woman's face lit up. She put on her glasses so that she'd be able to read Teréz's list in the market and stepped lightly down the stairs without holding on to the banisters. It was as if she had discovered a secret store of energy in herself and never mind the stairs. Teréz turned on the radio and went about her business, shaking her head from time to time. What a fool she was to leave the shopping to the old woman. She'd finish later than usual now. She had usually finished cooking by the time the old woman got home from her walk.

She had just finished the rooms when the old woman returned having bought everything on the list. Teréz thanked her, ran her eyes over the things on the table, and in her grudging good-hearted way went so far as to ask whether the bags were not too heavy for her before getting straight up and starting to cook. The old woman stood behind her at the open door, her face beaming. Teréz didn't have the heart to tell her to go away though it always made her nervous to have someone watch her cooking and there were times she had cut herself or grated her skin. If only the miserly old thing had bought fresh goods instead of the cheapest and the worst! The meat was streaky, all bones, fit only for a dog. But she said nothing, didn't even mutter. The old woman stood there for a while, watching her spellbound as the raw material was slowly transformed into food, then returned to her room. She was utterly exhausted and deliriously happy.

Teréz left the shopping to her after this, though her purchases sometimes annoyed her and there were times she quickly had to substitute one ingredient for another: the box of cocoa she left at the market, the mustard that fell out of her bag. She never criticised her for anything. There were other times she marvelled at how good she was and thinking so made her reflect somewhat sentimentally on her own condition. Why should she herself be a widow, and a childless widow at that? Just looking at the old woman could bring it on, this uncertain, mild regret. Teréz liked weeping; she delighted in watching films whose endings she never saw because she was too weepy. On the other hand she felt she was even with the old woman and was feeling pretty pleased with herself.

On 1 July, Teréz's birthday, next to Iza's usual envelope full of money on the kitchen table she found an old-fashioned silver brooch with the coral motif of a severed hand in the centre. Teréz turned it over and over in confusion; she didn't particularly like the pin but it moved her to receive it. She hesitated a moment before shyly pinning it on.

She had sent the old woman out shopping but it was the

caretaker who brought up the full bag, saying she had gone for a walk. When she didn't arrive in time for lunch Teréz became so anxious that she left the food on a low flame and went down to look in the streets, running round the block. She found her by the Corvin cinema, sitting on the steps with her eyes shut. When Teréz called her name she sat up in surprise and obediently set out after her back to the flat. Teréz wanted to tell her off for making her worry like that but she couldn't bear to, guessing that the old woman had been hiding from her to avoid the embarrassment of being thanked. The old woman deserved some respect for that. Who could have guessed she was such a sensitive soul? She gave her lunch and while serving it out, still with her back to her, feeling suddenly confused and shy, she thanked her for the gift. The old woman whispered something, her face and neck glowing with happiness.

*

After the first few weeks of disorientation, Iza too was beginning to adjust.

Surprisingly enough, Domokos played a part in this readjustment. One day, in the middle of a play, he turned to her and asked what she was going to do with granny. The question sounded flippant coming from him because she thought he wasn't really interested in anything beyond the form of his own utterances and had never detected signs of particularly charitable concern in him.

Domokos continued gently but firmly as Iza hesitated, watching the stage. 'Because if we leave her out of occasions like this you might as well have left her in the country and she'd be no less lonely.'

Iza leaned forward. A character was speaking a monologue on stage. Theatre was the art form Iza had always liked least. If ever she got the time she read sober works of realism and novels with sensible plots. It was only because of Domokos that she went to the theatre at all and the actress's long monologue irritated her. People talking to themselves were pathological, she thought. She didn't answer the question, which made it look as though it was not worth answering, but she simply didn't know what to say. She had been pondering the question for weeks. She didn't know the answer.

'Keep thinking,' said Domokos. He leaned back and said the actress had poor diction.

It was on that occasion that she first seriously thought that, given all the circumstances, she could actually live with Domokos. Domokos – and no one who had only passing knowledge of him would have imagined it – had been suggesting marriage for a while. Iza was reluctant to entertain the idea. She was in two minds because behind all her objections there was always the memory of Antal's hair blowing in the breeze and the trees in the copse bending with the wind as Dekker passed. 'I hope he doesn't write about this,' she thought suddenly and looked away from the stage to get his reassurance. 'You won't write about me, will you, Peter?' she whispered. Domokos's face clouded over: he looked older, much older. He shook his head.

Once she got home that evening she decided to write down how she spent her time.

It was like being a student preparing for exams again. She

took a piece of paper and divided the day into hours. Morning: rise, prepare, dash into work; home by late afternoon. She was usually tired after the journey then and not up to spending time with her mother. Certainly not up to taking her out somewhere. But by about seven, if there was nothing special she had to do, she could perhaps try sitting with her till supper time. After supper the evening would be her own since the old woman would go to bed then. She couldn't do this if she were on the afternoon shift, of course. She needed mornings free then to make notes, to work, or to write the odd article. She felt a degree of stage fright telling her mother this, worrying that she might not understand that it was the only way she could be fitted into the day, but she need not have worried: the old woman understood perfectly and responded to Iza's plans with such happiness and gratitude the girl really didn't know what to say.

Having put the plan into effect she was with her mother four times a week, visiting her as if she were a guest. The old woman always welcomed her into a tidy room and offered her some-thing delicious that ruined her appetite but which she didn't have the heart to refuse. Her mother had put on a little weight and started to look more like her old, rural self. The two high-lights of the day – running errands for Teréz and Iza's visits to tell her about life at the clinic – seemed to be enough for her to take new courage and gather strength. Iza's heart almost broke with pity to see how hard her mother worked to try to understand what she told her, how she strove to memorise the names and how proud she was of being able to refer back to a previous conversation. 'Is that the colleague of yours who got married in China?' Or, 'Did you find the book that vanished

from your table while you were in surgery?' Iza never felt at
her best in the hour or so she spent with her mother but she
always pretended to be. Her plans for the late evening had
generally to be postponed or cancelled – she only got out with
friends or went to the cinema on a Sunday afternoon, though
she hated going out in the early afternoon. As far as Iza was
concerned late evening, after supper, was the right time for
company or concerts. She might have been willing to give up
company but she couldn't do without the concerts, especially
on the days her season ticket was valid, so she put the old
woman off on those evenings, but she felt so guilty seeing her
ever more worn, disappointed face that she always made up
for it the next day: it was like catching up with homework.
Domokos, when he came, now tended to arrive after ten, once
Iza had finished her work and the house was quiet. The old
woman occupied the time between her two daily highlights one
way or another and slowly got to know the other inhabitants
of the block, at least those on their floor, always stopping to
talk to mothers with children. The women were fond of her.
The great city of her honeymoon had shrunk to one small part
of a single postal district, but one that was growing intimate,
village fashion. Teréz extended her brief to cover household
goods. People all over the area were getting to know the old
woman, the dairy shop even providing a chair for her to sit on
when she had to wait.

*

The summer was unbearably hot.

It was hard for the old woman and she had nowhere to hide

from the heatwave. It was almost dark before she dared open the shutters. She stumbled about blindly in the flat and instead of the rural scents of summer behind cool Venetian blinds she had to put up with the unforgiving heat. Iza did not suffer very much but her mother was struggling for breath. When Teréz saw how pale she was and recalled how she had been gasping since the morning, she didn't let her do the shopping, telling her it would be bad for her to be carrying things and that they'd have to tell madam-the-doctor. She took the string bag herself, pushed the old woman into the dark room, left her with a cool wet cloth on her forehead and ran off.

The old woman was for once grateful to her. She felt hot and weak, weighed down by her thoughts. She wanted to order a permanent memorial to Vince in time for All Souls' Day, the day of the dead, and closed her eyes trying to visualise the best possible stone and inscription. She had corresponded with Gica about it: the cloak-maker was a person of taste.

The heatwave lasted for weeks. It was possible to open windows in the evening but the fresh air didn't do much to cool the baking walls. Iza too lost weight and was planning a holiday. She first thought of going to Czechoslovakia to be in the Tátra mountains but then changed her mind. 'We won't go to the Tátra this time,' said Domokos. 'Let's stay in the country, rent a room somewhere along the Danube Bend, and take the old girl with us, she looks utterly washed out.' Domokos was careful not to use too many poetic metaphors when he talked to her.

So they planned ahead, the old woman most keenly, with one small regret, because she had no memory of ever going away except in her youth and she felt awkward about planning holidays now Vince was dead. At the same time, in her own modest way, she was happy to take a break from the unbearable oven the city had become. The time between Teréz leaving and Iza returning went all the quicker for the thought and she imagined how great it would be to spend the whole day with Iza and that mad writer of hers, who always greeted her, coming or going, with 'Your servant, ma'am.' For some reason she couldn't explain even to herself, she liked Domokos, though she often reflected on the irregular and quite wrong relationship between him and her daughter.

Teréz regularly finished an hour or two earlier now she did the shopping herself.

One afternoon, when Teréz went off having left a bowlful of apricots by her armchair, the old woman wondered how Teréz could get away so early and still be doing the shopping. Could it be that she had shopped on the way here? But then she thought how it was the same even when Teréz nipped out to the shops in the middle of the job. How could that be? She started nibbling at an apricot but it didn't taste like the ones back home used to, not quite ripe, a little bitter despite all the sun. Suddenly she stopped chewing. She realised why Teréz tended to finish so early nowadays.

It was shocking, in fact monstrous, for her to realise that she wasn't helping Teréz by doing the shopping but rather slowing her. The blinds were drawn, the temperature in the room stifling; the old woman was having one of those rare moments of perception when everything seems blindingly clear. All of a sudden she felt terribly ashamed of the way she had misjudged Teréz. Teréz was strong, thought the old woman as slow bitter tears crept down her cheek. Teréz only seemed stern and loud, in reality she was gentle and sensitive. The image of Teréz as a stern loudmouth was replaced by that of a tender young woman, transformed into an abstract idea of pure virtue, who had taken pity on her and was, as an act of sheer grace, sacrificing her own valuable time in order to help her occupy her idle hours. Teréz must clearly be doing a better job of shopping: being better acquainted with the covered market, while she was still working through the stalls without having fixed on any particular butcher or greengrocer, there being so many of them that she felt she had to try them all. She was more of a hindrance than a help to Teréz. If it weren't for the heatwave, and if Teréz hadn't been so prepared to take the task back, she would never have realised it. Never.

She didn't dare look Teréz in the eye the next day, though they had got into the habit of chatting by then, Teréz being happy to talk about herself and her dead husband while the old woman reminisced about Vince. There might have been twenty years or so between them but they shared their widowhood and that gave them some common ground. Teréz didn't understand why the old woman had become so morose and reserved. Once she even felt her brow to check she wasn't ill. She couldn't persuade the old woman to do the shopping, not even once the heatwave was over, and while this was a great relief to her she couldn't help but be curious. She felt offended, as if her kindness had been rejected, and paid no more attention to the old woman who was back to crouching in her armchair and to wandering about the streets, thinking how to let Teréz know that she felt she had no right to accept her kindness and that she would rather die than go on in the knowledge that she was hindering rather than helping anyone.

Then she started worrying about the same thing with Iza.

Iza continued faithfully visiting her in the early evenings, though she was tired, bleary-eyed and ever thinner in the face. On one occasion she caught a summer flu and sat further away from her, croaking and holding a handkerchief before her mouth, but she still came and made conversation. The old woman kept a beady eye on her in the half-light. Iza was always cheerful and never complained, the news from the clinic was invariably good, all going well, with the hope of a trip abroad. But later in the evening, when Iza thought she was asleep, the old woman crept to the door and listened as she rang Domokos. 'No, don't come now, I can hardly speak, I'm going to lie down. You must understand I have to be by myself, I can't go on like this. I'm like everyone else, I need a couple of hours to myself alone when I just lie there and look at the ceiling.'

Hearing this, the night that followed was like the night Vince died – long, too bright, unreal.

*

The city traffic died down but hadn't quite faded; it was never completely quiet on the József Ring, there was always some noise as if the heavy breathing of daytime work had given way to a light snoring sleep in the dark. The old woman did not take off her clothes when Iza left her, she remained fully clothed in the big chair, clenching and unclenching her fingers. Her mind was full of naive childhood prayers: *'Watch over me, dear guardian angel, prevent me from going astray, guard my every step, let me grow in the fear of God.'* She had a Catholic wet nurse in infancy through whom she learned to love the angels.

God was far off and male, the guardian angel was closer, more comprehensible, more tangible. 'My guardian angel,' thought the old woman. It was such a strange thought since the angel had neither age nor gender while she herself was very old; that guardian angel must be pretty tired by now – the guardian angels of the aged would have lost their own agelessness and hers would be gasping for breath, scuttling along with ever slower steps behind her. Iza had Domokos to complain to, that is if she ever told anyone what bothered her, but she wouldn't be able to help Iza, she might simply shed a few tears with her and stroke her hair as she did when Iza was a child, but Iza was grown up and what could she do to lighten her load now? Iza was tired, she was working hard, her mornings and afternoons were dedicated to the sick and what little time she had left she was giving to her, her mother, so there was only a tiny part of the day left for herself. She was having to slice up her days the way you slice bread. Vince was dead, Endrus was dead, the old town had gone, everything was gone. Even Vince's illness, with all the horribly demanding tasks it entailed, with all its dreadful obligations and the constant gnawing fear that filled her days, seemed something to envy now. Her helpless fingers trembled with the pain of thinking of it. Teréz would get on better without her. Iza could never relax when she was around. There was no Captain, no Gica, no Kolman, nobody who really depended on her for kindness or even conversation.

Maybe she was already dead and hadn't noticed? Could a person die without being aware of it?

Outside she could hear the clatter of a late tram. The old woman started calculating how long she might have to live.

Her parents had died early, so that was no clue; some naive instinct in her told her she would live to be Vince's age, approaching eighty-one. But how much better not to have to get that far! Iza could go and enjoy a holiday by herself and needn't tire herself out entertaining her mother in the evenings.

The next day when Iza dropped in she waited for her in bed and said she'd already had supper, that she was exhausted and would rather sleep than talk. Iza took her pulse, made her sit up and looked at her very hard. Her mother's face looked tired though she had days when she looked remarkably fresh too. Now she looked precisely her age, maybe even older than seventy-five. Her pulse was as slow as it always had been, maybe a little stronger but still regular. She didn't seem ill. 'Maybe she's bored with me?' wondered Iza as she took her leave and returned to her own room, humming to herself, opening and closing a few drawers and starting to dress. 'Maybe she is bored with these conversations every evening, maybe she wants to sleep? Maybe she has got used to life here and doesn't need me so much?'

She picked up the phone. The old woman could hear her dialling. She didn't get out of bed this time, she didn't listen or wonder whom she was talking to and what about. The lilt of the voice, the cheerful melody of it might as well have been scored on a stave: she could hear it as clearly as if she had been at the door. Iza was discussing something with someone and soon there was the sound of water running into the bath. Then the door opened a crack. She stayed stock still, pretending to be asleep. She could smell the cool scent of Iza's cologne. Iza stood listening for a moment while the old woman tried to breathe regularly as though she were gently snoring, then she closed the door. The front door needed to be closed very firmly and she heard the small thunder of it as Iza went out. She hung about by the open shutters looking down at the street as Iza passed in her white dress, her hair let down so she looked like a schoolgirl. She was running through the gate and jumped on to a passing tram.

After that she let Iza in only for a few minutes at a time.

*

Iza observed her with some suspicion at first but since she always found her asleep in the evening she slowly got used to doing other things. She wrote articles, had Domokos round, invited friends from work and went out more often. For a long time she only saw her mother on Sundays: the old woman was becoming strangely gaunt and hard-faced. Iza felt there was no love in her eyes and complained to Domokos about how distant and alien she had become, that she hardly ever spoke to Teréz, that she avoided her, that she did nothing but sit around and that when Teréz arrived she would immediately leave the flat and not return till lunchtime. Where on earth did she go and what's got into her to grow away from her like that? Domokos didn't know and said one would have to see her more often and talk more to her to understand. One Sunday when they were dining together at Iza's he went out of his way to be nice to the old woman, unusually nice, like a little boy, which wasn't hard because he liked her. He didn't know what to make of her though: she didn't respond to his jokes, she had little appetite and hardly touched her food but soon left them, saying she was tired and was going to bed. 'It may just be part of the ageing process,' said Domokos. 'While she was back in the village she was obliged to stay young to cope with all her troubles but now you have brought her up to town she is letting herself go. The world has shrunk around her. There are such cases. We will grow old too.'

'You never will,' said Iza, shaking her head. 'You are too irresponsible to grow old.'

That was what she said but what she thought was: 'You have less sense of responsibility than Antal.' She hated herself for always relating everything to Antal.

Domokos, who had no regular hours of work and who went to the café opposite Iza's block to write, promised to keep an eye on the old woman's secret comings and goings in the hours between Teréz's arrival and lunch, about which the old woman refused to speak. 'I just like walking' was all she'd ever say when asked, though they didn't believe her because it clearly wasn't true: the hours she chose were far from the best time for walking.

Iza simply stared at him when he told her that the old woman spent hours on the tram.

'She gets on the number 6 in front of the house, goes as far as Moszkva Square, then changes to the 59, goes all the way to the end of the line, then gets on another tram, travelling from one terminus to another and that's all she does for hours on end.' Domokos himself felt puzzled recounting this, just as he felt anxious following her at a distance seeing that she never once spotted him, never looked round when she was on a tram, not even at a stop. The old woman didn't speak to anyone, she had an empty string bag on her arm and stared at the streets without any expression on her face, utterly absorbed as though she wanted to ask the unfamiliar houses some questions.

'It's a harmless way of passing the time,' said Domokos, chiefly in order to reassure Iza who was clearly shocked and saddened. 'Cheer up! She's getting to know the town.'

Iza did not cheer up because she didn't understand. The old woman had never mentioned her journeys, it was as though she were guarding some state secret – in fact, she hardly ever said anything about anything nowadays. Teréz grew morose, unnerved by the great silence. Teréz wanted either friendship or war; the state of silence between them was unfamiliar territory and she didn't like her disappearing for hours. When Iza's holiday came round and the three rooms at Zebegény had been booked, the old woman announced that she wasn't going anywhere and would prefer to stay in town because the strange new environment would only exhaust her. Iza pleaded with her for two days, then realised that her mind was made up and felt ashamed that her joy at the news was greater than her anxiety and agitation. Two weeks by the Danube! Two free weeks!

She rang home every afternoon from Zebegény and received the same news each time: I'm fine. Teréz was on holiday too so the old woman did the cleaning and cooking for herself. By the time Iza got home she had lost more weight but seemed calm. She complimented her daughter on her appearance and returned to her room. It was a Sunday morning and Iza was really looking forward to telling her about things, feeling fresh, energetic and rested, smelling of sunlight. She swept up the post and went through to her mother's room.

The old woman was just preparing to go out. She said she'd hear her news the next time as she had to be off now. Iza stared at her in disbelief. Her mother picked up the empty string bag and left. Iza leant on the windowsill and watched her in a panic. It was no longer suffocatingly hot. Her mother was in the street, less scared of the traffic now because she crossed the narrow route to the traffic island without any help and got on to the number 6 tram.

didn't like it that the house had come into Antal's possession —
what was it to a tankardman's son and why would he marry
again after Iza?

It was not only Gica who came with the house, not just the
newsagent, but Kolman too.

Every time Antal got home, before he could even step
through the door, he had to stop because the grocer was
gesturing to him and sometimes ran over with a string bag.
Shopping had become more complicated since he lived here
rather than at the clinic. Gica claimed that Kolman had insulted
her and that she wouldn't do her daily shopping there, while
Kolman was upset that at the start, before Antal knew he was
upsetting him, he did all his shopping at the clinic buffet and
brought it home in his briefcase. One day Kolman stopped him
in the street and told him how much he was hurt by his lack
of patronage. Antal didn't want to offend him. 'I'm such an
idiot,' thought Antal each morning on his way to work when
he gave Kolman his shopping list, which was always the same
— milk, bread, butter, occasionally some sugar, salt, fruit and
green peppers — and which he would pick up. But he was not
really angry. Kolman beamed goodwill but it wasn't so much
him Antal didn't want to offend as Vince. Maybe, come summer,
he, like Vince, would offer cuttings and rosebuds to the girls
behind the counter.

He accepted the full string bag, the uglier of the old woman's
pair, an awkward, lumpy thing, with a design of orphan children, that she had stitched together from an old coat, its lining
made of waxed canvas. With his briefcase under one arm and
the string bag on the other it was difficult opening the gate
and no easier shutting it, so he put the things down as quickly

as he could on the basketwork table inside the entrance. Now, at twilight, the air was thick with the scent of Vince's roses, sweet as honey, the whole garden luminous in the dying light. Gica looked after the flowers: that was clear from the freshly dug earth and the traces of recent watering. Captain huffed and puffed his way out of the woodshed, old and clumsy now. At the bottom of the string bag lay shreds of cabbage – a secret treat for Captain, but he could take his turn.

Nowadays, after a good while, whenever he went in and closed the door behind him he felt an undefinable sense of well-being: it was what he had hoped for when he bought the house. Nothing disturbed him behind those old walls. There was no longer the heartache of missing Vince's familiar figure, instead it was as if he were still present and strangely alive in the rose bushes outside, his personality and his solid good humour preserved in the high brick walls overrun with ivy. When he first moved here the raw healthy smell of fresh plaster and paint filled the rooms, and he was often troubled by memories even though the house was quite different from when he and Iza lived in it, its character having changed, the old furniture having been cut up and used to make sensible, lightweight tables and chairs, everything more modern, more up to date, with less of the pleasant sense of timelessness of the Szőcs family home.

Iza's ghost was more stubbornly persistent than that of her dead father, or the old woman who had left with such a hopeful look on her face, clutching Iza's hand and hanging on to her skirt. At first he regretted tidying away so many years of struggle with money he could have spent on a new freehold flat in Balzsamárok without any memories attached and significantly closer to the clinic than this town house. He kept walking up and down the refurbished rooms without quite feeling at home. A strange double vision troubled him: there was the old furniture that Iza sold him for next to nothing, furniture that had long been rebuilt into something new that fitted into its new setting, the walls covered in bookcases – yet it took weeks for him to get used to it as his own home, weeks before he could open a wall cupboard and not think that piece of wood was from the chest of drawers where Iza kept her underwear. The girl had been too close to him to forget her now. The building work, the carpenter and the upholsterer, all took longer than planned and lasted till midsummer, even though every workman he hired had once been his patient and tried to work as fast as possible to please him, so it was the end of June before he could move in and August before Iza had become memory rather than presence, or at least no more a presence than the old woman with her kindly enquiring look and clever busy fingers, or Vince with his wise small eyes and peaked caps.

There was no such image of Iza, nothing as tender and charming; Iza remained a rather sombre memory, that is when he thought of her once he was in bed. It was a word here, a phrase there, he suddenly recalled.

But then she too faded away like so many things, like everything, in fact.

Captain panted after him up the two steps that led into the house. His mail was always addressed to the clinic, the only mail he ever found at home being the occasional business card and there was nothing today. Antal was tired, he had had a hard day. He was intrigued by the way his nervous system could adapt itself to such strange games: if Lidia were not on the night shift he wouldn't feel at all tired, they'd wander the streets together or sit in the woodland café and chat as they did on all their free evenings right into dawn. But Lidia was going to be working tonight and suddenly he felt drawn to the bed as he never did when there was something more important to occupy him, such as a new patient, a death, a particularly important meeting, an article that needed writing and could only be written at night for lack of time. Such things kept him going, but Lidia first and foremost. Above all, Lidia.

He bathed and changed his clothes. On the top shelf of the built-in wardrobe was a pile of old boxes that had belonged to Iza's mother, which Iza had given him for nothing. He smiled as he did each time he opened the wardrobe. Mama's odds and ends, Vince's stuff, his stamp collection, his glasses. It should all have been thrown out but he didn't like the thought of it. Such things brought him closer to those who were now far away and there was a lot of room in the wardrobe, so everything could be accommodated and it was only the ugly old paintings he consigned to the attic. Iza had also left him a complete kitchen set, old-fashioned, well-looked-after items that he and Gica arranged neatly in a cupboard. For decades Antal had possessed so few things that he was sometimes amused by the highly personal clutter that came with the house: a watering can, a block for chopping wood on, a pipe filter, a small axe. He left the pipe filter out because it had a heavenly smell, hanging it on a nail in the hall next to two of Vince's meerschaum pipes arranged in a cross, and Vince's cherrywood walking stick. When he grew older he might perhaps smoke a churchwarden pipe. The mixture of old and new gave the house an amiably quaint look, so cosy that when his colleagues came to visit they'd clap their hands as they entered, and Sanyi Vári gave a whistle and wondered why he had bought a bachelor flat on the fifth floor of a tenement block. The price he had paid for it would have covered the cost of Antal's house and everything in it. There was a welcoming air to the new place, something nice and intimate.

Captain wanted feeding so he put something out for him in the kitchen where mama used to, then he too ate, enjoying his yoghurt and happily munching away at the loaf Kolman had put aside for him. It was natural to have a ring on his finger by now, though he found it strange when they first got engaged, his eye constantly catching on the bright circle of it. It was distracting and felt uncomfortable when he was washing his hands, but he didn't want to upset Lidia by removing it. 'I like other people who look at you to know that you are already spoken for,' she said. Iza disliked symbols and never wanted an engagement ring but Lidia would have proclaimed her status as bride-to-be on public posters if she could. She was possessive in a way Iza would simply not have recognised, jealous for no reason other than the fact that Antal had been alive in the years before she met him. Sometimes she'd lose her temper with him but not for long and then she'd glow with happiness, a radiance she never lost because at last she had an object for her passion. Antal knew that if his life were at stake, Lidia was willing to kill for him, or, even while trembling with fear, would offer up her own life for his sake. He had never known anything like Lidia's love, a love so vulnerable it had no self-defence mechanism, and he responded to her devotion just as unconditionally, just as innocently.

In the first few weeks of their relationship, after she was given the painting of the mill and following Iza's attempt to offer her money, it was like trying to penetrate a layer of disciplined reserve and to overcome her shyness. But when the real Lidia emerged with her background in poor villages like Gyüd and Csordarét, with the kind of intense, all-pervading passion that he loved, he felt like someone in a foreign country who was finally being addressed in his own language. He answered her call immediately, body and soul.

The engagement party was held in the house. Women whooped when Antal produced two rings and placed them on the sideboard. Although everyone had known that, once the relationship between Iza and Antal had been established, the pair were bound to get married, no one had the least idea of the developing relationship between doctor and nurse. Antal was always going out with someone. So this time it's Lidia, they thought. As he was opening the champagne it occurred to him how little the previous owners of the house would have been bothered by this wild behaviour; Vince would have loved the dancing and cheering, and would happily have gone round the guests offering them his home-made walnut brandy, while mama would have been overjoyed to see so many people in the house, just as it used to be in Aunt Emma's day when she was still a girl with a mass of hair, young and full of blushes.

Iza would have been the only one to think it all – the engagement itself, the exchange of rings and so on – a waste of time, a lot of fuss about nothing. That night he hardly left Lidia's side and felt closer to her than ever. When the party was in full swing, when everyone was drinking and Sanyi Vári took out his guitar and sang the words of 'There's a Small House by the Mighty Danube' to a different tune, he took a walk in the garden with her. The house, the only real home he had ever known, was being given new life, not at Iza's instigation this time but at his own, the revived house being the fruit of his own labours, the product of nights mulling over a thousand details. He desired a house, this particular house complete with Vince's cherrywood walking stick and Captain who was hiding from the guests in the wood store, wheezing asthmatically as he always did when he felt hurt. Lidia was walking silently beside him letting him collect his thoughts. Iza was a soldier by comparison, a comrade who had marched along with him a while. It was not the same with Lidia. As soon as he began to love her he realised she would never walk either beside or behind him: Lidia was, in essence, part of him, *was* him, not as the result of some agreement but because they moved instinctively together.

Now he was preparing things. He had always liked this kind of mindless activity, opening tins, laying the table, doing this and that, the kind of things Iza dismissed but which were the joys of everyday living for him, something that assured him he had food to eat and that what he was eating was something he had himself bought, not what others gave him. He opened a drawer or two, then pushed them shut again. He never left the washing-up to Gica thinking it would be a shame when he had hot water on tap. It had long been his dream to have a home with a made-up bed and a table with a tablecloth on it, and when he entered on his internship he would often plan his house, should he ever acquire one, in great detail. Antal had been so poor he had only two ways of reacting to his early poverty: he could forget any dreams from those days and get on with life or bring those dreams to pass as thoroughly as he could. When he got engaged to Iza he felt that Vince's house was everything he was looking for. He was deliriously happy, almost lost for words when the old woman handed him the keys.

Back in spring when he first told Iza that he would like to buy the house, he noticed a gently mocking smile hovering about her lips. It was as if she were saying: *I don't want to spoil your mood. No doubt you enjoy paying a mortgage and there is probably something wonderful about the fact that the first real house you actually lived in now turns out to be yours to keep with no strings attached, and of course you will be pleased you won't have to whisper when talking or keep your voice down while making love in your room so the old folk shouldn't hear anything.* Iza's self-confidence was such that he sometimes felt warm clothes and heated rooms were wasted on him, that her spirit and willpower were sufficient. She was his defence, his shelter from cold weather. Normal ideas of polite behaviour were made for people weaker than she was. Antal was always sincerely happy to see her succeed.

Dorozs, the place where he was born, was an insignificant village. He was born close to the hot springs, in a sweaty hovel smelling of sulphur. Antal had no memory of his mother who had simply disappeared at some stage. 'She's gone up to town,' ventured his grandmother with no sense of certainty. Later, once he was grown up, Antal had some ideas about why she would have gone to town, to meet what fate, other girls from the village having met a similar fate.

He did know his father though, in fact he saw him die. Like most men in Dorozs he went round town in one of Dániel

Bérczes's carts, but he wasn't a carter, he was what the villagers called a *kupás*, or tankardman, someone who escorted the cart loaded with hot water, measured the desired quantity into a tankard and delivered it to the carter's clients. Dániel Bérczes rented the spring from the village council and had a hundred and fifty water carts to cover the locality. It took a lot of skill and courage letting the water out: the water was boiling hot and it did you no good just being near it, but the really dangerous task was to pull out the spigot and to stuff it back in again, then to carry the water to bathhouses or people's tubs without spilling any. Bérczes took no care of his carts and one or two were rickety, starting to rot. Antal's father died one day when, before setting off, he squatted under the cart to check the tap and the bottom of the cart split open, drenching him in boiling water. They carried him home where, strangely enough, he said nothing, but screamed obscenities for two hours before he died.

Antal's grandparents had too many problems of their own, so couldn't afford to spend days weeping and mourning, but sat up till dawn discussing how they might turn the tragedy to their advantage. Bérczes's lawyer forestalled them by paying for the funeral and a little extra, persuading the elderly couple not to make a fuss because it would only anger Bérczes, while this way he was well disposed and willing to address their interests. Antal's grandfather had already called on Bérczes that spring to enquire about a post as a park-keeper but wasn't taken on; now he received a message that he could start immediately and that there was a job at the hot spring for the child too. Antal carried mud into the mudbath but they didn't let him into the bathing area proper because there were a couple of cabins close by the spring. Even then the eight-year-old boy knew that it wasn't because he was a child or because it was a more complicated business standing guard over property than opening a cabin door. It was because they thought he might steal, because a very poor person is unfit to do jobs requiring security, because anyone who rents a cabin rather than spends time squatting on the muddy slopes of a spring must have valuables worth removing and therefore stealing. The old man was park-keeper, the child the mud carrier, both being paid positions, a situation envied by more than one water-bearing family in the Dorozs community.

The story of Antal's father eventually came to the notice of a left-wing newspaper in the capital and the matter was even discussed in parliament. Bérczes's lawyer turned up again and this time brought a journalist with him, one on a government-supporting paper. He took statements from the old couple and frightened them so much by noting down their stuttering attempts to speak that they left everything to the lawyer, who then reminded them that Dániel Bérczes was not only looking after the aged parents of the unfortunate victim: since the tankardman's son appeared to be quite intelligent he was also willing to pay for the boy's education and he could attend the famous grammar school in the nearby city as a boarder.

His grandfather listened and would have preferred some ready cash, while his grandmother just wept, though she tended to weep at anything. She was always frightened something bad would happen and indeed, there was reason enough to fear. She didn't know what it was but behind the timidity and despair there was something she couldn't name, a tremor no more tangible or defined than the shadow on the ground of a bird in flight. Antal didn't want to go. He screamed and protested, being only too happy as a lark, but the tears dried up in his grandmother's eyes: it was as if a thought had travelled a very long way to flash through her mind and she was the only one privileged to think it. She did something she had never done: she spoke before her husband had a chance to and said that the head of the household could remain as park-keeper and that they did in fact want to send the boy to school, so there was no need to make any complaint against Mr Bérczes, nor did they want anything else of him.

Antal kicked and carried on kicking when they deposited him in the cart. Bérczes's lawyer drove him into town, though he had to stop twice because the boy leapt off and, like a puppy, made for home. There was no package to accompany him because they didn't have anything apart from a certificate from his school to say he had done well in his four classes, a certificate that consisted of the teacher at Dorozs reflecting on Antal's none too visible virtues, since he could barely read or write and had none of the basic school requirements because he attended school for only a couple of weeks in late autumn and late spring, which was when he could afford the time and the shoes. The note omitted to mention Antal's minimal attendance because if the teacher had done so he would have been in trouble with the authorities.

The institution in which he became a boarder was a five-hundred-year-old Church school to whose governors Dániel Bérczes agreed to supply a vast amount of hot water in lieu of Antal's fees. In the first two years his teachers thought it a poor bargain because the boy knew next to nothing, was stubborn, rude, got into fights and was nothing like the idyllic image of the gentle, shy peasant lad he should have turned out to be. He hated study and would sneak out through the back door and wander around town – and whenever he saw one of Bérczes's carts entering the great arched gate with its statues of early Church fathers, Transylvanian princes and paintings of long-dead illustrious bishops, he burst into a stream of foul language that surprised even him, since the boarding school was a veritable paradise compared with Dorozs, and he had put on some weight and grown strong on account of those carts and that steaming water.

Antal spent the first two years of school just making up for what he had missed, but he did grow to like learning. He still waited each day for the Dorozs cart to arrive so he could swear at it, but he wasn't swearing at the driver or the tankardman, both of whom he greeted with greater respect than he did the masters at school. His classmates never laughed at him for this. Antal had great respect among them because he was an orphan. He swore and fought, responding neither to kindness nor to punishment, which was unexpected in a student whose fees were being paid not in money but in water and whose father had died in such dreadful circumstances. No other half-orphaned pupil could compete with him.

Bérczes took no interest in the child and never sent him a penny. Though the boy was provided with bed, board and tuition he remained alone in the building at Christmas and Easter. The servants all liked him because he was so bored he was ready to help them without being asked and because, when he was alone and the school did not want to keep the heating on just for him, he'd go down to the kitchen to sleep. In the summer holidays he'd hop on any cart that would take him home to Dorozs. At the end of the first year when he turned up with a dreadful report, dressed in the half-city, half-country-style clothes provided by the school, and glared at the strange dog lurking around the bathing area, his grandmother clapped her hands and wondered what to feed him since he had turned into a real giant on school meals. But he hadn't become a gentleman; he immediately kicked off his shoes, changed his clothes and ran out to the mud in just his pants to carry on with his old job. He brought home whatever he earned and they were genuinely sorry to see him go away again.

He was in his third year of school and aged thirteen when he really developed a taste for learning.

By that time he had caught up with his classmates and, as it turned out, he had an iron will to work and a remarkably good mind. He wasn't keen on literature, but geography and biology interested him, and he had a fondness for mathematics as well as for languages, which was unusual for the class; in fact, for anything that required logic. This sudden awakening of interest was part of a moment of enlightenment. It was as if a dark curtain had been rent open and he saw his mother, whose face he could barely remember, his father and grandparents, and Dániel Bérczes with his carts, just as they were in life, or might have been. Whenever the pre-ordered water carts from Dorozs arrived during the school's quiet hour he asked to be allowed to help with the tankard work. It was a dangerous occupation and the young teacher who gave him permission had no idea of the risk involved, thinking it was merely a strange game. Antal's entire life had centred on the hot spring, and the tankardman and driver both continued to believe that the little boy was rushing downstairs to meet them because the water was calling him, and that he would soon return to pick up where his father had left off – for why should he want to do anything else? Bérczes would surely get bored with his remarkable philanthropy and return the boy to the low station from which he had raised him, so it wouldn't do him any harm to get used to it now, since it was what he would do till his dying day.

A year later he asked for an appointment with the headmaster.

The headmaster was astonished. It was he who called the students in to see him and it wasn't his habit to grant them interviews just because they suddenly thought of something. But he knew Antal very well: collegues talked of him with a certain quiet irony at first but he had gained a growing respect. Besides, the school had never had a pupil who paid his fees in water and many of the resident staff were able to relieve their rheumatic limbs because he was there.

The head examined Antal as he entered and saw a thickset fourteen-year-old peasant boy of distinctly protestant look wearing ill-fitting clothes made of cheap but decent material.

Antal Antal, fourth-year student, was requesting that the board of the *gimnázium* give him the opportunity to continue his education by letting him pay his fees either by teaching younger students or through working as a member of the in-school service staff, rather than by having Dániel Bérczes pay them in lieu of a supply of hot spring water.

The head was a classicist, a passionate researcher into antiquity, someone who adored the heroic cast of mind and the high ideal of manliness symbolised by the classical world. His office did not oblige him to teach but out of sheer passion for the subject he taught an annual class or two and solemnly believed that the great figures of Athens and Rome continued to provide the perfect model for the younger generation. Antal was excellent at Latin, his all-consuming mind and his ever readiness to engage in analytical thought helping him to overcome any difficulties in learning the language. 'A sterling product of our education,' the headmaster thought. The headmaster saw the Capitol rise before him, the seven hills, and the never seen yet a thousand times imagined face of Romulus. Meanwhile the boy was seeing the body of his father with shredded muscles hanging off his arm. The name Dorozs, the place of hot springs, was fundamentally non-Latin but had its origins in the languages of the Danube basin, languages the headmaster couldn't identify. Antal had no idea why the headmaster seemed to be moved, but he felt his request was being warmly received and that made him happy.

The head thought of the director of the newly opened school in the next street and felt a certain pity for him that he could have no such experience. He stood up, patted the round head before him, quoted something from Horace and promised to have a word with Mr Bérczes, and that he would argue the boy's case before the board of governors. The child clicked his heels as his teachers had taught him. The headmaster felt moved as Antal left: the boy was a miniature *civis Romanus*.

As soon as he was outside the door Antal said something truly terrible about Mr Bérczes, the kind of thing his father was screaming on his deathbed, then leaned against the iron railings that ran alongside the wooden steps in exactly the same way as they had done a good century and a half ago when the school was first rebuilt after the fire, and kissed it as though it were a living creature with a mouth.

The head walked up and down his room, still in a state of high emotion, vowing to look after Antal's interests as long as he himself was alive. The head misunderstood the boy in regarding him purely as the product of his liberal but highly puritan education, or indeed as the embodiment of his own classical ideals with the result that when he died, during Antal's university years, he died not quite knowing who it was he had been teaching.

Bérczes was absolutely delighted not to have to think about Antal any more; the tankardman's accident had long been forgotten in Budapest and, being a businessman, he preferred to sell his water for a price. The *gimnázium* board was happy to see Antal through as many scholarships as necessary to top up his paid work. '*Sub pondere crescit palma,*' thought the head, who had been referred to as Cato ever since his student days at the school, as he watched the boy set out for his daily job, showing his special exeat at the door. Antal made a great impression on all his classmates, he hung on to his free tuition right through to matriculation while in receipt of a regular supply of underwear from the Women's Voluntary Corps. He no longer went home for the summer, the head assigning him to teach a class of failing students from the countryside, the sons of landowners and village registrars, so that when he arrived home in autumn he looked tanned and strong, every student of his having passed the repeat examinations. Mothers didn't like him because when one of his students didn't want to learn and would not be persuaded he would beat the boy, beating him without anger, with all the detachment of a doctor administering nasty medicine for the greater good of the patient.

He could never afford books: they lay beyond the limits of

his working salary. Newspapers, on the other hand, were afford-
able. Papers cost a few farthings and one could learn a great
deal from them, particularly about politics. The head walked
into the dormitory one bright day just as he was lost in the
news, reading the foreign correspondent's report with great
care.

The head didn't like his students reading newspapers.

His school was not of the old hidebound kind but a relatively
free-thinking institution whose broad views sometimes featured
too prominently, as a result of which it received far less state
support than it might have done had it been less liberal. At one
time it had suffered considerable trouble with the authorities
and the headmaster's immediate predecessor had been sacked
in 1920. This head was more cautious in his approach to
progress and was terrified that this boy, whom he had liked so
much, might be taking the first steps down a dangerous road.

Antal defended his hunger for knowledge and choice of
reading with perfectly reasonable arguments and wouldn't
relent even when the head extended to him the same rights in
using materials from the great and famous library as the masters
enjoyed. Antal replied that the great library was chiefly for
classical literature and he'd also like to read living authors
writing about modern things.

He's young, of course, thought Cato, only sixteen. Maybe
he wants to read some of those contemporary love poems,
verses so obscure that no one can understand them, the writers
themselves being snotty brats, people who read with their
nerves rather than their brains. But the boy wants his own
library and that is a worthy ambition. He thought of the infinitely many scrolls of Cicero at the bottom of the *scrinium*

and of Cicero's freedman, Tiro. Yes, it was a fine ambition and a pity to stand in the boy's way. The Mitasi lad is already chasing skirt and smoking cigarettes. This one wants books, so let him have the books. What time did Vince Szőcs tend to call in?

He knew the judge, they had been fellow students in this very school, it was just that Szőcs had studied law afterwards whereas he trained as a teacher. Szőcs was a quiet little chap, someone who was not too keen on Latin but did well enough on Roman Law at university. It was, again, one of the teachers who had taken him under his wing, the boy being an orphan. Once he qualified he became a clerk at court while the head started as an assistant master. One day, around Christmas, he appeared at school, swinging his walking stick, running up the wooden stairs, having returned because he liked the school, even the smell of it. From then on, until he was dismissed from his position, he always tried to drop in when passing, or to call on the head at the boarding house so he could take a look around. He was a loyal son of the school, always willing to donate something, a little shyly, whenever an unusually gifted student needed help. He said he didn't have a father himself and that others had brought him up, and that though he couldn't afford very much he would like to give a little something every Christmas as a present for the kind of penniless child he used to be. There was always an envelope in his hand that he would leave on the table before rushing off. Then the round little man would be gone before he could be called back.

So he appeared every Christmas, nor was it a negligible sum he brought with him. He liked to be told whom the money went to and was happy when the child was pointed out through the window, but would bolt if they wanted to introduce the child to him. When, in 1923, the head learned that Vince had been dismissed from his job, he thought he'd never see him again, but he appeared at Christmas as usual, in the evening this time, as if he didn't want to be seen by day, thinner, somehow older and more mature, as if it were only now that he had attained to proper manhood. He hadn't really seemed an adult before, not quite, maybe because he was generous in a way that didn't quite befit a grown man. The head was doubly pleased to see him this time because he now knew that Vince Szőcs was a man of principle, that the word of the law was sacred to him and that his sense of justice was not to be trifled with. He only regretted not having visited Szőcs when the man was first put on a pension; he would surely have appreciated it.

Szőcs didn't stay long and the sum was indeed trivial compared with what he used to bring. He apologised and said the money would be enough only for one or two books but there must be some students who loved reading. Then he immediately stood to leave. He was wearing a tattered coat and the headmaster felt he shouldn't have accepted money from him. But he did accept it and continued to do so each year. After the introduction of the *pengő* as currency in 1927, it was always the sum of twelve *pengő*, neither more nor less.

When the judge's envelope appeared as usual in 1933, the head called Antal. The boy didn't want to accept any money, not even when it was explained to him that it was for books alone, the kind of books that might form the basis of a developing personal library. Antal replied that he could only accept money he had worked for.

The head looked at him with increased respect and pointed through the window. The boy followed the direction of his finger to a grey little man in a shabby coat carefully skirting the mounds behind the column dedicated to the Dutch benefactor. 'That's the man who donated the money. That man there by the memorial column was a village boy like you who paid no fees because the village supported him,' said the headmaster. 'Ever since he earned a salary he has given something to the school. In 1923 they sacked him, so now he can afford only enough to pay for a few books.'

'They sacked him?' asked the boy.

The tone of the comment was indifferent, apparently unconcerned. The question didn't sound much like a question, it was simply the repetition of a phrase as if he thought it would be discourteous to doubt the fact.

'He used to be a county judge,' said the headmaster and offered the boy the envelope again. It would be awful if the boy thought Szőcs was a thief or a murderer and that the school was willing to accept gifts from criminals. 'They say it was on account of some particular judgment he made when there was a harvesters' strike in the county,' he added.

Antal Antal bowed and said he would be happy to accept the gift. The head gazed tenderly after him, as tenderly as if the boy were his own son. It was only after he had left, closing the door quietly behind him as he had been taught, that the head felt some unease, though he would have laughed off any suggestion that he had been scared by a look in Antal's eyes, a passionate look so different from the neutral expression normally worn by that adolescent face, which was only just now developing a bone structure. It was a gleam that went out as if by command, suddenly, according to some order emanating from deep inside him, from a place so deep a man might wonder whether the gleam had really been there or not.

Antal matriculated, but only with a Merit, because his result in Hungarian Literature let him down; he never could write a literary essay. The organisation of material into a three-part format bored him and he had absolutely no interest in the nineteenth-century epic's treatment of ancient national religions. Nevertheless the president of the exam board, one Professor Dekker – it being part of the school's tradition to invite previously outstanding students to be president of the exam board – read everybody's papers with a childlike intensity and picked out Antal's as the only one to give a complete picture of the literary treatment of ancient national religions, albeit in the form of an index or academic bibliography. In the oral part of the exam he noted the student's carefully measured, rather stiff manner of speaking, his sure grasp of every scientifically verifiable detail of the subject, and his reserved but polite reluctance either to enter into sentimental explanations or to paint vivid word pictures of historical tableaux. Antal hardly looked at him, having been absorbed by the preparation required and being preoccupied by other issues such as whether he would be admitted to the university, how much reduction he might expect in his student fees and whether Cato would succeed in securing him some much sought after university accommodation. It was a nice surprise to him, then, that after the results had been announced he was told that the president of the exam board had promised to support him. Dekker had heard the story of the tankard boy from the headmaster and also happened to be dean of the university that year, so when Antal appeared before him at the ceremonial welcome to new students, after the usual handshake he asked the boy to remain behind.

'I'd prefer it if you didn't get involved in politics,' said Dekker, examining his hands. He had unusually short fingers. They weren't doctor's hands, more the hands of a wrestler.

Antal looked him in the eye, then immediately looked away. Antal had a passionate interest in politics and knew nothing about Dekker yet.

'Study and think,' Dekker continued. 'That's not an order, it's just a personal plea.'

Back at school, boarders were always discussing world affairs, including the subject of the local socialist youth movement. Antal thought the professor meant that he should not get involved in left-wing politics, so he simply stood there and looked at him without saying yes or no. Dekker told him he could go.

It didn't take Antal long to orientate himself. In October, when he was asked to join the fascist student movement, he declined, saying he had too much to do, as most certainly he did: he had to look after himself now and couldn't rely on cheap sales clothes or college charity. Dorozs was slipping away into the past: his grandparents were no longer alive and he didn't have to support them, but the spartan mentality was his own and had little to do with having or not having a family to consider. Antal liked responsibility and though his relationship with his grandparents was functional rather than emotional, he still missed having a proper family.

Dekker's words at the enrolment ceremony made full sense to him in December when he stopped to allow the dean to pass him at a corner, raising his soft hat to him. They were in the university building, Dekker in his official garments, *plenis coloribus*, hastening to a meeting because, being head of every organisation within the university, he was obliged to attend such things. He saluted back by putting two fingers to the golden ribbon of his professorial cap and stopped. The corridor was lined with palms, the glass roof white with snow. Only the wall lights were on and the marble panelling glowed pale as butter. They could hear the shuffling in the great ceremonial hall beneath. They were alone.

'You're in everyday clothes,' Dekker remarked, looking at his hat. 'Are you not coming?'

He gazed in polite indifference at the professor's glittering outfit. 'I'm not a member of the movement,' he answered.

Dekker removed his cap and ran his fingers through his dense unruly hair. 'I'm pleased you listened to me,' he said and set off towards the stairs.

Dekker could never walk at an even pace, he either sauntered or rushed. At that point he was rushing. Antal watched him and felt he liked him. Later, in 1945, when Antal was the president of the committee examining Dekker's papers and a member argued that Dekker should not remain in his professorial chair, and that his activities before the war should count against him, Antal did not cut the man off but, once he was finished, revealed Dekker's work behind the scenes, and how golden ribbons and *dominus* caps were a cover for his faultless organising ability, his intelligent treatment of the fascist movement and his brilliant acts of clinical sabotage when the town was evacuated. Dekker for his part cursed softly and dismissed it all as nonsense. He hated being praised.

Antal's love life was very simple. Suddenly, what had been very difficult at boarding school became very easy in the medical faculty. He had great fun with provincial female medics who, in 1935, the year Antal entered university, were still a little drunk on their own courage in taking up such a daring career rather than spending their time in quiet university libraries and were all too keen to prove how unrepressed they were. They wanted to show that nothing about nature and the body scared them.

Antal took from them what they were willing to offer and responded with whatever courtesy seemed due; he danced with them, he helped them in class discussions or when they were in trouble, and patiently heard them through whenever they bawled their eyes out or complained. The university was located among centuries-old oaks and was comprised of four faculties, and the students' rooms were mixed up, not organised by faculty. Antal got on with all his room-mates but chose his friends carefully. The leaders of the youth movement left him alone. Dekker's patronage protected him from the loudmouths and his excellent marks, combined with his fierce independence, excused him from taking part in fascist activities. On one occasion when he was accused of something, the leader of the movement spoke in his defence, asking how in heaven's name could he be a member and take a full part in it when he was earning his living by teaching Jewish children, and receiving his fees from all those rich lawyers and doctors who wouldn't hire him if he were member of a well-known anti-Semitic organisation. Antal's taste and judgement were formed in his boyhood. He and his friends watched the Hungary of the Thirties and the rise to power of Hitler like circus lions who knew they'd have to jump through the flaming hoops before long, and that they'd need all their strength for the moment. At the funeral of his old headmaster he sang the hymns of mourning along with the rest, and tears ran down his cheeks as he stood by the bier and saw for the last time the simple champion of Roman virtues who felt more at home in the ancient world than among the children of his contemporaries.

It was at this funeral he met Vince Szőcs.

He recognised him immediately, though he looked thinner and more exhausted than he had that winter when he was shuffling in ordinary shoes past the column with its statue of the Dutch donor. He stood at the very back, more outside the funeral hall than in, as if he feared that his appearance might cast a bad light on his late friend, and once the procession started took care to walk at the back of that too, constantly looking round as if ready to scuttle off among the graves at the first awkward moment. No one took any notice of him and when anyone did his face betrayed nothing except the obligatory normal signs of mourning.

Szőcs was not alone; he was accompanied by a girl of unusual slenderness. She was taller than him and Antal couldn't work out her age. She was too thin, her waist was far too long, her legs were like the legs of a thirteen-year-old as were her clothes, her gloves far too big so they slopped about on her hands as if they had been borrowed, and her black handbag was creased.

Her brow, her entire face, but most particularly her look threw him into confusion: it was the face of a young soldier on sentry duty, it was how she moved beside Vince, unblinking, her gaze moving around the mourners. She moved as though she were escorting a seriously ill patient, watching the time and keeping an eye on her surroundings, the road and the place generally, worried in case the air was too chill for someone who had hardly recovered. Later, when he tried to conjure Iza's face it was this young, timeless face he kept recalling, that military look, Iza as the line of defence, Iza with the floppy gloves and unusually white lips, walking side by side with Vince.

Antal was with Dekker who, by this time – in view of Antal having reached the final year of qualification – had started addressing him as *te*, the familiar form of you. It was clear by now that he wanted to train him up as his assistant and they had various passionate conversations about politics. Dekker didn't look up but stared at the ground, finding the whole affair boring and painful, his view being that death was a purely personal matter and that any ritual associated with it was a form of superstition meant to make people feel better, a sort of communal sport. Nevertheless he came along because he liked the old Calvinist citizen of Rome and because they were once classmates who went to the same inns and bawled the same drinking songs. He trod through the autumnal slush muttering to himself: why didn't they simply do as old Cato might have wished and burn him on a pyre according to Roman custom in Donor's Square where a toga-clad *histrion* wearing a Calvin mask might imitate his familiar gestures in the authentic way? It was Antal, not the professor, who noticed that Vince Szőcs wanted to speak to him.

It was impossible not to notice. From the moment his shy glance fell on Dekker it had not shifted. Szőcs was whispering something to his daughter who had been standing straight enough before but now stood even straighter. She was like a tall exotic flower growing before his eyes. Antal slowed until they were almost beside them and Dekker slowed his own steps to please him. It wasn't proper to say anything and, fortunately, there was no need to since the professor finally noticed the judge and greeted him warmly. A look of uncertain pleasure, a kind of hope, flashed across Szőcs's face. The girl took an appraising look at the professor, the way one looks at goods in a shop: what was he worth?

Antal rarely felt obliged to take any particular action but, when he did, he followed his instincts. It had been just this kind of instinct that prompted him to knock on Cato's study in childhood and to offer his own work rather than Bérczes's deal as the basis of his scholarship. It was the same instinct that led him to lowering his defences in the third year of his studies when Professor Dekker brewed him coffee in his office for the first time, and he understood what the professor expected of him and what kind of opinions he actually held. Now the same voice told him to go and join the Szőcses. The girl, that strange girl with the long eyes and the bearing of a junior cadet, was clearly the judge's daughter, the judge who, year after year, gave him twelve *pengő* to spend on books. Surely Cato must have told Szőcs who was getting those books?

Dekker stopped him. He said goodbye to Antal, telling him they'd meet at the clinic, because he had something to discuss with a friend. He stepped back and took Vince Szőcs by the arm. He never even looked at the girl. The minister had started on his funeral song. Dekker took no notice whatsoever but was explaining something to the judge whose face went ever redder as he listened and the sudden change of expression conjured in Antal a sense of what his face might have been like in happier, more confident days. Antal imagined him in his youth, with a rakish smile, right here in the same place when the cemetery was just a wood, at a picnic perhaps, lying under the oak, swigging from a flask and passing it on to Cato, laughing, red in the face, his expression full of hope.

The headmaster's burial took place without either the judge or Dekker noticing it. The girl turned her head towards the grave but did not join in the prayers, her face stiff as a mask, as if she and the priest were citizens of different countries, but she didn't want to insult the priest who, in her eyes, was a diplomat representing a different political system with which she did not agree but which she felt obliged to respect even while maintaining her own opinions. Dekker and Szőcs continued talking together after the burial, discussing something near a crypt, a little apart from the others. It wasn't a situation on which he could intrude and be introduced to the girl.

Antal returned to the university in a temper and bolted down his food in the canteen. He wasn't due to give private coaching till the afternoon so he hung around the noticeboard on the mezzanine. It always amused him that here they were in the middle of the semester and all his friends received letters but no one ever wrote to him. He glanced at the table of repeat examinations, the rector's announcements and ran his eyes over the names of the incoming students. They had already accepted enough applicants to overfill the faculty, so the graduates would have to be sent out to territories recovered under the Second Treaty of Vienna: to Transylvania, to the Czechs, to the Serbian town of Nagykikinda or to the Ruthenians, as if people didn't know that a posting like that would last only a couple of years until the territories passed to someone else again. There was a single name in the right-hand column of candidates not admitted, a rare event because it was extremely rare for someone who had got this far to be rejected. The faculty had turned down the application of Izabella Szőcs.

He entirely failed to concentrate on what he was supposed to be teaching that afternoon. He knew it was Dekker's habit to call in on his ward last thing at night to check over the most serious cases and he knew he could catch him at the main door. He was counting how many hours were left before he could see the professor and discover whether the connection between Izabella Szőcs, Vince Szőcs and the conversation at the funeral earlier in the day was what he thought it was. 'You're not alone, young soldier,' thought Antal. 'If you get here Dekker will support you and, believe it or not, I will too, not just for your father's sake but for the strange look in your long eyes and for that extraordinary authority you seem to radiate, an authority not often found in young women.'

Once Dekker arrived he told Antal everything without being asked, how the next day he would talk to the rector and tell him he wanted to accept the daughter of an old classmate of his, someone the institution was too scared to admit for fear she would be a bad influence. If her father is such an honest man, why does she need a diploma?

They'll admit her on the second round, said Dekker, and clinked his cup down next to the toy elephant. Dekker wouldn't have a skull on his desk like some of the others and whenever he found one on someone else's he would pick it up and sniff it as if he suspected it of being newly dead, giving the owner a few anxious minutes in the meantime. Antal knew that what he promised would be carried out: it was 1941, the country was now firmly involved in the war and people tended to shout a little louder but everyone was in awe of Dekker who wore his academic cap upside down on formal occasions and whenever the Germans won a major battle would go around singing 'Another war, yet more disaster, down the chute and ever faster', and when the rector took him up on this he would reply with a straight face, saying, 'I was drunk.' It was common knowledge that Dekker only drank milk or fruit juice if he could help it and that, when young, he had received a grant to study in Scandinavia where his friends got him used to such drinks rather than alcohol.

Two weeks later he saw Iza coming up the steps with a very old, much battered briefcase under her arm. She was wearing the same short coat she had worn at the funeral. He sat in the finance office and waited for the girl to complete the forms and pay; there was no bursary of any kind for her. His heart ached for her when he saw her measure out the hundred and four *pengő* and the enrolment fee. Vince Szőcs had been forced into retirement, yet he brought twelve *pengő* each year as a book prize! What had they sold to afford this? Or maybe they were not eating or heating the house this month?

When the girl stood up he followed and called to her in the corridor. 'Hello, fresher!' he said. 'I am your official class mentor. Introduce yourself to your senior.'

Iza looked him up and down but did not answer. She took a glance at the signs by the stairs and set off towards the medical wing. Antal went with her. Iza pretended she didn't see him. It happened to be a break between lectures, the lecture hall doors were open and second-year students had just ended their theory session when Ulla, Ulla Deák, winked at Antal. Seeing the lechery in her sleepy eyes, a lechery based on memories of the previous summer, he was so cross he hardly acknowledged her. Iza simply carried on, glancing at the doors with the professors' names on. She stopped in front of Dekker's office.

Antal was right behind her. Dekker hadn't come in yet. He was expounding something in Room 26, the great hall, whose doors were still closed. Once he was in the swing of things Dekker took no notice of bells and carried on despite the noise of the corridor, too absorbed in his teaching.

Iza knocked.

Antal took Dekker's key from his pocket. He was free to come and go, to tidy Dekker's papers. He opened the door to Iza. 'Do come in,' he said.

The girl did not step in but stared at the stone floor as if trying to decipher some secret message there. Antal closed the door again and stood beside her. Although there were only five centimetres between them so they were almost touching, Iza's tense refusal to engage in conversation made it seem as if they were miles apart. Later, years after, even once Iza was no longer his wife, he knew this was the moment he fell in love with her and that he wanted to live with her.

Dekker arrived at last. When he opened the door to the girl he invited Antal in too. Iza blinked and gave him a cold, formal nod but did not extend her hand.

'Antal will be ready to help you in everything. Listen to his advice and learn from him. No need for thanks, just go to your lecture.'

He lit a cigarette and addressed Antal through the smoke as they were leaving: 'Look after her, young man.'

Any other girl would have laughed but Iza's face remained cold and hostile. There was nothing he could ask her, she was impossible to speak to.

They walked past the girls' room and Ulla's face flashed by again as she looked through the open door. She noted Iza's ill-fitting coat and the old briefcase, but she didn't look happy. Ulla too had noticed Iza's long eyes and bright lips, and marked the awkward, nervous way Antal was following her, desperately hoping for encouragement. The stone floor was loud under their heels, the halls were finally empty and the buffet was filling up. Antal knew the girl would have no money but he also knew it was pointless offering her a drink since she wouldn't accept it. The thought stung him terribly, yet he was proud of her.

They had to stop by the great hall. The blue booklet with the first-year timetable was open in her hand: Iza was preparing for her first class with such calm assurance she might have been in her old school not at her first university lecture. There were only two minutes before the bell. Iza's lip trembled. Now she would say goodbye and close the door behind her.

'I know your father,' said Antal.

She turned to him. The blank face was gone. The soldier turned into a smiling girl.

'For years he would bring me books at Christmas. Did you know?'

The girl shook her head. He put his left hand to his throat as if not trusting himself to say the right thing, worried he might be talking about things of which it was wiser not to speak.

'He gave twelve *pengő* to the school each year; and every year after year six the headmaster gave it to me. Did he not tell you?'

The girl's eyes told him he hadn't.

'One time he came I saw him. He was younger and more mobile then. He ran among the snow drifts on Donor's Square as if he were afraid that someone would stop him and thank him. Are you still not talking to me?'

The young soldier's face softened a little, creasing like a child's. 'Every month he got three *pengő* pocket money from mama,' she said. 'One he gave to me, one he used to buy a newspaper on Sunday because he really liked reading the papers but I didn't know what he did with the third. Was he saving it for you?' She was using the *te* form to him now as naturally as if he had been her brother.

'Let's go to the cafeteria,' said Antal.

She'd only just enrolled and was already late on the course so it wouldn't matter as long as she attended her first class at noon, he said. They could go to the cafeteria, have coffee, smoke a cigarette, even eat something, then go for a walk in the wood. As long as she attended the physics class from twelve till one that would be enough for today. He'd go with her, he thought. He'd go with her everywhere. He'd be the first to take her to the dissection room with its cadavers.

Iza put her blue book into the briefcase and walked along with him as he suggested. She was tall, a touch taller than he was, and wore no hat – her hair was brown, brown as a school-girl's, a child's, without any hint of gold, like a Biedermeier painting.

They ate a slice of cake and Iza asked for sparkling water, sipping it with great pleasure as though it were fine wine. She refused a cigarette but was happy to accept a stick of chocolate and carried on chewing it when they went out to the university woods.

The wet weather of the funeral had been followed by a minor heatwave. The sky was blue and no breeze shook the dying leaves. It was mild weather: birches and firs looked hazy and uncertain between sturdy oaks. There were benches on the hill and a brook at the bottom of it, both artificial of course, on a bed of lowland sand. Iza sat on the railings of the little bridge dangling her legs, leaving her briefcase on the ground beside her. There were carp in the pond, plump brown carp, and she threw a few clods of earth at them.

'I'll come to visit you on Sunday,' said Antal.

Iza said fine.

'You won't forget that Dekker said I was to look after you?'

'No.'

Her skin and hair were gently scented with a little-girlish smell of soap.

'Dekker is a good man. Listen to him. About everything.'

The older ones would tease her, call her fresher and give her every kind of nickname, he thought. He was more concerned for her than he had ever been for himself. How to look after her? What could he do for her? How to shield her from all the likely dangers? It would be awful if some fascist in the youth movement were to pin a crane feather in her hair and declaim how Hungary was just about to win the war and reclaim all the territories lost in 1919, from the Carpathians through to the Adriatic. He took the hand with the chocolate in it. She didn't mind.

'Don't get too involved with politics.'

The girl immediately vanished; it was the young soldier who stared back. The chocolate in its silver foil hovered between them in the air. She didn't eat any more but snatched her wrist from Antal's grasp and threw the chocolate to the fish in the pond. She leapt off the bridge railings, picked up her briefcase and set off for the main building. She didn't say a word until they reached the edge of the wood, then stopped and looked at him again and spoke very clearly as if she wanted to emphasise every word to him. 'Politics will be my life as long as I live,' she said.

He knew it was crazy but at that moment he was sure he would marry her.

3

He married her on a sparkling wind-blown day in the autumn of 1948. There was something deeply moving in being fully aware of the character of the girl he was marrying, that, in the seven years he had known her, he had seen her study, pass exams and move among the sick and dying. He had danced with her and had provided her with leaflets that informed people of the true state of the war, leaflets that she would slip between notices advertising canaries or reliable guard dogs. It was good to know that he wasn't marrying her just because he had fallen blindly in love with her or because he physically desired her, but because they were intellectually matched, because Iza was a person you could respect, someone from whom you could learn.

And of course it was good that he could marry her at last without any further complications.

He did in fact feel a fierce physical desire for her right from the start and tried to tame the desire so it might become a less passionate, more brotherly, protective relationship, which shouldn't have been too difficult since her waist was so thin and her limbs so childlike he felt ashamed even to have noticed that adolescent body. But once he got over that he was surprised how passionately Iza responded to his kisses and how womanly her body became once she was in his arms. He was never in any doubt that he would marry her as soon as he could, but he also knew that he wanted to live with her till then. Iza was not Ulla. He couldn't imagine taking her down into the club room and making love to her on the billiard table or under a tree in the wood.

It was hard not having a home. They lost weight and felt on edge. Dekker's office, where the girl often called to see the professor, offered a solution. Not that Dekker noticed. He had long been a widower; his personal life had more or less finished with the sudden death of his young wife and he devoted himself entirely to his work, to saving his students from the pointless war and to ensuring that as many young people as possible could see the situation of the country for what it was. Dekker would turn up at the clinic at the most impossible hours and was to be found in his office only after he had finished teaching. He never noticed what went on there and he thought of his two young protégés merely in terms of their respective specialisations: Antal, once he was qualified, became his assistant and Dekker regarded him as a highly promising surgeon; as for the girl, she was clearly interested in rheumatological therapy.

When he saw them kissing by the statue of the local poet he was genuinely happy that matters had taken this turn and that he could give Iza, now in her last year, an appropriate wedding present; he had already taken steps to ensure the girl's position and once the wedding day arrived she had a post at the clinic too. He was their witness and wanted to take them for a meal after the register office, but Antal said they couldn't deprive the old couple of their proud day, so they all dined at home. Vince, now rehabilitated, was the head of the house and seemed to have grown half a head taller. He was wearing his new blue suit, offering them drinks, while the old woman, now laughing, now crying, rushed around in a tizzy. Dekker left immediately after the meal saying he didn't want to see them at the clinic for at least a week.

It was most unusual, almost incomprehensible to others that, now they finally had some money and when the doctors' trade union had offered them rooms in one of its holiday flats in the mountains, they should turn down the offer. Iza declared that honeymoons were a stupid bourgeois tradition and Antal echoed her saying they'd be stupid to go away now when, for the first time, he had a proper father and mother.

The old woman shook her head and didn't dare say that she was a little embarrassed to be with them now. The physical aspect of the relationship to be conducted under their roof made her nervous. Vince thought of Pest and his own inordinate pride on knowing his way around the streets while his wife pottered along next to him, giggling and confused; how satisfying to feel expert and knowledgeable about the world, to point out the famous sights, to take his wife's arm solicitously at crossroads and to escort her to the other side. He would have liked Antal to take Iza away somewhere, to *lead* her to places, to direct her attention to things she might not otherwise notice, but he soon lost confidence in the idea. Iza wasn't the kind of person who could be led anywhere and was certain to know her way around Pest better than Antal. She was unusually happy and beautiful on the day of the wedding, her face radiant with love and satisfied ambition. Vince watched her as she moved about the room, brought in something or took something out; he admired the certainty of her movements, the way she sparkled with good cheer, a cheer that hung around her like some portable effulgence wherever she went. She had never been shy: she was a young woman fully confident in her own being. Vince laughed at himself. No use expecting her to be naive; young people who had lived through the Second World War would not be fazed by something as ordinary as a wedding – nor, if by some chance they were born female, would they blush just because they were marrying a man. He couldn't understand his own confused state of feelings but would have liked Iza, on this special day, to look just a little overcome.

Later, on just another such bright, blowy morning when the three of them were left alone, Antal took the two suitcases that contained all his belongings and Iza closed the door behind him, hanging up the now unnecessary fourth set of keys on the hook beside the three others, and went about her business with the same straight face though he would have preferred to see her crying. But Iza did not cry. She put on an apron, tied back her hair and set to tidying, rearranging the room that used to be theirs, carefully wiping the wardrobe that had been Antal's just a few moments before. Vince followed her, carrying the dustpan behind her just so he could be with her. Right now he was watching her squatting down, rolling up the rug at the foot of the bed. Vince was shorter than Iza and felt unnatural looking down on his daughter as though she were a child now. He simply felt a peculiar, quite inexplicable desire to see tears in her eyes again.

As a little girl Iza was just like any other, that is insofar as he remembered the girls from his own childhood: she laughed when she had cause to, she cried when she took a fall, when she broke a cup and when she was afraid. What had happened to that little girl? Of course, it was much nicer for everyone that there were no scenes at Antal's departure and that the atmosphere in the house had hardly changed or that, at most, it had cooled a little, as if someone had left the windows open when airing the room so the walls and furniture felt the winter chill wafting in. But Vince would have given years of his life – even those precious much-loved years following his rehabilitation – to see Iza in tears as she rolled up the rug. Antal was not short of tears when he left, weeping, kissing their hands and faces. His shoulders sagged as he was carrying his cases: they seemed burdened with a greater weight. His lips trembled and he was gulping as he looked back at Iza. If the divorce had been Iza's idea Vince might have understood their contrary behaviour, but it was Antal who was filing for divorce, Iza had merely agreed to it.

*

Antal soon realised he was born for domesticity and that he would prefer to live with Iza in a proper family home rather than continue in their previous romantic circumstances. He felt his attachment to Iza would grow ever deeper once they conducted their lives in a regular manner and was therefore more than happy to receive her family in lieu of a wedding gift. He could talk about a great many things with his fellow boarders and about practically everything with his closest friends, but it was only with Iza that he could talk about Dorozs.

Dorozs was a secret, a project so important he couldn't set about it soon enough. Antal was preparing himself to meet

Dániel Bérczes and to discuss the hot springs where he was born. The idea had never been to surprise old man Bérczes in his garden and stick a knife in him, even to start belated proceedings against him. Bérczes, if he thought of him at all, was just the symbol of an unsustainable form of being, a living mechanism for transporting hot spa water by horse-drawn wagon rather than by proper engineering. And yet the idea that the spring might be confiscated from Bérczes and that the strength and intelligence of his servants might be better employed, to a more humane end, was quite dizzying to him. If they could not bring the dead to life or compensate them for those terrible years of their lives, at least the future of Dorozs might be ensured. He knew his own passion would not be enough to see him through the campaign to save his village. Now that he could discuss it with his new wife he was happy beyond measure.

Once a week Iza went with him to Dorozs and looked up those of Antal's acquaintance who were still living. She explored every nook and cranny of the bathhouse and took samples of the water to analyse in town. As concerns the tankardmen, it was mostly their sons doing the work now. Men didn't tend to live long in Dorozs.

Antal felt more inhibited visiting the tankardmen's houses than Iza who was visiting them for the first time. He had clear memories of Vince's house at night, of Iza bending over a crude map of Dorozs, the arc of her neck, the angle of her head, her eyes focused on papers listing social organisations, checking through documents required by the ministry, the text of which he had had to write. Dorozs would be his life work. It would be what his life was about, the sum of all he had achieved. It was his hopes for the future. Dorozs might be saved from the likes of Bérczes. The village might be restored to itself, people in their thousands might be cured by its waters. He would far sooner the record of such cures became his father's memorial than a few useless wreaths.

It was the map of Dorozs and the profile of Iza as she studied the analytical results of water samples that appeared before him that night. He had woken with a start beside her and had just released her from his arms that felt cool even after love-making. It was that face he saw confronting him in the darkness as he heard a suppressed cry rise within him, warning him: you must leave this woman. It was like stumbling across a second self inside him: one self embraced Iza and shared his thoughts and feelings with her, the other was watching them both suspiciously, its eyes never flinching.

Iza was never so cheerful as when they were fighting the battle for Dorozs. She was like a bird full of joy, he had never heard her sing so much. When the old woman dropped a beautifully made pancake she was tossing with a single flick of the wrist, Iza consoled her by telling her of the wonderful sanatorium that would cure her incipient gout. Iza was brilliant in the evenings. It was as if she had received a wonderful present as she rushed along beside him, or by herself, to organisations, offices, even up to Pest, rousing the villagers of Dorozs while convincing experts and politicians in the capital. By the time nationalisation came along there was no social or health organisation that hadn't heard of Dorozs, and the order authorising the conversion of the bathing area was the first act of the government.

They were already married by the time they started building the sanatorium. The night before work began Iza went to bed at eight and slept like a child till ten in the morning. 'See how strong I am?' she asked with closed eyes as she woke and reached for Antal as usual to draw his hand to her face. 'See me, how strong I am?' She tensed her body and stretched out. She still looked remarkably fragile and it was hard to imagine her setting forth to battle for Dorozs with hands as thin and a body weighing under fifty kilos. Suddenly he felt frightened analysing her words so intently, so suspiciously.

The old woman knocked at the door and asked whether she should bring them breakfast in bed on this special occasion. She had seen in the paper that the bathing pool in Dorozs was to be replaced by a sanatorium fit for international visitors and that work on the country's most modern project had begun. She was full of laughter and congratulations, and remembered the hotel at Szentmáté with Aunt Emma and how cold the stone flagging was even in summer. Iza sat up, rested the tray on her lap: there was fried bacon on it, her favourite. 'Enough congratulations,' she said to her mother. 'Hurry to the kitchen and get rid of the bacon. Vince has a weak stomach but he can't resist bacon and it's very bad for him.' The old woman obediently trotted out and could be heard arguing with her husband about the bacon. Iza meanwhile cut the bread into slices and carefully dipped it into the fat. 'Do you love me,' Antal asked her, almost unwillingly. She smiled at him by way of answer with guileless bright eyes. He sensed the danger like a storm about to break, he could feel the wind rising before it. Yes, Iza loved him. It would be so much easier if she didn't. But he loved all three of them: Iza, Vince and the old woman too. When one night he finally told himself he was leaving, his heart beat so he thought he would choke.

For years the four of them had lived together with only a wall between them. The old couple had seen them exhausted, distant, nervous at times and in bad moods, for neither Dr Antal, Professor Dekker's assistant, nor Dr Iza, the rheumatologist, found it easy when a patient died or proved incurable. They had seen Iza and Antal arm in arm by the Christmas tree; they saw how they watched over them when they unwrapped presents Iza and Antal had spent half the night wrapping. They had heard them singing together, preparing for this or that conference, one interrogating the other, and even heard their occasional arguments, Iza putting her case calmly, politely and intelligently, Antal beating on the table, but it was always clear that it was some idea, some topic or other that was the cause. It was this, not Iza, that annoyed Antal. They never saw them fight in the ordinary sense. Neither was jealous or ill-tempered: they trusted each other completely. The judge and the old woman, happy in their own marriage, lived in the atmosphere of another good marriage. It was like a double line of defence.

In the period preceding the divorce the old couple spent a long time wondering whether they should try to make peace between them, but they left them to it. Iza never asked for advice, not even when she was a little girl, not once she had taken over the family's affairs. Of course, they couldn't hide the fact that they were sad. Once Antal disappeared from the house, both of them felt it was the end of something, the end for ever – maybe it was the child Iza who had died, a child who remained a child for them when she got married, because she was living with them under one roof and they could see her in her nightgown with her hair pinned up for a bath, running here and there in her slippers before bedtime. No one was really surprised when she told them that she was changing jobs; the old couple never even exchanged glances when she announced it since they had often whispered about it in bed. She's off to Pest, ah, well, she's off to Pest, it's probably for the best. Of course it was hard watching her get into the taxi and drive away. They hugged each other, hoping to feel less desolate about her going if they clung together. 'Life too will take leave of us one day,' thought Vince. 'As suddenly as this, not looking back. I'd prefer it if I didn't notice it and was unaware of the hour.'

*

Now, lying down in roughly the place where the old couple's beds used to be, Antal no longer thought of Iza but of the old woman. He felt the same sense of panic as he did every time the thought occurred to him. 'Has she discovered it?' he wondered. 'Does she know, and if she does, how is she taking it?' Antal had no memory of his mother's face; in his grandmother's wrinkles he read unhappiness, suspicion and fear; it was only in albums and museums that he saw the much admired image of happy, smiling mothers, and now here she was, radiant, before him for the first time. How strange it was tracing elements of Iza in his mother-in-law, to detect behind her uneducated exterior her natural intelligence, her good temper, her unstinting appetite for work, all aspects of Iza too. What restless hands, what a complicated, clever little mind, what heaps of goodwill, what endless curiosity and constant readiness to help! How good it would be to speak to her, thought Antal, but the old woman needed neither his company nor his help.

The old woman left the task of negotiating Vince's headstone to Gica, the cloak-maker, who was almost bursting with pride at being entrusted with the task and because she was the only one with whom she was in regular correspondence, exchanging drawings, bills and ideas for inscriptions.

She wrote to Kolman just twice, as she did also to the teacher and the newsagent, but not once to Antal, nor did she answer any letters, except to Gica. It was as if she had suddenly grown tired of letter writing or had nothing to report.

If they do instal a headstone, thought Antal, Iza is unlikely to come down but the old woman is sure to be here. In fact, he could have written to her and offered her a room for the night but she was bound to reject his offer. He picked up a magazine since he liked reading in bed. He had the walls freshly painted when he moved in, the bunches of flowers disappeared, as well as the golden medusa-shaped patches, everything boldly replastered. The rooms somehow grew around him, but Antal spent ever less time comparing and recalling: the house was his, he had discussed the furniture and its arrangement with Lidia and it was Lidia who took flowers from the garden into the clinic. Antal's memory of the hot spring was of a bubbling inferno, a steaming, heaving mass of mud. He was a qualified doctor by the time he first saw a mountain stream. He knelt down beside it and let the ice-cold water run through his fingers. He could have wept at the sheer beauty of it. His fingers grew numb in the miraculous childlike gurgling of water as it thrust onward. The stones at the bottom of the spring were bearded, a bush bent towards it, an unsuspecting bird perched on its branches. Whenever he thought of Lidia he pictured her beside water, ever supple, full of life, and heard the throbbing of the millstream in that frozen image of the old photograph.

The evening was unusually quiet, with the promise of rain. Captain was snuffling around in the garden. The old woman had always taken pity on Captain and let him in. 'A rabbity old dog you are and rabbit stew is what you're fit for, pickle and all,' Iza would say, laugh and lift Captain by the ears, Captain's paws waving in panic as her fingers held him gently but firmly. She never hurt him. Everyone looked away because Iza was right, of course, rabbit-dogs didn't belong in the house, even when they are clean and relatively intelligent. It was just that . . .

Rabbit stew with paprika or with pickle, people here or there, the Dorozs sanatorium, Vince's headstone, the old woman in the Budapest flat. Iza took care of everyone and if she ever left anyone out it was most likely to be herself. Someone in the canteen yesterday had stopped in mid-sentence while talking about Domokos and Iza, and Antal was astonished how little he himself cared about her and the way she organised her life. Instead he thought of Domokos and was shocked: he had read his books and admired that clear, promising prose he had often seen in books and in the papers. 'He's not going to marry her?' he had worried the day before. 'For God's sake, he's not going to marry her, is he?'

Captain was scraping at the door. The scent of Vince's sweet william and night-scented stock wafted through the open window. Iza no longer lived in the house but Vince's spirit still hung around the place, as did the old woman's. Antal got out of bed and, cursing all the while, looked for his slippers to let Captain in as the old woman would have done. The house was empty now, there was no need to go on tiptoe.

4

She no longer received letters from home though that didn't surprise her because the only letters she answered were Gica's. She often thought that the Kolmans must be puzzled by her silence and she imagined she knew how they'd explain it since she couldn't explain it any other way herself. They must think she was too comfortable, too lazy, enjoying the good life. 'Iza would have written,' the newsagent must be thinking. 'Iza was never too proud.' And Iza would in fact write, letters would come and go, there's no obligation. Iza would never leave loose threads.

What could she write to them?

How could she explain to old friends how she lived and what went on around her? Should she talk about Teréz, the sameness of day after day, about the enormous trams that slipped through the streets of the city? Should she write about Domokos who was calling in more frequently now, even when Iza was away, and would sit and chat with her? If she wrote half the truth it would seem like bragging, but if she wrote the other half, about the feelings behind those of comfort and security, she wouldn't be able to face herself.

It was impossible to correspond with people back home. Opening the window into the light shaft she could see the same frosted glass in the window of the flat opposite. When the neighbour, the bus conductor's wife, was airing the opposite flat, she always said hello back and asked what they were having for dinner that day. The conductor's wife was blonde and chubby, fond of singing and would switch her domestic appliance on and off, machines very similar to the ones in Iza's flat.

The old woman, who was frightened of all machines, found a curious way of making the acquaintance of the refrigerator. She discovered that the fridge made a sort of animal noise, a low purr. It startled her at first, but then she imagined having a conversation with it and would sit beside it, feeling she was not alone. The noise reminded her of some kind of cat but since her last pet had been Captain, a dog, a soft thing as far as she was concerned, it represented a clumsy white version of Captain. On one occasion she spilled cherry soup in it and tried to wash it up because she was afraid of being told off. Iza went quite pale when she saw it, because of course she hadn't turned the electricity off first. 'Look, my dear,' said the girl. 'This is not a block of ice. Never even think of cleaning it with a wet rag. Never mind if it leaves a stain.' She pulled out the plug of the fridge and the purring stopped.

After that she no longer tried to make friends with the refrigerator and directed her desperate efforts to understanding how it worked, so that she might prove herself capable of operating it. The trouble was that Iza never had the time to explain and she was reluctant to ask the conductor's wife. She took much more care touching it now and would simply sit beside it, comforted by its benign hum.

She did not dare ask Iza about Domokos and marriage. She wasn't even sure of her own feelings about it yet, whether she would be happy if they did get married. At the beginning, when she first became aware of the writer's visits, she'd have been pleased if they did, it was after all a sinful and illicit relationship, but because there was no one from her old circle of friends to remark on it she did not feel too bad about it in the end; people seemed to regard these things differently in Budapest. Domokos liked her and, if she didn't feel uneasy about his profession, she would have been readier to return his signs of affection, but Aunt Emma had told her that writers drank and, though they seemed all right at first, sooner or later they came to a bad end; besides, she found it unnatural that he didn't have regular hours and a regular place of work, which meant that Iza might have to earn a living for them both. She didn't share these thoughts, of course, and nobody asked her opinion or advice. One day the conductor's wife shouted across the light shaft wanting to know if she had a good recipe for pastry, one that didn't use too many eggs, and that made her feel good for the first time in a long while, because she still remembered one of Vince's favourite cakes, the cake that Iza stared at with such longing when she was a child – how cheap it was to make, how delicious and how easy it was to convince those who tasted it that they were eating a real delicacy.

She felt happy each time she saw her neighbour's cheerful face. She only regretted that the young woman was also a conductor and had little enough time to spend in the kitchen. If she were around more she could ask her for news of the world. Since Vince had died she was no longer able to follow events. Not that she was particularly interested in politics, though Vince often read the paper to her, but somehow she felt at home in it even when she didn't fully understand everything and only skated over things. Now she desperately yearned for information; ever since she had moved to the capital, to the industrial hub of the whole country, she had been aware that there was something vital missing in her field of vision, that there were people here of a kind she had never personally encountered.

Insofar as the old woman had ever really known anyone, it was individuals such as shop assistants, conductors, postmen and small traders. She had never really encountered class or spoken to blue-collar men apart from those working on her house to fix the wiring, but even they were born on the outskirts of this or that town and spoke just like local peasants. Workers in the pharmaceutical factory, the recent and only genuinely industrial building in the area, never came round their way. It was terribly difficult in Pest to tell who were the workers because everyone dressed much the same. When she was off on one of those circular tram journeys and the tram rattled past a factory during a change of shift, she had no idea what they were manufacturing inside, she just looked back from the tram window as long as she could and thought she ought to ask someone what they were producing there and who lived in the area, but the tram swept on and she immediately felt ashamed of thinking such a thing. Iza had no time for her, let alone for strangers, and who would understand why she was interested in this or that particular matter?

After a time she stopped looking out of tram windows and

stopped thinking about anything at all except herself and her memories. Domokos's visits were starting to irritate her because when the writer did drop in to see her he brought her cakes as if he were dealing with a greedy child and would pull up the footstool next to her, which irritated her even more, because that was where the child Iza used to sit, right next to her, with such a longing look, the Iza who was interested in everything and who was getting to know the world, whose questions were inexhaustible and impossible to answer. And the writer kept asking her things, always about the past and she was always having to answer him, not ask questions of her own. She hated his questions, the peaches he brought, which were the size of fists, and those slices of melon sprinkled with rum. She was angry and bitter every time they spoke of the past because the past was the past, it was gone, vanished along with Vince. Vince was still alive then and Iza depended on him for so much. When Domokos asked her about the town's past political affairs it struck the old woman that answering questions was regarded as her way of earning her keep, but she felt ashamed thinking that and blushed bright red.

It was on her seventy-sixth birthday that she really got to hate the writer once and for all, on an evening Iza had promised the three of them would spend together. They'd play board games for proper prizes and they asked her to go and get some prizes to play for because she was the one who had most time to spare. When Iza was a child she used to like playing board games. She'd sit down happily with the pair of them, and she and Vince would cheat so that Iza might win — because Iza didn't like losing and would go quite pale and cry when she did. Miraculously, in view of all that moving, the board game had been brought to Pest and the old woman got fully absorbed in shopping around tobacconists and bazaars for all the silly little things they could use as prizes.

It was the big day. Teréz brought flowers and Iza greeted her with the old children's greeting. The old woman had wanted to thank the well-wishers in the most appropriate way so, the day before, she went over to the conductor's wife and baked some sweet pastries so as not to upset Teréz or mess up the kitchen. The young woman watched silently as she went to work. She taught her how to use the oven and when her visitor asked how much she owed for the electricity she burst into laughter, then suddenly grew serious, grabbed her round the neck and gave her a big kiss. The old woman looked at her and saw her kind eyes fill with tears. She was so flustered that she tried to open the door with her elbow but was so clumsy she dropped the prettiest, reddest bits of pastry on the floor.

Domokos came over in the evening to offer his congratulations and what should have followed was the offering round of the pastries and the board game, a nice family gathering to remind her of old times. But Domokos arrived out of breath and started whispering to Iza while holding a large parcel wrapped in tissue paper under his arm, a strange, frightening-looking package. Iza came into her room and announced that Domokos had managed to get tickets to the Margaret Island open-air concert with Feltrini conducting, just when it seemed impossible to get any. Some friend of his had worked a miracle and now they really had three tickets so they should quickly get dressed. The old woman would come with them, it would make a wonderful night.

The party had to be cancelled, of course, which was a real shame but at least she wouldn't have to keep bending over and tiring herself out. Yes, the pastries looked delicious! And look, Domokos had bought her a present to make up for the games. She must hurry and get dressed because the taxi will soon be here, and they have to leave immediately.

Iza was already in a rush, not waiting for an answer, changing her clothes. Domokos came in, peeled away the tissue paper wrapping from whatever it was he had brought her and revealed his present: it was a cage with a bored-looking cynical-eyed bird in it. Domokos would never forget the terrified look on the old woman's face as she saw it. Not knowing how to react, he gave a shrug and left the room to smoke a cigarette.

The old woman carefully covered the pastries with a table-cloth so that no fly should get at them. (There were no flies in Pest, not one, but the old woman was used to flies in summer and from June onwards she always put up a long strip of sticky-backed flypaper that hung on the lamp above her head.) She took out her black outfit. 'We're not leaving you alone tonight,' said Iza, looking radiant. 'Of course we're not leaving you behind, dear! I'm taking you to a concert. I want to show off my beautiful blue-eyed mother!'

There lay the deserted pastry, her wrists still aching from mixing the dough, and nobody wanted it. She thought the bird was giving her the evil eye. 'This bird is supposed to be company for me,' thought the old woman as she wriggled into her clothes and squeezed her feet into the black dress shoes she had last worn at Vince's funeral. She immediately felt weepy at the sight of them. 'This bird is to be my companion. I am supposed to talk to it.' Iza was slamming doors. Domokos's breathless voice was urging them to hurry, so they were all breathless by the time they got to the taxi.

There was a great crowd at the island venue and the old woman felt colder than she had expected to. She didn't really like classical music and there was no Vince to whisper in her ear and tell her what was beautiful about it. His descriptions were so clear. Handel was all scarlet ostrich feathers and silk ribbons fluttering in the wind, great silver trays blazing with candlelight. Wagner was trees creaking and snapping in the storm, foam running up the foot of a cliff, waves sweeping round rocks, black peaks reaching to the sky. Vince was no longer there, it was only the music with no introduction and no commentary. She heard it but didn't listen or think anything, she only saw Domokos holding Iza's hand, Iza gazing at the conductor, her mind entirely on the music, both of them enjoying the concert, every so often glancing at her, she being the person for whose sake they had arranged this wonderful night. They were treating her like they would a child with a present. Why wouldn't they just let her be?

The old woman was thinking of her pastries, of the liqueur she had bought specially from the grocer and the little glasses she purchased to replace those they had given as a gift to Antal so he wouldn't have to use Iza's heavy cut glass. This was all because she wanted to offer them something of her own, the things that were now covered with the tablecloth. It was useless now. Domokos saw she was cold, took off his jacket and wrapped it round her. Those who noticed him doing it smiled, while she, for the first time, noticed how bright Iza's eyes were when she glanced at Domokos. It was a look she had once reserved for Antal alone. 'I see you are just as good,' said Iza's eyes. Domokos straightened up, his strong, broad-shouldered body snug in his immaculate shirt. Those who looked on didn't mind him being in shirtsleeves. This writer fellow must be a decent man, they thought. He is giving up his jacket to help a shivering old woman. Everyone was happy and satisfied.

The orchestra struck up and the music swirled among the trees like flocks of birds. It was a Beethoven evening, but all the old woman kept thinking was that it was too loud. She raised her head in fright, as if she were in pain; there was no Vince to tell her what to hear. 'Listen, Ettie, can you hear how earth, heaven and God himself are being called to answer?'

After the concert Domokos ran ahead, his white shirt blazing in the distance. Iza's face had taken on a tender look, her lips were swollen. She was always moved by music and followed the arcs of melody as keenly as her father had done. Domokos rushed back triumphant, having succeeded in finding a taxi again. He seated the old woman next to Iza and climbed in beside the driver.

The old woman wondered what would happen if she suddenly had to get out of the taxi and find her own way home. She had never been on the island and because of all the bright advertisements could not even tell which way the taxi was going. She really wouldn't know which way to go, she thought. 'I could do with some coffee,' said Iza contemplatively. Hearing this, the old woman's tiredness suddenly disappeared because she felt everything might be all right again once they got home. Never mind about the board games, it was too late for that, but perhaps they could still eat the pastries and she could brew them some coffee. Then Domokos suggested they could go for coffee at The Palm and she slumped again. They took her home and kissed her goodnight. Domokos escorted her up in the lift because there were times the old woman was a little clumsy with her fingers and couldn't open the front door. He even put the light on for her and gave her another kiss. He told her the bird's name was Elemér, then rushed off.

The room was hot and stuffy. She swept the pastries from the plate, put them away in an old shoebox lined with a napkin and stuffed the board game away in the bottom of the wardrobe where she had found it. She covered the birdcage as she had learned to do at Aunt Emma's where it was her job to clean the cages, folded away her birthday dress and lay down. She had completed her seventy-sixth year. Suddenly it felt shocking to have lived so long. She thought of Vince, of Vince's grave and the headstone on which she had arranged to have her own name engraved under his. Gica had been so precise in her descriptions of it. The bird was a little restive in its strange new environment and made soft nestling noises the old woman didn't like.

She put up with it for a fortnight but every time it made a noise it reminded her of the humiliation of packing the pastries away into the shoebox, of that incomprehensible Beethoven piece and the cancelled board game. One beautiful summer day she decided to let the bird fly away. It didn't want to go and she had to frighten it through the open window with a towel. She was a little uncertain and felt a stab of guilt seeing the bird roosting on the boughs of a dry tree, looking depressed. It was like someone who had lost not only his home but all hope, who had given himself over to fate. She leaned out of the window, worried that she hadn't thought the matter through. Condemning anyone, even such a soulless pariah, to homelessness was a terrible thing to do. She called the bird and tried to tempt it back, while down below trams clattered on in the busy traffic. She kept sight of it for a while, the simple colours of its plumage glimmering through the boughs, but then Teréz arrived, saw the open window and made a gesture of hopelessness, muttering something about how that didn't last too long, then closed the door and advised her not to lean out too far in case she got dizzy and fell out. In any case, said Teréz, the doctor would no doubt bring her mother another bird.

But Iza didn't bring any more birds and Domokos felt a little hurt. 'I really wish they were speaking a foreign language in my presence, the way I did with her father when she was just a little girl. It's not worth bringing me presents, I am so clumsy,' thought the old woman. The empty cage vanished. Domokos threw it on to the tip. It was just another thing weighing on her heart after that. Sometimes she woke in the night and saw the bird, whose name she never wanted to use while he was still with her. 'People shouldn't call birds such extraordinary human names,' she thought, while imagining Elemér in hiding, sticking his small beak under his wing, a creature with fewer possession than even she had, with not a roof over his head and nothing to eat, all because she didn't like him being there, near to her.

The old woman lost weight. She spoke less and less.

That frightened Iza, and Domokos, who had, surprisingly,

been annoyed by the old woman's thoughtlessness, felt less angry. Iza said she had expected that Vince's death, leaving her old house and moving from the country into the capital would be something of an ordeal for the old woman, but she didn't think she'd find it so hard to adapt. After all, she didn't have to worry about anything and there was no way of ensuring that she could fill the day with the same things she used to in the old house. In any case her mother was no longer as capable and young as she imagined, and the managing of a Budapest household was quite a different matter, simpler in some ways but also more complicated, and in the end it was a hundred times easier having Teréz run the flat. She could work better and rest better too with Teréz at her side. She didn't need to ask her gerontologist friends for advice in order to know that the old woman needed something to do in order to exercise her remaining energy, that work was the strand that connected the old to life. But she really couldn't leave the housekeeping to her: she wasn't up to doing perfectly ordinary things. One day she bought a lot of wool and gave it to her mother suggesting she might knit a cardigan for her. The wool was a nice lavender-blue colour. She and Domokos spent an evening making balls of it for her. The old woman thanked them, turned and turned the clever little nylon pack with a hole in it for the yarn so it shouldn't get unravelled, but didn't go on to take Iza's measurements. 'Mama knows I am just giving her something to do,' said Iza, 'She knows I'd never wear it because I could buy a nicer one in the shop. What to do?'

'Why not get her to apply for a job,' Domokos suggested. Iza was shocked at first, then gave it serious thought. There was no chance they could just turn up somewhere and ask for retirement employment for her. She couldn't take on proper work and even if they did employ her, she thought, her mother tended to be careless at times. She could perhaps look after children but you couldn't know what kind of family would employ her, and she might get into an argument when they asked her not to tell the children stories about angels, because all mama's stories involved angels with long blonde curls who looked to see what the little boy or girl was doing and either rewarded or punished them. You also had to consider what people might think if they heard that she was making her mother work when she herself was earning good money and her mother was in receipt of a bigger than usual pension. Domokos was lying on the sofa eating a cantaloupe, practically assaulting it, tearing it from its rind. Normally he was a most refined eater with delicate manners, but occasionally he liked to behave as if he hadn't yet grown up. 'Well, if there's nothing suitable,' he said, the mouth smiling but the voice serious, 'then just try to see more of her.'

'Idiot,' said Iza, 'I have no life of my own as it is.' She threw down the newspaper she was leafing through and went over to the window, clearly angry.

The next day she called at the Women's Association.

They knew her there and held her in great respect, inviting her to all their receptions, even asking her to give advice and the occasional talk. Iza got straight to the point and told them what the problem was. The official gave her a big affectionate smile. 'What a splendid woman she is,' thought the official, 'she spares absolutely no effort.' She took out her files and leafed through the possibilities. She couldn't work as a voluntary nurse because not every block has a lift and she was no longer young, neither her heart nor her legs were up to it, and besides there was her effect on sick people to consider. Children were too unruly, too exhausting, and if her eyesight was poor she might lose them in the playground. She was simply not strong enough for housework. On the other hand there was assembly-line work in a factory that produced plastic goods. It was positively relaxing, light and pleasant piece work, more like playing really. It wasn't something you even had to look at to do, eyesight was not an issue, it was relaxing. Does the old lady have a sewing machine? Yes, said Iza, she used to but it was an old thing they had brought up from the country so she would buy her one. Mama could work at the factory, or at the association itself, where there were many people aged seventy or so, but if that was too tiring she could work from home and keep herself busy there.

Iza rushed home. The old woman listened patiently and thanked her for going to so much trouble. She said she'd go to the association, take a look around, but it wouldn't be worth it yet — not yet — because Vince's headstone would soon be ready and she had to travel down on the day it was to be installed. Iza would come, of course, and Domokos too once everything was prepared. She didn't seem to be too worried about sewing. Her hands were still nimble, she said, and when they were very poor she had stitched a good many toys for Iza.

Iza relaxed — it was at least a gleam of hope. Why not let her pay a visit home, let the old woman go and pray for the departed according to her faith. Domokos said he wouldn't go. He said he never went to cemeteries of his own free will and would have to be carried to his own, but if Iza wanted company he could go down with her, not to the cemetery itself, but to the town at least. It was bound to be refreshing for her to see the changes in the area, as well as old familiar faces.

Iza spoke to her mother about it. 'I won't go to see dad with you,' said Iza and her voice quavered a little so she sounded almost childlike. 'I loved him very much and it's very hard for me to think of him as no more than a grave.'

'Then don't bother with the train,' said the old woman immediately. There were no changes involved and she'd find her way home. Gica would look after her. She could stay with Gica. It would be perfectly natural to do so. She hated the hotel. She wouldn't stay with Antal because the house no longer belonged to them but to Antal.

Iza bought the sewing machine and brought it home. The old woman took a long, careful look at it. Her old one stood there. It wasn't the sort with a cover, one you could fold away; compared with the new one it was clumsy and ugly. She didn't know how to open the new one or how to use it. She put it in front of the window, covered it with a small embroidered tablecloth and never gave it another look. When Iza looked in to give her a kiss, she found her in the armchair again just gazing out of the window. She was looking with intense fascination at the transport workers moving the tram tracks, the way the machines raised the old asphalt surface and the workers picked up the cobbles, under which for a moment she glimpsed the earth that was as brown and gentle as anywhere out in the country where the roads were not surfaced. 'It's not easy,' thought Iza, then kissed her again. 'Not easy for her, nor for me. But maybe it's just a little easier for her. She can give shape to her loss in headstones and wreaths. It would do no harm to give her another examination before she leaves, though. She is dreadfully thin.'

5

The stonemason had promised it for August, but the headstone wasn't ready until the very end of October.

The old woman was clearly happy thinking of the journey; she was brighter and more talkative. Iza arranged her baggage, removing from the suitcase a range of useless items her mother wanted to take. The way Mrs Szőcs packed you'd have thought she was going for weeks in the country, not for three days. Iza removed two changes of shoes, an enormous bath towel and put the washing powder firmly back in the cupboard. Gica could lend her a bath towel and one pair of shoes on top of what she was wearing would be enough, what was the point of taking so many for such a short time? If she really needed washing powder she could call in at Kolman's and buy some. On the other hand she should take her shawl because it would be just like Gica not to put on the heating even when there were visitors.

There were gifts in the suitcase too. After considerable thought the old woman had decided to give Gica a lead-crystal ashtray that weighed a ton, which annoyed Iza though she didn't want to be carping all the time. It was not just that Gica didn't smoke but that she frowned at anyone who did. The old woman had bought the ashtray because she liked its colour, it was such a dignified object, so heavy and priestly looking, with its black-and-white stripes. Maybe Gica had a customer who smoked and if she did it might be nice for them to drop their ash in such a gentle, pious-looking vessel, not in some light, brightly coloured and frivolous piece of pottery.

Iza didn't say anything. She could have picked up something very like this once she got there, but there was no arguing with her when she was determined not to understand that she might not find a porter on her arrival. Her luggage was rather heavy to carry down to the tram stop as it was. Furthermore, the journey from the capital to the local station being about four hours, the old woman tentatively suggested that she'd like to take some food. Iza bought her a packet of biscuits.

The old woman was unusually agitated on the afternoon before the trip. She kept running out into the hall and opening and shutting the kitchen window, before retreating to a corner in a bad mood and watching everything from there. She fell silent after supper, as if in mourning, finally reconciled to her fate. Iza blushed with embarrassment when the conductor's wife called at ten o'clock with some red roast chicken and a few pastries. 'Sorry to be so late, ma'am,' she said, 'but I couldn't come earlier because the little girl had a tooth coming and was so grouchy it was hard to know what to do with her.' Iza brought in the food to her mother and put it on the table. The unusually old face with its unusually youthful blue eyes took a quick look at it, then turned away. She looked very pale. The alarm clock set for dawn was ticking quietly beside her. Iza had arranged for a telephone wake-up call but the old woman didn't trust it to wake her in case something happened at the exchange.

'The whole block will be laughing at us,' said Iza, 'and, what is more, you are hiding things from me. That's not very nice of you, dear. Do you imagine you'll be travelling by mail coach? It's only a four-hour journey! One roast chicken and a kilo of sweet pastry! Where will you put it? Will you eat it now? Because you might as well eat it. Why didn't you ask Teréz to make you a little something if you thought the biscuits might not be enough? Why ask Mrs Botka, whom I hardly know? Did you pay her for baking?'

The old woman didn't answer but drew the eiderdown up to her mouth, which made her look so strange Iza just stared at her.

'I'm off tomorrow anyway,' said the old woman without any show of emotion. 'Leave me alone.'

Iza was almost in tears when she closed the door. She rang Domokos who, of course, was not at home though it was gone ten. Leave her alone! What had she ever done to deserve this? She was just making sure her mother would not be too exhausted with all that silly weight she felt obliged to carry. It was the first time she had been so hurt and offended. Maybe it wasn't such a bad thing if her mother went away for a few days. Mrs Botka would tell Teréz what happened tomorrow. She wouldn't keep quiet about it, of course, they had had a disagreement before, something to do with shaking out carpets, and she'd be all too happy to annoy her.

The old woman was just waiting for her to leave so she could get out of bed. A less than perfect napkin would have served the purpose but she couldn't find one, so she wrapped the chicken, which was already in greaseproof paper, in a linen headscarf. She went to the cupboard and took out an old beer bottle filled with tea that she had managed to brew using the quick boiler she still possessed without either Iza or Teréz noticing. The smell quickly dispersed in the air that had turned unusually chill in the last few days.

She didn't sleep a wink because she didn't trust the alarm clock either and she didn't want to be late for the train. Iza's phone rang a little earlier than hers did, but then the alarm clock went off too. She felt proud to hear it. It was at least forty years old and what good service it had done! She slipped it into her string bag next to the food. Maybe Gica had no alarm clock. How would she wake up in time for the homeward journey then?

Iza had calmed down by the morning but she decided not to show it. Let her mother know what she thought of the roast chicken affair! When Domokos arrived with a taxi for them and she opened the old woman's door to get the suitcase, she stopped on the threshold. She thought it was only a suitcase her mother was taking, now there was a string bag too. How would she be able to get up into the tram at the other end? She asked her but the old woman looked at her coldly as if she were an interfering stranger. The look in her eyes scared Iza.

'I'll get a taxi,' said the old woman. 'When I arrive I'll get a taxi.'

Iza shrugged. She didn't believe her mother would call a taxi and pay ten forint for the very short journey to Gica's. No, she'd rather tell a lie so she could take her roast chicken and get her way. Once they got to the station and her temper had cooled, as it usually did with a little time, she pulled herself together again. Surely she couldn't let her mother set off on a journey like this with that miserable string bag?

'Mama,' she said and took hold of her arm. 'Leave the food behind. There's a dining car on the train and you can eat all the way if you want. Don't be so difficult.'

'No,' said the old woman. She pushed away Domokos's helping arm and clambered up into the carriage by herself. They didn't say anything, but got on the train with her, put the suitcase into the rack and the string bag into the baggage holder above her head. The old woman took the seat facing forward. Domokos gave her some magazines to read. She thanked him, then she linked her gloved fingers to signal that she no longer required their company. She wore a blank expression. It was barely polite.

They stayed with her until the train was about to start, Domokos even succeeding in making her laugh once. Iza opened her handbag and slipped her another three hundred forints just in case she suddenly needed something at the other end. The old woman stiffened again, her face filled with suspicion. She glanced at the fat woman opposite who was reading a women's magazine and didn't even look up. 'She is worried she might be robbed,' thought Iza, shaking with nerves.

Two minutes before departure they kissed her and were obliged to get off.

Domokos pulled down the window for her so that she might be able to wave and she did in fact rest her elbows on the open window to wave her black, lace-edged, scrupulously clean handkerchief. Iza's eyes glistened and Domokos knew why: the face looking at them was polite, indifferent, without any expression, nothing suggesting either that she was leaving with a heavy heart, or that she was pleased to be on her way. The old woman was waving without any feeling at all, the way she had been taught in childhood. Iza burst into tears and covered her face with her handkerchief. There was a great deal behind her frustration: roast chickens, alarm clocks, even the woman on the train, chewing nuts and reading the magazine. The train set off and disappeared. Domokos drew Iza to him and kissed her. He had never kissed her in such a public place, nor would Iza normally have allowed it. This time she did. It felt good. The station seemed a neutral place.

Iza knew her face must be smeared with tears and wiped them away. 'Is he sorry for me?' she wondered in a panic. 'Does he think I'm someone to feel pity for?' She was in a mess, a blend of joy and uncertainty, it was like stumbling about in the dark with strange soft objects stroking her face and brow. 'I could marry him if I wanted,' thought Iza and the thought made her feel stronger, washing away the anger and sorrow that had taken control of her when the old woman left. 'Yes,' she thought, 'I'll marry him.'

The ring road was loud with morning traffic. Domokos's ginger hair and amber eyes comforted her with their familiarity. He was holding her hand as he always did on busy roads, watching the traffic to see whether they could bolt across. Domokos liked playing this kind of game, enjoying the excitement of cheating traffic cops. But Iza still felt he pitied her, and her own feelings were a peculiar mixture of relief, nervousness and confusion.

*

The train seat was comfortable and there was a small lamp above her to use when it got dark. She clung to her handbag with both hands because she sensed the woman chewing American peanuts was giving her a good look now and then. It was a long time before she finally resolved to go to the toilet because she feared someone might steal her luggage and leave the train with it, but slowly she relaxed. She had a brief conversation with the woman opposite, who asked her if she didn't mind her smoking as she fancied a cigarette, and it turned out the woman was a teacher or an inspector of some sort on her way to examine a school in the provinces. That set her mind at ease. She liked and trusted teachers, and the woman had a half-price ticket so she must be telling the truth. She didn't feel hungry, of course, but she was thirsty so she took a few gulps of her tea. She was glad she had brought it. She had been on train journeys with Aunt Emma when the train was held up for a long time and it was good to have brought food along then. The thought of the roast chicken filled her with an extraordinary sense of security. It might not be required on the journey but even if not, at least she could surprise Gica with it since she felt awkward about staying with her for nothing. Gica was poor.

She spent some time looking out of the window. The train was fast but did make a few stops. The landscape was foggy and grey at first, then the clouds broke and suddenly it was bright. When Iza took her to Pest the express had been too fast and she didn't see very much. This time she could take in some of the places they passed.

The landscape wasn't as she remembered it, everything was more orderly somehow. Instead of scattered farmsteads there were chimneys and long buildings that looked like stables or would have suggested stables had they not looked so much like public buildings. Every so often she spotted a school in the middle of nowhere and, at the odd crossroads, a brand-new house set in a brown field. 'Everything has changed,' the old woman thought. 'I can't tell what is what any more, only that nothing is as it was.' She did not recognise the bridge over the River Tisza, the bridge being new and of a strange modern shape, and a couple of hours later she got a fright when she thought she saw the same bridge again and seemed to be going in the wrong direction, heading back to Pest. The school inspector had long got off but the new passengers looked re-assuring enough and were talking about canals. She took a long look out of the window again but there was no canal anywhere to be seen, nor had there ever been any kind of canal in the area. A lot of people took their leave at Dorozs, huffing and puffing, making a fuss. The train stopped for only two minutes but that was enough to crowd the station.

A few miles from her place of birth she was alone in the compartment.

She kept looking out, her eyes hungrily seeking the familiar. Soon she recognised the acacias. They came just before the quivering woods full of anaemic trees. If she could call out to the bushes they would answer, she felt. She linked her hands as in prayer. She was back home, in the county that had seen her grow from a baby into a young woman and finally enter widowhood. Vince seemed much closer now than before. It was this soil in which he was laid. The landscape was a part of him.

The conductor called in to announce that her birthplace was the next stop and lifted down both her suitcase and the string bag without being asked. She was radiantly happy and at peace.

It was like the last time she went to church, when they christened Iza. Everything seemed to hover around her. She blushed. Her breath came faster. She recognised the railway buildings and the neon sign for the station, which was turned off now, of course, and she almost stepped from the still moving train. Someone handed her her luggage and she stood on the platform, unable to move at first, gazing around her in the wind that was not a light breeze but a biting lowland gust that had a familiar smell. It smelled of home. She didn't notice how heavy her suitcase was or how the string bag was dragging at her arm, she simply drifted out with the crowd. In the square was the statue of Petőfi raising his arms to the sky, his eyes in a wild reverie as if to announce the great poet's immortality. It was a gesture as simple as a bird spreading its wings. She sniffled a little, wept and glowed, telling herself she was home again.

There was a great crowd of people at the tram stop so she let the first tram go and managed to clamber on to the second. No one thought to help her and she had to grapple with the suitcase by herself. She succeeded in blocking the door for a moment in doing so and the conductor barked at her, as did the other passengers, so that, in her panic, she caused an even greater obstruction until, finally, a boy snatched the suitcase out of the way to let other passengers on. Hearing annoyed voices, she immediately pulled herself together. This was even more familiar than the raking wind – they were telling her off. 'I've caused trouble,' the old woman thought in shame. 'I'm always causing trouble.'

She had secretly been hoping that Gica would meet her at the station but the cloak-maker wasn't there, so she had to make the five-minute journey by herself from the tram stop to the house where she was to stay, which was no easy job because the luggage was heavy. She kept stopping and changing hands, looking out for the street. How much work they had done around here. They had even fixed the pavement since she left and there were new postboxes along the way. There had never been such bright red boxes here before.

She proceeded carefully because she had needed to take care down this road in the past, ever since a wartime shell had ripped up the cobbles. The road was smooth now. 'Vince,' she whispered to herself. She inwardly repeated her husband's name as she walked, continually swapping the weights. Once she crossed Budenz Alley she'd be in sight of the house.

She trudged along the narrow terraced street and stopped on the corner. She dropped her luggage. She didn't put the bags down, she dropped them as though she wanted to dispose of them. The house she had lived in was no longer there.

She stood and sobbed. Of course the house was no longer hers but she did want to see it all the same, having imagined in Pest how she would feel, and it was precisely from this angle and distance that she had wanted to see it. It was the spot where she used to rest on returning from the market. The disappointment was so bitter she could hardly move; she couldn't understand what had happened to the house, how it had managed to disappear. A great tide of anger was rising in her. The house was in Antal's possession now – Antal had made it disappear somehow. Instead there was a strange building standing in the place between Gica's house and the other neighbour.

The old woman had never worn her glasses in the street because, out of an innocent kind of vanity, she wanted to keep her short sight a secret. Iza had insisted she wear them in Pest but as soon as the train started she had put them away in her handbag and she didn't want Gica to see them. It was only when she got much closer to her old house that she saw what had happened: Antal had painted the fence and repaired the front walls. The colour had changed, as had the surface, and some rough yellow material now covered the old greyish-white wall. Instead of shutters there were blinds, the same blinds Iza had in Pest. The letterbox was now framed in some sort of metal and the dragon-shaped spout had been painted red. It looked almost alive, like a real animal.

She could have walked through the gate if she wanted to because she still had the old keys at the bottom of her handbag. She hadn't meant to hide them from Antal – it was just that she didn't go home after the funeral so she couldn't hand them over to him. If she wanted to she could go in, see the rooms, the garden and Captain too. But you don't just walk into other people's houses, you need a permit to enter an old relative's home too; it would be like breaking in.

The newsagent was absorbed in his sports magazine and didn't even look up, which was a good thing because she didn't feel strong enough for a conversation. She turned her face when she passed Kolman's shop too and hoped they wouldn't notice her in the noontime traffic. Kolman was used to seeing her in her old coat, not in this new one with its otter-fur collar and that modern hat pulled over her eyes. Iza had taken away her old coat and bought her a new one in its place. She felt she was being ungrateful for not liking it, but she only liked decent, well-worn clothes, honest signs of poverty, believing, with Vince, that it was bad to rouse other people's jealousy and that, as two helpless elderly people, it was best not to look as though they were comfortably off. They were always anxious about being burgled. Had they not needed Captain as a guard dog they wouldn't have had a dog at all. Kolman didn't see her and she arrived at Gica's door undisturbed.

She had just put on the heating.

Everyone recognised that Gica had principles – she herself regarded her poor lifestyle and empty woodshed as principles – and she was of the opinion that overheating rooms was bad for your health and that she would only start heating the house once the snow started falling. The old woman had heard this innumerable times from Gica, and had experienced it too whenever she dropped in to see her about something: the fire really was not on till November was out, except for the tiny flame in the boiler; but this time she was convinced Gica would overcome her principles and have a warm room ready for her. After all, people behave differently with guests than they do by themselves.

Gica told her she had received Iza's telegram only in the morning and that she hadn't got the fire 'blazing' until she arrived just in case the visit had to be postponed and the fire would have been on for nothing. The room felt damp after the central heating in Iza's flat; it was cold and smelled of smoke. Gica was delighted with the roast chicken and was pleased to receive the pastries and the ashtray, though she was less enthusiastic about the latter. She said she expected to see the old woman in better health and asked if she had been ill. The question surprised her. She sensed that Gica was in some way getting at Iza and she set feverishly to praise her daughter.

Gica was full of news. She had harsh words for Kolman, who was so puffed up with pride he could no longer see straight.

When it came to the bathroom she apologised for not heating it but the boiler was out of order. The old woman shivered at the thought of bathing in cold water and felt ashamed at her own obstinacy; she had stuffed the bath towel into the suitcase after all and it had turned out to be useless. She went out, fussed around the freezing bathroom, but her fingers went numb and she was hardly able to use the towel provided. Feeling ashamed of herself for doing so she turned the control on the boiler. Water came out, of course, the boiler was working. She blushed on Gica's behalf. It was dreadful that just for a couple of kilos of fuel Gica was prepared to bath in the cold.

Gica was friendly and full of conversation. She said she had finished her shift early at Antal's so she could be at home when her friend arrived and asked if Ettie fancied nipping over to see what had happened to the house since it was sold. The old woman rejected the idea and said she would rather go to the stonemason's, as planned. They had agreed in the post that as soon as she arrived they would pay for the headstone, which the mason would then drive over to the plot while they bought a wreath and some flowers. Then they'd walk down to the cemetery and inspect the stone in place. By the time All Souls' Day arrived they could have lights around the new headstone. 'Will you stay till then?' Gica asked, closing her friendly round eyes when she answered yes.

They went the back way, that's to say not towards Budenz Alley but down Dobos Street, where in the last six months new buildings had been constructed on the old vacant sites. The houses were just like the ones in Pest, thought the old woman. Each multi-storeyed building reminded her of what had once stood there: they had all been single-storey, one was the rope-maker's shop, the other belonged to the man who made sieves. Now there were neither houses nor workshops, but offices and a clinic of the sort Iza worked in.

Vince's headstone cost a fortune and when she saw it she felt cheated.

Iza did not interfere in how she spent her money but the old woman felt that anything she received for Vince's possessions or the old furniture should be spent on him, so she had ordered black marble, the most expensive in the mason's shop, and from all the plans and drawings faithfully sent to her by Gica she chose the most showy. But now that she stood before the grandiose black stone with its overwhelming carved roses, the stone on which their two gilded names appeared next to a bare date, it felt sadly like bragging. The old woman knew nothing about art but she sensed that what she was looking at did not represent Vince, not even her own sadness, that it represented nothing, in fact, and that it was, in short, clumsy and vulgar.

Iza! Iza again! The comfortless truth of her words. Iza with her cigarette as she waved her hands about in the dusk: 'Forget the headstone, mama, just get the grave dug and forget memorial stones. What do you want one for? A wooden memorial is more like him, less loud, more modest.' But the old woman wanted to do something special for Vince and had spent a fortune on the black marble she was now sadly contemplating. When she was a young girl she had had angels carved for Endrus's headstone, light and charming figures, and for years – for decades after – she felt they were like playmates to this tiny boy. At night, when the body was not subject to the normal laws of decay, she imagined the stone angels playing with Endrus, all flying together. Now that she was seventy-six, looking at the new headstone, she knew the dead really die and that there was nothing you could give them by way of commiseration, no sadness, no love.

Gica's face was bright with pride and the stonemason was strutting around beside them. It was years since he had been given such a satisfying task. The last time was a good fifteen years ago, the headstone for a bishop, another commission with Gica acting as go-between. He felt a little wounded by the lack of enthusiastic praise. The old woman had said a rather hasty goodbye. Other mourners usually stayed longer to admire his work. 'Maybe in the cemetery,' thought the mason. 'Maybe she'll be more talkative there and be less stinting in her praise. The stone will be in place by four this afternoon.'

On the way back the old woman thought of Vince's arms, so much thinner than they used to be, and how his body had practically wasted away. There had been nothing in the drawing to suggest that the finished memorial would be so huge: everything in it looked delicate and small. 'You're no good at proportions,' Iza had said and showed her on the wall what three metres would be like. 'A stone that size? What for? It can't be nice!' The old woman didn't believe her and thought she was exaggerating. She was out of sorts at the florist's choosing the wreath but eventually succeeded in finding one Vince would have liked if he were alive because it included fresh-smelling pine cones decorated with resinous young pine buds and red berries that reminded her of the rose hips she used to make jam each autumn. Apparently Gica felt that she too ought to buy something since she had, after all, been involved in the choice of headstone, so she bought a wreath bristling with chrysanthemums so purple the old woman couldn't bear to look at them. Vince had hated scentless flowers and would often say that purple chrysanthemums were like red cabbage.

They dined on the roast chicken, the old woman and Gica taking just two bites each. Gica made some *rántott leves*, beating two eggs into the soup and it was good, nice and warm. Gica talked chiefly about Antal, saying she didn't have to tidy much after him; he was clean and decent and not at home much, usually only after supper. He had renovated the furniture and the place looked nice and modern. Captain was spending a lot of time hanging about, but there was no getting rid of him because Antal was fond of him. The main room was pretty well as it was. It was where Antal kept the bits of furniture he had not had renovated.

She didn't want to listen to Gica talking like this because the house was calling her again, the house where Captain was still snuffling around the place and the flowers on the windows would be coming into leaf as they did this time each year. Gica said it was likely she wasn't going to work for Antal much longer because the doctor was getting married, to a nurse, and she wouldn't like to get in the way of the young lady.

The old woman wasn't interested. Iza had Domokos now and Antal's love life was his own affair. It was going to be all too tiring to keep track of everything or even imagine it. If she felt anything at all it was a kind of faint joy that Antal, who was a good boy, was free to go his own way.

The afternoon was a trial to her.

When she saw the grave with its overlarge headstone that she had chosen with such love, such care and such inconsolable sadness, she felt that this was the moment Vince really died, that now he was undoubtedly, eternally dead. While there was only a wooden headstone there she didn't consider the loss to be beyond doubt, and there was a moment at the funeral when she thought everything going on around her was a mistake because if they levelled the soil again and pulled out the wooden memorial Vince might step from the grave, shake off the earth and admit he was joking, then they'd go home and she'd serve up some dinner. But the gold letters of his name surrounded by those black carved roses, the two clear dates and the text reading: *Died 7 March 1960* was incontrovertible proof that it had really happened; now that the fact had been declared it was for ever. The old woman felt that the ton's worth of marble that weighed on him had ruined his last chance of climbing out and escaping, that there was no hope left that he might suddenly take flight from among the clods in a sweet resurrection.

She thought of Iza, of how right she was not to want to see this, and she bent her head and covered her mouth with her handkerchief. Gica linked arms with her, thinking she was unwell, and could see that she was almost incapable of taking a step. The stonemason's wounded pride was somewhat mollified because he saw the stone had made a great impression.

It was cold at Gica's, much colder than in the morning when she was still warmed through by excitement and expectation, as well as by the weight of baggage she had been carrying. A weak fire was licking at damp bits of wood and the old woman opened and immediately closed her suitcase as she remembered that she hadn't packed the shawl after all last night – she didn't want to hurt Gica's pride by suggesting that she didn't trust her hospitality in preparing a warm house. One of Gica's cloaks lay unfinished on the sofa. She pretended she wanted to examine it more closely so she pulled it over her, drawing the plush silk up to her chin. She gazed at the fire: not even its colour seemed quite real and it didn't warm her. Gica was quiet, she too must be tired. They didn't talk.

Antal arrived shortly after six.

As Gica ushered him in she was muttering something about what a pleasant surprise it was, how she wouldn't have believed it and what honour he was doing them by calling, and of course she told him dear Etel would be visiting. Gica was watching the old woman's reaction as she was saying this and saw how tears sprang to her eyes the moment she saw Antal. There was no Iza here to restrain her so she hugged and kissed Antal as she would her own child. Antal of course looked at her in two ways as he always did. 'Just watch their eyes,' Vince would say. 'Both Antal and Iza look at you in two different ways: they see you as their mother but also as your doctor. You can never be sure which pair of eyes they are using at any one time and what they see there.'

Antal was shocked by what he saw though he didn't show it, having learned over the years to keep his diagnoses to himself and to keep the conversation down to polite enquiry in case he worried his patient. The old woman was half what she had been. She was still beautiful, the constantly laughing eyes were still there behind the tears, but they weren't entirely trusting. She was like a child that had been hurt. The hat and coat that Gica had left on the bed were brand-new and quite fashionable, as was her dress, but her cheerful babbling, that used to remain bright even when she was troubled, was slower now, more guarded. The old woman had no stories to tell, her answers were vague and noncommittal as though she had got used to the idea of never answering yes or no to anything. As she was speaking Antal was suddenly overwhelmed by sadness. He stood up, bent over her, hugged her and gave her a kiss. The old blue eyes, wrinkled and already shining, went misty for a moment, then she was Mrs Szőcs again. He could see her withdrawing.

It was dreadfully cold in the room, quite unpleasant.

The doctor lifted the cloak off the old woman and gave her his coat instead. He picked up her suitcase and string bag. 'Come on, mama, it's very cold here. I'm worried in case you get chilled down. You could roast an ox in my place. I heat every room and you know how much I like to be warm. You can spend the night there. I'm sure Gica won't mind.'

The old woman didn't budge. The wrinkles around Gica's neck multiplied as she dug her chin in. 'The wretch,' she thought, 'look how he takes charge! He earns a fortune, it's no big deal for him to throw his money around and indulge himself. He really upset the Szőcses that time. Etel won't go with him. That's obvious.'

Antal himself wasn't confident that he could persuade her. But he took one more look at the familiar face and saw the eyes weren't set on anything particular, that they were empty and indifferent.

'Do you think so?' asked the old woman uncertainly.

'Of course. Say bye-bye, mama.'

'Do I want to?' the old woman asked herself as if she were a stranger. She felt Antal putting his scarf round her neck. Gica was pulling a face. 'I don't know whether I want to or not. But I mustn't resist, I must never resist anyone. I am always being told what to do. Antal is young and knows better than I do.'

She kissed Gica, muttered something about the chicken, then

set off obediently to follow the doctor. The key – Vince's old key to which they had tied a piece of national tricolour for identification – turned in the gate. A light went on above and she blinked at the unexpected brightness. They never used to have a light bulb there and always had to feel their way along on dark winter afternoons.

From the garden she could hear the patter of small feet, the kind of small steps one might hear in a half-dream. Captain appeared just as he used to, sniffing at Antal and grunting. The old woman waited. Captain looked at her, unsure who she was, and drew back when she leaned down to him. He didn't recognise her. That didn't hurt. It was as if a part of her had been frozen – she didn't feel it.

The old items were still there under the arch of the gate, but they had been tidied up and the broken wickerwork on the chairs had been mended. There was a light for the yard too now, a strong bright light so you could see Vince's old rose bushes in a semicircle waiting for the snow. There was straw and newsprint to cover them, they were wisely keeping their heads down. This was as she remembered it, precisely so in fact, it was the sight that used to greet her at this time of year, not that this had any particular effect on her now. She followed Antal up the stairs that Gica had scrubbed to a brilliant shine.

There was light everywhere. The hall was white as snow with some strange green hangers on it much like at Iza's. All the doors had had a fresh coat of gloss. The two small rooms had fitted furniture and the same natural-coloured suites as in Pest with a lot of lamps and many clusters of flowers, the flowers still the flowers she used to tend. The carpets were purple and green, and there were the same low tables along with small nesting tables as at Iza's. The windows were covered in canvas curtains with mysterious abstract patterns. It really was warm here, wonderfully warm. Wherever she looked it was all so utterly changed from what she remembered that it made no impression and had no effect on her.

Antal opened the door of the big room, the door behind which Iza used to live with them. Here was Iza's old room when she was a girl, the one that got the most sunshine, the nicest room, the one with the view of the roses, that glittered each summer like a glass bowl in a rose bower. Antal put on a light, deposited the string bag and suitcase, and allowed the old woman to enter before him. He watched and waited.

Her face did not move, nor did the expression in her eyes change for a moment as she gazed around her. The doctor in Antal expected a reaction and was horrified when there was none. He wanted to get hold of her and shake her but he dared not touch her.

Her steady blue gaze took another look, a very slow look around the room. The curtains she had made back in the days of Aunt Emma, curtains woven of dreams and plans for the future, were still hanging in the window, and Vince's old bed stood in the corner, its belly much swollen with cushions piled high. The plush red footstool stood before it and the dog with the mother-of-pearl eyes. Practically every piece of furniture that remained was here, as well as the smaller objects she was once fond of, the chipped blue vase with its decorative birds, the little glazed sideboard within which Vince's Meissen mouse sat with its broken tail. The rugs too were the old ones, as was the fire screen and the lacquered fruit basket on top that used to be packed with slices of melon that mysteriously warmed to a pleasant temperature whenever they made a fire. Scarlet watermelons warmed through . . .

'I love this room, mama,' said Antal. 'You can stay here. Would you like a bath?'

He didn't wait for her to answer, but left her there. The old woman heard him moving around in the kitchen; she heard the clatter of cutlery and the old student song he was singing that was hauntingly familiar. It was as if it were Vince singing out there. He too was a man about the kitchen while he was healthy, always humming while working.

She unbuttoned her coat and sat down on a chair. Her first thought was that she had been right to bring the bath towel after all. She stretched her legs and looked at her shoes; they needed a brush. In recent years they had considered the hall too cold and had sneaked the cleaning materials into the bedroom, stuffing them into a cardboard box inside one of the bedside tables. She automatically opened the door of Vince's without any hope of finding anything there. She was simply following some old blind instinct. The box inside was new, a lacquered red box, rather jolly, but the old brushes, creams and cloths were there in it.

She squatted down and examined the brush. Slowly, very slowly, as if someone in a forest were calling her by name, she raised her head. She had to answer the call. That was how Antal found her, listening like an animal distracted by a distant shuffling.

The towels – not her old much-patched damask ones but fresh flannel ones with cheerful patterns, just like at Iza's – were hanging on the old hook and the bathroom was pleasantly warm. She was surprised how dirty her hands were despite washing at Gica's house, but of course that was in cold water. Antal was running to and fro, whistling, and served her dinner in the kitchen. Antal's was exactly like their one in Budapest, her old oven was gone, the food was warming on an electric cooker and here too the sideboard was part of the same unit as the sink. She tapped at the synthetic material that served as cover. 'It's my old cupboard under that,' she thought and imagined the wood could feel her fingers even through the plastic. Antal served the meal; Gica used to cook his dinners, not every time, just now and then, and this happened to be one of those times. The marrow stew was tasty, as was the rissole, much nicer than the roast chicken they had for lunch. Antal was still eating a lot of bread with his meals. They didn't speak but ate quietly.

'Mama,' said Antal after they had finished. 'Are you very tired tonight?'

She was almost dizzy with exhaustion but she didn't dare admit it. She said no.

'I was chopping wood today and grazed my hand. I hate leaving the washing up for Gica. I'd love you to do it, that is if you don't mind.'

She stood up without saying a word and collected the dishes. Antal noted how she looked at the taps as if startled by them, how she hesitated before turning on the hot water and then the sad attention with which she rinsed, raising the plates every so often, which were the remaining relatively whole parts of her old dinner set.

'Gica is very clever but she could never do a job as thorough as you, mama.'

The words came at her slowly as from an infinite distance,

their meaning taking time to reach her ears. Yes, Gica was a good girl, but she was never quite clean enough, not ever.

'When mama does the washing up it's as light as bubbles.'

'Light as bubbles,' she heard and something echoed inside her, repeating, 'Light as bubbles.'

'I hear Iza is getting married.'

She didn't reply to this. He too was remarrying, said Gica, there was no point in complaining about each other.

'I hope mama will spend some time here.'

'Some time,' said the echo inside her. 'Some time.' People were pleased to see her. For some time. Again she made no answer. It had been a pleasure working with those threadbare old tea towels, they soaked up the water so thoroughly the backs of the plates were like mirrors: you could see your face in them.

'I have an idea I'd like to discuss with you. You can decide whether you like it or not. The fact is I'd very much like you to stay.'

Decide something? Her?

She spread out the tea towels and closed the cupboard drawer. Antal kissed her hand, the way he always used to by way of thanks for a button mended, for fresh socks, anything. But the Antal standing beside her was not a jot more real than any dream might be. Only one thing was real and true, it was the plates, the clean glittering plates. The work that somebody *genuinely* needed her to do.

'You know how to use a boiler, don't you? I have to go out somewhere now but I'll try to get back early. Till then why not have a bath and lie down, then when I get back we can move on to more serious matters. Your arrival has been a blessing, mama. You have no idea how much I was hoping you would come.'

He turned and came back with his coat, but as usual without a hat. The words with which he had left were still rolling around the old woman like smoke.

In Pest it was always Iza who prepared the bath for her, fearing that she'd feel dizzy in the steam, or scald herself when using the boiler. She wanted to tell Antal that she was longing for hot water but that she was not allowed to take a bath alone – but she didn't dare say anything. Antal kissed her and told her to shut the door and the gate, and that it was perfectly all right to lie down since no one would call now and Gica never came at this time. He hurried off, whistling exactly as he used to. Captain was snuffling outside and had started scratching at the door, so the old woman let him in. Now that they were alone the animal came closer, sniffed at her ankles, then stood on his hind legs and looked into her face.

The words spoken by Antal were echoing ever louder around her; it was like hearing bells. The old woman knelt down without touching the dog, just staring at him, the great wheels of past and present spinning around her. She no longer felt tired. Everything was becoming clearer to her: she recognised the house, the old furniture and could feel the old walls beneath the fresh plaster. The house greeted her and spoke to her. She left Captain who, half in fear and half out of sheer instinct, started following her, hardly believing his eyes and senses, then sniffed right round her and began leaping about in the happy way dogs do. The old woman worked her way through the old rooms which, behind their green and purple curtains, were their old selves, then stopped on the threshold of the third room where Antal had put her baggage and leaned against the door-post. The experience of *coming home*, that the idea of home still existed, that the house was still here and that the past, like some kind of living being, could turn round, face her and call her by name was almost too much for her. She who had been practically dumb for several months answered the call within her, her mouth still closed.

*

Antal was rushing down the street. Running did his muscles good. That was how he left the house that morning too, the morning when he knew he had to leave Iza and run for his life. The sky seemed to be trembling that day. The streets felt different now, the air was damper. It thickened around him, felt oddly stiff, had become rather milk-like and at the same time darker. The lamps were withdrawing into themselves, all light was turning inward.

'She will kill her,' thought Antal, 'the way she almost killed me.' The old woman's life was hanging by a thread. Iza had let go of her for a day or two but once she returned the old woman would die within two or three months. 'If I can find that thread and haul her back by it, she might yet survive.'

It was good to know that he'd soon be seeing Lidia, holding her hand, touching her, feeling the coolness of her skin. It was good to know she existed, that soon they'd be living together and that if he woke at night out of a bad dream it would be Lidia's voice that awakened him, Lidia who would listen to his dream. There was hardly room on the tram and he had to travel on the step, tense but in good spirits, anxious as usual when he hadn't seen her for a few hours, but also because he was full of urgent plans he wanted to discuss with her. How good that he could discuss even Iza with her. With her and no one else!

When he got off at the clinic he was cursing and could hardly see the trees. The windows of the building had disappeared, everything was lost in the sudden fog and had to be guessed at. He found Lidia in the canteen, just coming to the end of her supper. She glanced up at him when he entered, then snatched her eyes away from him again and stared at her fork instead. 'She doesn't even dare look at me,' thought Antal. 'It's all in our eyes.' He sat down beside her and waited for her to finish.

He'd never forget that journey home, the way they made their way back in the dense blankness along the ancient path through the woods, the memory of which was now entirely filled with Lidia and no one else. Iza's breath had drifted away and was long gone. They walked through the fog clinging to each other, skirting round benches and trees, Lidia's face at one point coming very close to his so he could hear her rapid light breathing and know the girl was happy and excited. Lidia was glad to hear what he had to say and thought his suggestion was a wonderful solution. She told him about Vince and how they first started a conversation about Gyüd and the mill and the old woman. He could feel Lidia's thin arm through her coat. They guessed what Mrs Szőcs might think when she saw Lidia, whether she would remember her and, if she did, what it was she might remember. 'It is as if she were asleep,' said Antal. 'Don't mind anything she says. Think of her as being in a dream, but she will wake. She will have had a bath and is probably in bed, sitting there, propped on pillows with the glasses she only wears for reading, because she is vain, at the end of her nose, leafing through magazines. I hope she has found them on the windowsill. She will be willing now, you'll see, though she wasn't at the time of his funeral. But things have happened since then.'

In the street they brushed up against strangers, asked their pardon and laughed – it was simply impossible to see. The fog was no longer white but yellow. They tapped around the gate until they found the lock. Their skin was damp too. It was as if everything had been dabbed with wet cotton wool.

Inside, the lights were on in every room. The bathroom door was open, the tub wiped clean, the steam of the hot bath still hanging in the air, an unfamiliar bar of soap was on the basin and the drying rack was out with an enormous flannel sheet on it. Antal turned the lights off one by one. They found Captain behind the flower stand in the hall, ill-tempered and restless.

'Silly boy,' said Lidia, full of affection. 'Dumbo. Come here!'

Antal knocked at the third room. There was no answer. He knocked again, still nothing.

'Don't disturb her,' said Lidia. 'She must have fallen asleep. It can wait till morning.'

'You didn't see her face,' said Antal. 'Wait, I'll wake her up.'

He opened the door. The bed was covered with Aunt Emma's brilliantly snow-white sheet, the bed itself unmade. Iza's suitcase unpacked. The old woman wasn't in the room.

IV

AIR

She hadn't had an accident while taking a bath.

She took a long time and much pleasure in soaking herself. When she was finished she did not lie down but got dressed again and examined every part of the house once more, even looking into the pantry, opening the refrigerator and raising the lids of the pans. Back in Pest she found it hard to sleep when Iza was away and stayed awake until she got back. It was as if some terrifying monster were waiting to pounce on her in the busy and secure tenement block. But she felt no fear here even though she was alone. Antal hadn't told her where he was going and Gica never ventured out after dark, so she wasn't expecting her to call to see what she was doing. Captain, who had grown fatter and kept looking at her, stretching his fat neck as if trying very hard to draw memory from an almost exhausted well, was not a credible guardian of the house, but she wasn't afraid. It might have been the walls or the standing clock that had been left behind, the one that was bound to remain here as Iza didn't like it. She had hated it even as a child and would cry in anger whenever she heard it, point at it and hide when it was ringing. The old woman discussed it with Vince. It was unlike the child to be afraid of a clock. Endrus and every other child would clap to hear it, not Iza.

The ticking that to anyone else meant 'Life is passing' said something else to the old woman: it said time had stopped. After all these months the world seemed real again and the shifting soil that so often gave way under her was suddenly firm. The old woman started thinking.

It had been weeks since she had thought anything at all; at most she had remembered events.

The recognition that she was still capable of desiring things and that she could feel an emotion other than sadness shook her. She lowered herself into the rocking chair and rocked to and fro. If she did talk to anyone these last few weeks it had been to Vince, but now she began talking to herself. What she had to say in herself and to herself caused her so little pain she was surprised how easy it was.

She picked up her coat and the string bag that seemed startlingly light now the roast chicken and the pastries were gone. She took her handbag too, not because she thought for a moment that she would need identification papers to walk down the street, but because that was what she had got used to with Aunt Emma. Handbags were always to be carried. She put on her hat, adjusted it in the mirror and, for the first time since her arrival, decided to wear her glasses. Captain grumbled and ran after her, so she bent down to him once more and lifted him into her arms. She could hardly hold him, he had grown so fat. Gica was hopeless with animals and overfed him. She gave the dog a kiss between the ears, startling Captain who snatched his head away and snuffled, his eyes wild.

She hesitated at the top of the steps.

She had failed to anticipate the fog. She thought the moon would be shining. She had no idea why but it was the moon she longed for, so intensely now that she could only blink in disappointment at the brown half-light. The garden seemed to be moving in the rolling mist and the tower of the nearby church was quite invisible but for a faint circle of light. 'Oh, heavens, I am so ashamed of myself,' said the old woman to the Iza inside her, 'if only you knew how ashamed, Izzy!'

The key turned easily in the lock as though months hadn't passed since she last used it. The street looked unreal. She couldn't see Kolman's shop: it was like walking by a river without a further shore, only seeing people once one actually bumped into them, a head, a coat or a hat suddenly emerging out of the fog. 'Sorry,' the old woman kept saying at every encounter, 'I beg your pardon!' The pavement was wet and black, the lamp posts ghostly presences.

It wasn't even eight yet but there was hardly any traffic. Cars nosed carefully forward in the fog, the trams kept ringing their bells. There was something liberating about not having to watch out for everything, feeling no fear as she turned down Könyök Street, passing the enormous shadow mass of the church, then crossing the square in a chaos of flashing lights, ringing and car horns. She advanced calmly and gently, the slow-moving vehicles swimming through the fog now behind, now ahead of her. She found her way back to the safety of the pavement, but then was lost in the swirl of people leaving the cinema. She sensed the pulsation of the crowd but could only guess why people were rolling in such droves from the concrete gateway of the Hunnia. She never walked like this in Pest. She drank in the damp brown fog, opening her mouth wide as if she were choking. She had rarely felt as fresh as she did now. She bit the fog as she had done in childhood, when she tried to catch the falling snow between her sparkling teeth.

Where was Vince?

He couldn't be in the cemetery under that ugly headstone. But he must be somewhere, she had already felt his presence when the train entered the county. He was floating around her, his laughter blown this way and that by the wind. He must be here somewhere, hiding in the fog. She had felt close to him in the house too, Antal's house, but he was not quite close enough, just out of reach. It was her own self she discovered in Antal's house, not Vince.

While Iza was growing up, other little girls would come round to play, hiding things. 'You're getting warm, no, colder,' and when the object was close to being found, the little girls would cry, 'Very warm! Hot! Hot!'

Back in the house it was only 'warm' or 'lukewarm'. Not 'cold' because his cherrywood stick was still hanging on the wall and Captain was there too, and the rose bushes and the tulip onions deep in their pots. But there must be somewhere *warmer* and one place that was the *warmest* of all. Not in the cemetery, oh, no! And not in the house.

At the terminal there was the usual tram waiting to leave for the woods and she got on. She had no small change, only notes, and the conductress grumbled when giving her change. The old woman gazed at her affectionately, hearing the extended consonants of her birthplace. They didn't talk like this in Pest. She clung to her handbag and looked out through the window, reciting to herself the street names and tram stops that she couldn't see except as a vague change of light behind the glass. Now they were rattling by the post office, there was the Calvinist church, the old county hall, the town hall, the grammar school, the Kazinczy statue, the war memorial and the hospital. That shadow was the baths. If it were possible to see anything, she would have been able to see the mill too, the steam mill behind which there was an overwhelming scent of flowers every summer when the wind was from Balzsamárok.

The conductress called her for the first time since she got on. They were at the end now and were were about to turn round. Why didn't she pay attention? She would have liked to tell the conductress that this was where she had wanted to be from the start, but she didn't think of it because she was old and tired, and had got out of the way of thinking. The tram vanished, the passengers dispersed, somewhere dogs were barking.

She was feeling closer to Vince now but it wasn't because she felt familiar soil under her feet: the old track had vanished and had been properly surfaced. There was a bar with lights on along the road and she tried to look through the window but couldn't see much, just some backs and shoulders, almost everyone in some kind of leather coat. 'Poor thing,' she spoke to the Iza inside her. 'How dreadful it must have been for you. How awful.'

Balzsamárok no longer smelled of flowers but the old woman remembered past summers when it was heady with scent. She hadn't yet entered the denser fog hanging around between the gardens and southern edge of town but Vince was already there, not quite next to her but very close. The last time she was here was the day he died, when they were laying the foundations for the new estate. The houses will have been built by now.

Someone slipped by her, a big man in uniform.

'Is this a good place to cross?' she shyly asked.

'If you're crazy,' the stranger answered gruffly. 'It's mud up to the knees there.'

She wasn't worried about the mud, it was just the entrance to the estate that bothered her; the last time she had walked that way there were two bollards in the way but they were nowhere to be seen now. The road was indeed muddy but she did not lose her footing. Blindingly bright lamps lit the road; not enough to light the whole estate but she could see perfectly well where she was going.

A dog started barking and she was frightened for a moment, then took courage again; the sound grew louder but no nearer. There had been a nightwatchman here ever since they started building and the dog was tied up. But there was something dreadful about the sound, something unreal and overlong, not quite animal but something mechanical, like a machine continually howling.

The nightwatchman appeared to see what the dog was howling at. He looked up at the old woman and greeted her. He was smoking a pipe and was bored and cold. Any company would do. 'He won't harm you,' he said. 'He's just a lot of noise. He's all right.'

The old woman returned his greeting and stopped. There was an enormous electric light shining above his head and the nightwatchman could see how carefully she was looking around.

The buildings were all ready bar one. They were just lacking windows, none of them being glazed, the last building being complete to the fourth floor. A group of identical accommodation blocks squatted over the levelled fields of Balzsamárok, four to the left and four to the right. The old woman gazed at them in amazement. The roof of the fourth on the left was lower than the rest and somehow different, as you could see even in the fog that was thinning somewhat now: it looked unfinished, rather dented. The sky too looked crooked as though weighed down by the fog; it seemed to hang between the walls. The old well was where it had been, it was the only thing that hadn't changed apart from the sky. She knelt down beside it and admired its nice red stone rim, shiny and damp from years of water washing over it.

'Fancy a drink?' asked the nightwatchman. 'I have a spare mug.'

'No, thank you.' The old woman turned the wheel and it moved as smoothly as it had ever done. The water rushed on, white and sparkling, eternally young. She said she didn't want a drink, she just wanted to see the well.

A woman walked past and greeted them as people in the country do even on deserted streets. She was pushing a bicycle, then vanished down another street leading out of Balzsamárok, down Rákoczi Street. The dog started barking again and this time it would not stop.

'May I sit down here?' the old woman asked.

She felt the presence of Vince so intensely that she was sure that if the nightwatchman went away, returned to his cabin or simply turned round, Vince would immediately appear beside her and tell her what to do.

'Doesn't bother me,' said the nightwatchman.

He turned away. There was nothing to steal except a few bricks and an old woman like her would hardly be able to carry those off in her black string bag. Everything else was safely locked in the store and there was the dog to guard that. Why on earth an old woman should want to sit by the well in this fog was beyond him, but maybe she was going to live here and it made her happy to be thinking about it.

He returned to his dog and adjusted its leash. It was listless and would not respond to his touch, though it was normally pleased to be patted. Night somehow brought them together; they were the only two beings in the world because they had this special role and responsibility. Day would split them up again. By day the animal would be just an ordinary animal, and he merely a man who slept, ate and lay in bed until it was time to start working again. But at night such distinctions were swept away and it was good to know he was not alone. The dog was restless, no longer howling but whimpering. He gave it a slap on the head to try to make it shut up.

Vince was here, so clearly here that she didn't need to talk to him. She couldn't see him but felt his presence and it was as if this was the very opportunity her confused thoughts were waiting for. Slowly the darkness in her mind lifted. She didn't tell Vince how hard it had been waiting for him, and how impossible it was to describe the dreadful emptiness of life without him because Vince knew all that, and he wasn't going to say where he'd been and what he'd been doing. Strange how quickly he had become part of the new estate. There was nothing frightening or disturbing about him; everything was as natural as it had been throughout their lives together; it was just that he had turned into a house, a set of buildings, a light bulb. The strange thing was how easy it was to assemble him from such tiny fragments.

How could a man turn into a building? What material might he be made of? It was a pity he couldn't speak and tell her what she wanted to know. Now she would have to discover it for herself and, if she had time, she might yet do that. He had offered her this happy opportunity of doing something for herself, of working something out. He just set her on the road to it and once she got there his small bright eyes would be laughing and sparkling with joy that she had managed it all by herself.

'How dreadful,' the old woman said to herself as she turned the wheel and watched the water run, white as a long goose neck. 'It's so hard living with me, I am such a burden, I don't know what to do.'

The Iza that lived inside her furrowed her brow. 'I am tired,' she said in a high, sharp voice.

'That's another thing, the way I tire her out,' the old woman explained to Vince, 'though she is such a good girl and she works so hard. And if you knew how much money she gave me, my bedside table is full of hundreds. I am so ashamed to be doing nothing for it.'

Vince had vanished.

He had disappeared as abruptly as he had appeared the moment before. It was as if the estate itself had vanished, the buildings dissolved into soft blurs. Now she was angry and it didn't help. She suddenly felt cold, her bare hands were sparkling and had gone numb with the water. The fog looked dense again and angrier. The dog was howling.

Voices were approaching up Rákoczi Street, boys and girls arm in arm. 'Young people,' thought the old woman. 'Young people don't see the fog. They're walking towards the university, laughing, laughing just like Antal did when he was young, like Iza used to. I'm so stupid. Vince is not answering.'

She sat and stared at the ground. The mud round the well looked deeper, so she cleaned her black shoes. Their edges were shining in the dark. She wasn't tired but felt a strange tension as if she could see and hear more clearly. Someone was shouting, a door was being slammed, the low bells of the bar could be heard here too. Something was squelching in the distance, coming closer. The dog was quiet but that scared her more than when it was howling.

'Are you going to sleep here?' asked the nightwatchman, if only to pass the time. If people wanted to sleep by the well that was up to them.

Someone was squelching their way towards them singing a melancholy song. 'A white dove flutters over the village,' he sang. The old woman imagined the dove but the one she saw was silver, not white, and the way it flew was more like an aeroplane than a bird, somehow unnatural, in a straight steady surge. The walls of the village were all alike too: all had tiled roofs, all with verandas as on the news.

'Hey,' she heard the nightwatchman call. 'Not that way! Straight on! Rákoczi Street is that way. Where do you think you are going?'

She had always been scared of drunks. Her feet had gone a little numb now so she had to lean against something for a moment, and when she stood up again the waterwheel made a splashing sound. She gave the nightwatchman a guilty look but he was occupied with the young man who was explaining something to him in the middle of the road, pointing towards one of the buildings. He cut a clumsy, awkward figure in the fog, like a starving bear.

'I should be on my way,' she thought. Nothing worked the way she wanted it to, not nowadays, absolutely nothing. The figure of Vince was retreating into the far distance. The nightwatchman was telling the young man that he wasn't allowed to go near the buildings, and the drunk was bellowing something about having been allotted a flat here and that no one had the right to stop him going to see how the building was getting on. Something creaked, a board somewhere. It startled her and she set off in fright towards the buildings.

'Get moving, young man,' said the nightwatchman. 'Get on or I'll set the dog on you.'

She took great fright at that. What if the dog didn't know it was the drunk it had to follow and bit her instead? The old woman started running towards the identical houses. There used to be an unpaved crossroads here, maybe they had laid a better path and if she crossed here she might arrive at the tracks and back on the main road. She could wait there until it was all quiet again before returning. She tapped at the walls of the new houses, the walls as cool and damp to the touch as Vince's face when he died. Even the light resembled the light on Vince's brow.

'Go to hell!' she heard the nightwatchman bawl. 'I wouldn't show you round at this time of night, not if you were the angel Gabriel.'

'An angel?'

She slowed down. There was a plank laid over the mud and she walked along it, astonished at how clever she was, watching her feet with innocent delight as they avoided any contact with the mud. Wearing her glasses made her feel more confident. The builders must use this plank to push barrows along on the way to the last, unfinished building. She kept on walking to get away from the loud voices, getting an awful scare one moment when she seemed to pass very close to the dog. She saw it and stopped in terror but the dog for some reason fell silent at her appearance and just looked at her with dull eyes, almost frightened. Then it made a noise at her, as if wanting to say something, but it sounded nothing like Captain. She switched her string bag to the other arm.

'Go to hell,' she heard again. 'Where has the old woman gone? You haven't frightened her away, have you?'

'Don't be angry at me,' said the old woman to her inner Iza. 'It's just that I haven't found out anything. Papa exists, but not the way I imagined. Papa has turned into a house, and a road, and concrete, and won't answer.'

She went on trying to think how to do something for her daughter who, now that she was inside her, in the fog, was a child again, a child with curly locks, in an apron, with a runny nose, her mouth open and bitterly complaining. 'You're such a nuisance,' said the child in a thin little voice. 'I don't get a moment's rest because I spend all my time worrying about what to do with you. I have a job to do, you know!' It was so odd the way this image and this voice failed to match, the laced-up boots, the lisping voice of Iza and words like 'nuisance' and 'job'. 'I have no life of my own. You are so clumsy. Clumsy. You have ruined my life.'

'My darling,' thought the old woman. 'Poor Izzy.'

The nightwatchman and the drunk were still talking to each other when she arrived at the fourth building and saw, to her disappointment, that there was no way out on that side. They had put up a wire fence. She had to retrace her steps, back past the dog. She was scared.

The plank divided into two in a V shape. The end that lay on the flat soil led back over the mud – the part she had walked on before – the other was at a slope into the unfinished building that still lacked stairs. There was scaffolding there now, forming a kind of ladder. If she were younger she could run up that ladder. She used to love running along planks with her arms stretched out.

Vince was back again, angry with her about something and she couldn't understand why. There were so many things she couldn't understand. It hurt her that he should be angry and her eyes filled with tears. How could she possibly know what to do if he didn't tell her? It was obvious that she couldn't do it alone! Vince should remember that she wasn't very clever.

The nightwatchman's voice was very loud and angry now. He was almost shouting.

'Go break your neck at home if you want, but not here where I am responsible for everything. Get lost or I'll ring the police! Filthy drunken pig!'

The words were swallowed by the fog and swirled about in the half-light. Vince was suddenly gentler and the Iza inside her also grew nicer, her round eyes bright and full of longing as they were when she was small, asking for something, for quince, or honey with nuts.

'You have a guardian angel, Ettie,' Vince once told her, 'an angel who goes around with you. And you know what? You are the only person in the twentieth century who still has a guardian angel.' Now she could see the picture that used to hang over her bed, the face of the little girl gathering strawber-ries, a face whose Old German sweetness vanished, replaced by a wreath of wheat-coloured hair from under which her own wrinkled face looked out, and she saw that, in place of the little basket the running girl had carried, there was now her own black string bag. At that moment she realised what she could do for Iza, the Iza that lived inside her, not the stranger rushing about in taxis or the one who talks in whispers to Teréz and looks up from her books with such a stern gaze. Vince was no longer at her side but this time she didn't call him. This was a moment when she had to be perfectly alone.

'Go,' said the old woman to her guardian angel, the angel in the picture. The angel looked back at her and swept off. The plank was bare, utterly bare, the end that led upwards vanished into the mist. The old woman took off her glasses, folded the pink arms and put them into her handbag, then started up the slope.

For the first time in her life her guardian angel was no longer looking after her.

2

Iza woke at nine the next day, cheerful and satisfied. She had
never liked Sundays when she was a girl and was soon bored
without the weekend bustle of the town. Once she got a job,
though, she learned to appreciate those lazy twenty-four hours
with their unstructured freedom and to take pleasure in a break
that had once been unwelcome. This particular Sunday, when
Teréz wasn't due to come in, when her mother was elsewhere
and Domokos was at some reader-writer conference, felt like
an unexpected gift to her. She lay in bed, not even raising the
blinds, watching the light filter in between the slats, and adjusted
her head on the small pillow. She took a simple pleasure in
being alone, in not having anyone requiring her company,
especially in not having to put up with someone else's melancholy, unwavering attention in the next room radiating towards
her just as she was trying to relax. She was delighted to see
how utterly restful it was without the old woman shifting and
stirring, shyly opening the bathroom door and tiptoeing around
the bath, then the inevitable clatter, because the more care she
took with her movements the more likely she was to knock
something off. It was almost frightening to feel how much
better it was to be alone.

She had put aside this time to think the matter through

without interruptions. The medical report that had been sent directly to her after her mother's check-up was reassuring and she genuinely believed that the cooperative work she was offered would bear fruit eventually. There was also the hope that her mother would return from her visit to the country refreshed by the change of scene and more cheerful. Domokos's absence did not concern her. She was used by now to his irregular hours and to the fact that he didn't always need to be with her as Antal once did.

She planned not to dress, just to laze about till the afternoon, flip through journals and magazines, listen to some music, then, after dinner, go for a walk somewhere, in Óbuda perhaps, the most ancient district of the city and a subject of endless interest. She took her time enjoying breakfast, feeling light-hearted and self-confident as though she had succeeded in outwitting some hostile power that had never really let her rest. Her mother was living with her and was safe. She didn't need to worry about her any more and, with a bit of luck, everything else would sort itself out, including the kind of life she might live with Domokos.

She was just making tea when the telephone rang to indicate a long-distance call.

At first she thought it must be a mistake. There was no reason to expect such a call, but then she turned the gas down under the water and ran into the hall. Maybe she had misunderstood something and Domokos was not in Pest but somewhere in the country. He might be ringing her from there. It must be him, who else could it be? It was only twenty-four hours since she had last talked to the old woman, it couldn't be her. Her good spirits vanished. She hated long-distance calls and her heart always beat a little faster when she heard that broken ringing pattern. That was the way she heard about the death of her father. The old woman had rung her often enough wanting advice, about what she should do because the coal was mostly powder, because someone had undone the ties holding the trees, because someone had stolen a saw or an axe, because Vince wasn't well, because there was a new postman and she didn't want to leave the pension money with Kolman.

She wasn't worried so much as annoyed because Domokos should know, even if they hadn't discussed it, not to call her on Sunday, though at the same time one might feel stupidly pleased since one was, you know, important enough to the man to make him ring after all.

When the operator said it was her hometown on the phone she felt cheated. There she goes, ringing from home again, the same obstinate old woman with no respect for her privacy or her Sunday rest. Angry tears gathered in her eyes as she tried to work out what her mother had forgotten, what she had immediately to send, what had been left out of those two heavy bits of luggage? Her umbrella?

She could hardly hear Antal's voice. They both had to shout in order to understand each other.

They had to try the call again.

The reception was good this time, relatively clear. It was as if Antal were in the next room. Antal spoke just two sentences in a choked voice then, before she could enquire further, he put the phone down. The operator was surprised at the brevity of the call and asked if they had finished the conversation. Iza put the phone down without replying and it continued to ring on and off, as if the operator couldn't believe that someone would make a long-distance call for just two sentences.

Her legs gave way and she slumped down on the chair beside the phone in the hall. She couldn't believe what she had heard, it was impossible to take it in without any explanation. She thought Antal might have been weeping as he spoke and that he had put the phone down because he hadn't the strength to hold it. As if by instinct after several years of medical practice, she bent her head back and gently massaged her neck with cold, almost straight fingers. She had never in her life been so close to fainting. She breathed deeply and eventually stood up. She couldn't begin to analyse what she felt, she was struggling just to stop being sick. Her tears began to flow and she was astonished, not so much to find herself weeping, but at how she wept, with what screams and howls. She stumbled over to the medicine cabinet. Iza was prepared for all kinds of practical illness at home and between the kalmopyrin and the diacilin lay a sealed packet of tranquillisers that she had some difficulty opening. She took one pill, then returned to her room and lay down again.

She was already aware that she was feeling shock and despair as well as sadness. Her screams had been not quite human. She was like a wild animal that had climbed a tree in a forest thinking it had escaped the hunters, then suddenly heard them closing in again and had to run for its life once more. But where to run – Iza shuddered – where can you go where the hunter can't find you? She covered her tear-swollen face with her hands. Some time back in her youth she had been immensely proud and would never admit that she was depressed or suffering in any way. Being entirely by herself in the empty flat, there were no such constraints; every old wound inside her, every scar that she thought had healed over, suddenly opened up; she was back in the house with the dragon-shaped spout waiting for Antal to finish packing; she was hearing Dekker's voice telling her, 'Vince has cancer, Iza. If you love him wish him a quick death.' How alive that medical report felt in her fingers now!

She tried in vain to conjure up her mother's face. It was as if someone had stolen it, snatched it from her grasp, leaving only an outline, her bent shoulders and the angle of her neck that had changed so much in the last three months. The old woman was always looking down recently, never looking up at the sky. The sense of being alone crushed her: it was as if a heavy stone had fallen on her. Being alone was no longer a pleasure. Now it was good to know that Domokos was in some specific place, that she might be able to reach him, share her grief and ask him to travel home with her. She washed her face, tidied her hair and got dressed. The pill she took was taking effect. How useful, she thought, hating herself. A person feels she is falling apart, then one pill and it's already better. The panic that had seized her subsided. She rang the director of the clinic – she was perfectly calm by that time – she wrote a note for Teréz and packed her things for the journey. She did what had to be done. The flat seemed very spacious all of a sudden, as if the knowledge that the old woman would never again sit silently in her room and would never again be clumsy with the blinds and pull them right off had somehow increased the size of the rooms. It was very strange realising that she had neither mother nor father now. It felt new and raw, like drawing her fingers along both edges of a knife.

She slipped on her coat. Domokos had told her where he

was going today; it was just that she hadn't been listening because she wasn't interested. She was too happy thinking of the free Sunday before her and didn't want to hear. But if she thought very hard, she would remember what he said and where he was going. She did indeed remember.

She called a taxi and they soon arrived at the conference. There were a lot of people in the factory culture hall, everyone in good humour, all in Sunday best. There were no tickets and no one on the door, it was a free event. Domokos, who was normally quiet, was showing an entirely new side of his personality here, almost too happy and talkative. He was leaning against a table, waving his arms around, telling stories about his childhood, incidents he had never mentioned to Iza. People smiled at him and asked him questions as he went on. The door creaked when Iza entered. Domokos raised his head but did not register her appearance at first, but when he saw who it was his expression changed, he lost his easy unselfconscious flow, and was clearly startled and confused. The audience, who had turned round at the unexpected opening of the door, also grew more solemn and couldn't understand his confusion. After all, it was just a woman coming in, someone who might have been from anywhere, from the Central Library or the Writers Union. She closed the door quietly and sat down in the back row.

Domokos, who had lost his thread between two interconnected sentences, announced that he had answered almost all the questions, took a quick bow, shook hands with the people to the right and left of him on the platform, accepted a small bouquet offered by a frightened little girl and went over to Iza, took her by the arm and looked into her face. Iza's eyes immediately filled with tears. The audience looked at them as if they had been forced to witness some shameful event. Before Iza arrived their mood had been sunny and confident, a mood that defied autumn, but now it was as if everything had clouded over. The barely finished speech was no longer part of a pleasant morning's entertainment. 'That was not very nice,' thought the librarian. 'That sort of thing shouldn't be allowed to happen.' It was disappointing, frightening and incomprehensible. She felt sad and tired.

Domokos's car was parked in front of the factory, on the left of the square – he had bought it only two days before and they hadn't yet had the opportunity to sit in it together. He drew Iza to him and pushed away her hair as he might have a child's. 'What's the matter?' he asked. 'Where would you like me to take you?'

It felt good to be with him, inexpressibly good. Antal seemed far away again. Antal was different, more impulsive and more difficult at the same time.

'Home. Not back to the flat. *Home.*'

She had never referred to her birthplace in those terms but Domokos understood. He sincerely had no idea what could have happened to upset her so much and when he discovered it his hands simply flew off the steering wheel. He listened, let Iza cry, then stopped off at his own place first and left her for five minutes so he could pick up some necessary things, then they drove over to Iza's and rang for the janitor so they might use the lift. 'He understands,' thought Iza. 'He understands how I couldn't bear to go up for my bags alone, that I can't bear to be in the flat now. How strange. How does he know? Because he's a writer? Or because he loves me?'

The lowland journey wasn't particularly autumnal.

Every season was a visual experience for Domokos. Whenever he left the capital the winter seemed to him a drawing in chalk, spring a watercolour, summer an oil painting and autumn an etching or a linocut. But he had never seen an autumn landscape like this before. This was autumn in oils, the land summery, the sky a deep blue with some leaves left on the trees, not yellow but obstinately green, the ploughed earth a cheerful brown, no wind and the sun burning through the windscreen, the field of golden marrows brilliant, ready for roasting.

The writer sat up front, Iza behind, huddled in a corner. Domokos took an occasional look at her in the mirror. He felt he hardly knew her face, let alone her being. Who was this woman? She looked younger today than before, as if she were twenty-four or so, awkward, childlike. 'Who is she?' thought Domokos. 'Who is this Izabella Szőcs? And what happened to the old woman? 'Mama's dead. Come at once.' Then Antal put the phone down. How did she die? In what way? Why? She had had her check-up just three weeks before, Iza had showed him the report: she had an old person's heart, an old person's lungs, her blood pressure was appropriate for her age, but otherwise everything was fine. Had she got overexcited by the headstone and suddenly felt unwell? Had she been hit by some vehicle, the poor thing was after all quite clumsy so it wouldn't be out of the question. He could see half of Iza's face in the mirror, her lips open as she wept. He quickly looked away, he was so sorry for her. 'Will ours be a good marriage?' Domokos wondered. 'Will this woman make me a good wife? One thing is certain, she is dedicated to her work, she'd leave me in peace and she wouldn't nag me about wanting to go to the opera or demand to have friends round when I was working. Is that enough?'

They stopped halfway to have some lunch.

Domokos, who normally had a healthy appetite, ate a couple of cabbage pancakes, then pushed the plate aside while Iza made do with soup but drank thirstily, finishing off an almost full bottle of soda water. The Tisza was green, an oil-green river with thin waves wrinkling its surface between brown reed banks. Domokos had never been here and felt he might have enjoyed it more another time; now he only knew that this sparse landscape was strange and moving.

What could have happened?

Iza had always talked perfectly calmly about Antal. There was never any hint of passion when he came into the conversation. Now she was explaining how Antal had to get involved in everything that happened in the street. It was small-town mentality. Domokos wouldn't understand it. The fact was, whatever had happened, Gica could only rush over to Antal and tell him because only he and Kolman owned a phone.

It was the first time Domokos had heard anything about Iza's background and it was startling, not to say frightening. He had heard Dekker's name before, knew everything about Dekker, but not about Kolman, the newsagent and the cloak-maker . . . 'I don't like meeting Antal,' said Iza, and that struck him, though Domokos was not a jealous man in the normal sense of the word and had no strong feeling of possession either in terms of people or things, thinking that people had the right to be wrong, to have shameful memories, even to cultivate their obsessions. He had never minded Iza mentioning

Antal but didn't like it that she was afraid of meeting him. Why would it be bad to meet him? It's not unpleasant meeting most ordinary people, just boring. What kind of man was Antal and why did he want to be involved in everything? Was it just that he was a small-town person? Antal was the doctor who had tended Iza's father. Antal informed Iza of her mother's death. Antal bought Iza's family house. Is that what being involved meant? He'd have to take a trip to some small provincial town else he'd never be able to imagine how such people lived.

Passing through Dorozs, Iza averted her eyes and was silent. Domokos drove down the main roads and took a long look at the unusually beautiful sanatorium, wondering why no one had told him about it. Dorozs was doubly painful for Iza, because of Antal but also because of her mother. The old woman had stood here, her face younger and smoother, her skin more glowing, her gentle features ever young, her eyes always bright, waving and rushing to her when she came to meet her! No more now – it was the end of that. 'Where do the dead go?' Iza wondered. 'Where has my father gone? Where's my mother?' She felt ashamed asking such naive questions. She knew too well what a frail structure, what cheap deteriorating fabric it was she worked with day after day. Where do the dead go? Precisely nowhere. The hot springs of Dorozs were now in their red stone caves surrounded by a ring of concrete on which visitors could stand and peek in towards the source. Antal had been a child here, his silly little feet sinking into the mud that burned his soles.

Iza's birthplace wasn't like the image Domokos had formed of it from her descriptions. The high street was exactly like any other busy city road with precisely the same shops as you find in Pest. Billboard after billboard announced the national conference of agronomists.

'Which way now?' asked Domokos when they reached Kossuth Square. It felt strange to her saying turn right, turn left, as they swept down the streets of her youth. The town that had changed a great deal since she was a child yet was exactly as she remembered it. Domokos saw how her lips began to tremble as they passed a big school and turned down Budenz Alley where the street they were looking for suddenly appeared. He glanced at the gate of number 20, Iza's old house, but Iza got out at 22 and began tearing at the bell cord. No one answered; the gate was locked. The moments he spent standing beside her, reading the name: *Margit Horn, cloak-maker,* and listening to the ridiculous tinkling that sounded quite profane, far from the mood that seized them both, would be etched on his memory. Years later when he thought back to Iza, it was that face he always saw, that hollow, scared, intently listening face as she reached up for the bell pull, the way children do when reaching for anything just a little too high, and kept tearing at that piece of simple wire, quite without hope, as though she were ringing an alarm.

Gica wasn't home. They had to try Antal's.

The gate was open. 'Now we'll meet,' thought Domokos. 'What will he be like? What effect will he have on me? Will I hate him?'

He took to him immediately. He liked the confidence radiating from the compact body, the thick eyebrows and the wide mouth. It was almost a pretty face but there was something good about it, something clearly, unmistakably decent. It was just that Antal looked more careworn than Iza. There were shadows under his eyes, and he looked exhausted as though he hadn't slept.

'I wasn't expecting two of you,' he said, without any animosity in his voice, nothing as if to say, 'Oh, I see you are together, I know what's going on.' 'The hotel is no good. I've already rung, there is an agronomical conference going on and the ministry has taken all the rooms. On the other hand Dekker has offered a room so one of you can go there, the other can stay with me. Mama . . .'

Iza was looking at him as though she couldn't hear him. Antal broke off.

It was the first time in many years that Domokos listened to anyone without direct literary interest. Normally he studied everything, processed the information and stored it away in his imagination. He made no mental note now, did not try to register it in his memory. He looked at Antal not as a writer might but as another human being.

The word Balzsamárok meant nothing to him, he was astonished that the old woman should have been found there at night after she had fallen from one of the floors of an unfinished building. How concisely he expresses himself, thought Domokos. He is always careful to say she died rather than she had an accident, though that is what must have happened otherwise she wouldn't have been found on a working building site.

'Balzsamárok . . .' Iza repeated. She was looking at her gloves. Her voice and eyes were those of a stranger.

Antal told them how he had brought the old woman over to his house, how they had dined together and how he had then left her alone, and later how they had looked for her at

Gica's, at the teacher's house and at Kolman's, in fact everywhere that she might have gone on such a foggy night. Their first thought after her unexpected disappearance was that her memories might have been too much for her and that she simply had to go out. Iza's back felt stiff and she leaned into her chair. Antal, they learned, had rung the police and it was the police who informed them at about eleven that she had been found and that the ambulance had taken her to the clinic. 'What is this talk of "we",' Iza wondered. 'Who was he with?' The nightwatchman at the building site said nothing would have happened had not the old lady been frightened away by a drunk. She was just sitting there thinking, turning the wheel on the well. It was foggy yesterday, unusually foggy, and he couldn't see where the poor thing was running.

Domokos felt pity for the old woman but was noting the details: the fog, some well or other, the lovely name of the place, a drunk waving his arm . . . such memorable images! Iza didn't look up; Antal was breathing quite heavily.

'We all have to go to the police station tomorrow,' said Antal. 'It's unavoidable, I'm afraid. You'll sleep here, won't you?'

The question was addressed to Domokos who thought it perfectly logical that he should stay here and felt happy to be doing that. But Iza wouldn't have it. Domokos must go to the clinic to Dekker's. *She* wanted to sleep here. She was almost hysterical in her insistence, her voice rising, imperative. Antal looked at her, then closed his eyes, his lashes long, like a child's, dense, dark curves. 'She doesn't want us to be here together,' thought Domokos. 'She doesn't want me to talk to Antal. But why?' He tried to decide what it would mean to him if Iza slept in the same house as her ex-husband and was surprised to find that it didn't mean anything. Really nothing, it was just that he felt like spending some time with Antal himself. He had long wanted to get to know a real doctor, a true hippocratic who took his oath literally.

Antal was clearly not keen on the idea but made no objection. He said he'd escort Domokos over to Dekker's and told him he could get some food there. He could take the meal up to his room if he wanted. Iza would presumably eat here. She shouldn't let in anyone while he was away, not if she wanted some peace. Gica had a key and might want to call. Don't let her. Bolt the door.

Antal was there when Domokos kissed Iza goodbye. Iza noticed how little it annoyed Antal, what little effect it had on him. She heard them closing the hall door and heard Captain barking, a sound that suddenly cut her to the quick. Then she heard the two men's voices in the garden, their immediate camaraderie breaking into conversation. 'Domokos never speaks to me like that,' thought Iza.

She felt sorry now that it wasn't she who would be spending the night at the clinic, though the thought of being under one roof with whatever remained of the old woman was no more tolerable than the thought of Antal and Domokos growing friendly, sitting up and talking through till dawn. Once she calmed down she simply shrugged and hated herself for her cowardice, for not daring to go out to Dekker's, for not daring to leave the two men alone. After all, what could Antal tell Domokos that she herself would not? She had never told him anything but the truth: Domokos knew that it was Antal who left her and not the other way round. Though if they had stayed here and if it were she on her way to the clinic now she would have the bitter smell of the wood for company.

Now everything was coming alive around her. Objects started speaking. It was the kind of dusk Vince used to call golden, the descent of the internally lit warmth when the heating in the house is on and when you know it will be biting cold by the evening. The objects, Antal's new things and her parents' old ones, were so alive around her she could almost hear them breathing. The small black sideboard had turned back into a bar cabinet; when she opened it she found her father's funny thick drinking glass. 'Balzsamárok,' thought Iza in her exhaustion. 'Oh, the poor thing!'

She couldn't bear to sit down. She went into the next room where Antal slept and looked at his books. He had as many now as he did when they were married. She clearly couldn't spend the night here, but there was the third room where they once lived together. If Antal hadn't brought the old woman over, if he hadn't worried that she'd be cold at Gica's . . . But Antal was always too sensitive. The old woman should have stayed in the cold house; at least she'd be alive.

She crossed the hall. Vince's cherrywood stick and tobacco filter hung next to the small hooks where mama's amusing cross-stitched, nylon-backed, polka-dot brush holders were ranked with their sacred texts. She opened the door to what had been her parents' room and searched for the light switch.

She hadn't yet turned it on but was already aware of her mother's scent. Everything in the wardrobe smelled of lavender, the whole room swimming in that clean, heavy smell. The bed was untouched, the suitcase – closed but unlocked so as not to crease the clothes and let them air – stood there like an animal watching, waiting to be called. The string bag had gone, only its contents remained here and there, a folded kitchen towel, the tin of pastries, empty. She hadn't even noticed that the glass with the remnant tea was missing in Budapest. She had no idea it was here. 'She cheated me,' thought Iza as her tears started again. 'She had made tea. They sell sparkling water on the train but she wouldn't believe it.'

She opened the case, then immediately closed it again: there were personal items there she couldn't bear to look at. It was not only that the room was almost as it used to be when her father and mother lived there, it was as though everything that had vanished was in good repair, including her childhood. It was as if the old woman had only popped out for a moment. When someone pushes a case under a bed there is nothing to show the stay is merely temporary. She returned to Antal's room, couldn't even bear to think of eating and lay down. By the time Antal had returned and put on the light he found her there crouched on the bed, open-eyed, smoking a cigarette and staring at him.

'I can't sleep in there,' said Iza.

'Fine, then stay here, I'll move.'

For a moment, for one crazy unforgivable moment as he leaned over to pick up two half-read books, she thought he'd stay with her. They had never had twin beds, nor a double bed wider than this. Domokos and the old woman were both a long way away. If Antal were to draw her to him one more time, if he were to embrace her, if she felt him next to her again, the terrible tension, that inconsolable sadness, would pass.

He did not stay with her, just leaned over, put his hand on her brow and quickly took her pulse. She snatched her hand away in anger and disappointment. He was touching her like a doctor, the way he used to touch her mother.

'Do you want a sleeping pill?'

'No,' she said crisply.

'Goodnight.'

The door no longer creaked as it had done in her father's time; it opened quietly, but she was immediately and simultaneously aware of both past and present, of the smooth movement of the door and the creak that was no longer there. She shivered under the eiderdown. Two humiliating negatives. It was a mild night, unexpectedly much milder than most autumn nights. She seemed to hear great wings beating softly over the garden.

3

She fell asleep about dawn. A host of memories and images kept hovering and flittering around her.

Vince's proximity was what least scared her because her father's death was *logical* and he died in a manner appropriate to his circumstances, not in Balzsamárok while a drunk and a nightwatchman were having an argument. She thought a lot about Domokos too, about how far he was from her, about where he was sleeping, about the far end of the path through the woods, about the clinic and the narrow divan where the professor would sometimes doze off after he had spent the night tending a particularly sick patient. It was as if she had become one with her mother during the night, as if mama had entered her, and that, from a place inside her, from somewhere between her tendons and sinews, she was speaking in broken words, in sentences that sounded in her ear. Only one person was distant from her and that was the person sleeping in the next room, Antal. He was further off than the vaults of heaven.

She woke in the morning tired and this time she wasn't able to avoid Gica. Gica burst into tears when she saw her, her face and clothes smudged with tears. For once Iza was glad of her awkward presence because the cloak-maker kept telling her how happy darling Etel had been, poor soul, and what a dreadful tragedy the accident was. Under normal circumstances Iza would not have had much time for Gica, finding her obsessions, like her vow never to buy any item of clothing that wasn't black, or never heating the house before the first fall of snow, however cold the house was, rather infuriating. She was surprised by the warmth of her feelings now. Gica was an old and lonely spinster leading a difficult life but she had at least known the old woman and could understand her.

Antal was making coffee just as he used to — it was always he who made the morning cup of strong black brew when they were married — but he stopped with the flask in his hand as he saw Gica. The cloak-maker was babbling and visibly shaken. She had brought over the remaining pastries and partly consumed red roast chicken defrosted on a plate, and handed these over to them as one might hand over to the family a bequest, something that had accidentally come into one's possession, like the loved one's last message from the world beyond. Here it was: a piece of chicken and some sugared pretzels. Iza couldn't bear even to look at the food and apparently Gica hadn't been able to eat it either, though she usually snapped up anything that came free. Only Antal reached for one of the pastries and bit it in half to go with his coffee. It was something he would never be able to taste again. He ate sadly and respectfully. Domokos arrived at nine, having crossed the woods. He was very happy with the accommodation at the clinic. He had even managed to have a brief conversation with Dekker. Gica's eyes practically devoured him; the sight of Iza's fiancé down from Pest almost alleviated the sense of mourning.

They drove to the police station in Domokos's car, Gica

285

nearly fainting with delight at travelling with them. Iza was anxiously keeping an eye on Kolman's shop as they got in, wondering whether he would rush out and mutter some conventional words of consolation, his eyes full of tears, tugging at his moustache. But this being a Monday, Kolman hadn't appeared yet. He spent only some half an hour about noon serving at his counter. Iza breathed a sigh of relief once they passed Budenz Alley; it was a lucky escape.

The first person she saw at the police station was Lidia.

Lidia was wearing gloves now, though it was her fingers Iza remembered, the way they closed then suddenly straightened when Iza gave her the envelope full of money after Vince's death. 'Is it a photograph?' asked Lidia and Iza felt a kind of cold fury rising in her. Just because, due to some misunderstanding, this girl had been given the painting of the mill, why should she imagine she was owed a photograph too? But if she wanted to call the money a *photograph*, that was up to her. Iza very much looked down on those of her colleagues who hoped to receive a gift from dead people's relatives as a reward for taking charge of some particular patient, but she also knew that this girl had done more than was necessary and had given a lot more than her profession obliged her to. One had to respect this in some way and respect it she did.

Antal was standing beside her and blushed when she handed over the envelope, which made the moment particularly awkward. Lidia didn't slip it into her pocket as she was supposed to do, but opened it, there in front of them, with some strange eager look in her eyes, and Iza couldn't tell her not to do it, not in front of Antal at least. Everyone knew Lidia was not supposed to accept money. Lidia's fingers ran along the edge, revealing the hundred-forint notes. It was shocking because the expression on the nurse's face clearly showed that it really was a photograph she was expecting and desiring, as though she had some personal reason to possess a keepsake of Vince's face, the way he looked when he was still healthy. Iza was amazed to see how white Lidia went on seeing the money, and how Antal turned his back, walked over to the corridor window and looked out. The nurse put the envelope down on the top of the radiator and left without saying anything. The envelope immediately started curling with the heat. They were on the ground floor on corridor B, close to the furnace, where the heating was at its most intense.

Once Lidia's steps had receded down the corridor Antal turned back, picked up the money, opened Iza's handbag and put the envelope back in it. He made no comment. Iza felt as if she had been given a beating and put in the stocks in a public square. What did the nurse want? It was common practice to slip underpaid medical staff some money after a completed course of treatment or a death. She hated feeling obliged. And why did Antal seem to agree with the nurse and remain silent like that, his lips twitching? What did they want from her anyway? Who were they to lecture her on medical ethics? She was being ethical. Iza was genuinely grateful to Lidia, had great respect for her inexhaustible energy and conscientiousness and was aware how much Vince too liked the girl. People knew that. She had been so consumed with shame that she hardly said goodbye to Antal, but ran outside.

*

Oddly enough, Antal was recalling exactly the same moment. Lidia was standing exactly like that now, in this corridor, by a radiator and there was a slip of paper in her hands now too. It was the summons to appear. He had searched for her for ages that day in March but she was no longer on duty and no one in class could tell him where she had run off to. He found her in the pharmacy when he happened to look in for something. She was behind the counter helping a chemist friend out of sheer goodwill. He went over to her and without saying anything put his hand on her shoulder. He could only see the back of her neck as she leaned forward, rinsing glass containers in the sink without a cap.

There must have been a good reason for Vince to have left the painting of the mill to her.

Antal was bothered by the thought that the girl might be feeling that it was a simple financial transaction, that the family was offering her five hundred forints to compensate for her sleepless nights and patient attendance at Vince's bed. Their fate was more or less decided at the point when the girl turned round and looked at him, her eyes filled with tears. Lidia was the first person to whom Antal had tried to explain Iza, the first to whom he could show sympathy and more by addressing her wounded feelings, by breaking the silence. Lidia had to know that he wanted to do something real for her, not in terms of money but by offering her something she could accept with a brief thank you.

They went home together, their first non-professional conversation being long and occasionally halting, and, as they crossed the wood and walked along the main road leading into town, Lidia's tears were still running. The road smelled of earth and roots, the boughs above them nervously shuddering.

There were eight of them here now: Antal, Domokos, Gica, the nurse, a shaggy old man wearing a woollen jacket and a shepherd's cap with a shining raincoat thrown over his shoulders — clearly the nightwatchman — and a leather-coated, freshly shaved, thin young man who stared at Iza, then muttered something, his lips trembling. 'The drunk,' thought Iza. Now she was in full mental control, in startlingly clear control. The sleepy medic in charge of the ambulance the previous night stood next to her.

The officer who received them was sensitive, friendly and clearly full of sympathy. He said something about his own mother, what a blow it was for him to lose her, what it meant to his children, and he took a long time shaking Iza's hand. He frowned but thought it perfectly natural that Iza should not be alone but be accompanied by Domokos. The girl in uniform sitting by the small writing desk stood up. She too shook Iza's hand. Iza's expression froze: it was awful all these strangers being a part of her grief. They should ask her what they had to ask, then let her go; they shouldn't feel sorry for her or look at her with such sad eyes. It was bad enough without that. Lidia didn't shake hands with anyone, she merely nodded at Iza. Domokos was counting flowers on the windowsill and examining the small water sprayer. Who looked after these plants so carefully, the man or the woman?

What on earth was Lidia doing here?

Gica was the only one who could see that the nurse's presence did not feel entirely natural for either Iza or Domokos.

'Antal's little fiancée,' she whispered in Iza's ear. 'She is going to live in that nice new house.'

Lidia did not look as though she had won a prize. There was nothing radiant about her, nor did she stand close to Antal. She stood where she was and kept her eyes down. So, thought Iza, this was the explanation of that odd 'we' yesterday. She had heard of the thick fog that night, a deep yellow fog, and could imagine Antal and Lidia going from door to door, ringing at every house, anywhere that might conceivably have taken the old woman in. When Antal had left the old woman after supper it would have been to fetch Lidia. They would have come home together. Having sorted the facts into a reasonable story, Iza looked at Lidia with different eyes, not as when she had first come in this morning, nor as in the past, when she tried to give her that money.

It was the second time fate had brought her into direct contact with the girl. Fate seemed to have drawn a tight circle round the pair of them and she couldn't step out of it. That in itself was not the problem: her own anger was. It was like being cut to the quick by a thorn. Antal loved the girl, she could see that in his eyes, he showed it in the way his face flushed and how his voice changed when he greeted her. His thickset manly frame relaxed a little, it was as if a light were shining through him. What could Lidia give him that she couldn't? As they sat down, Domokos took her hand. His were warm and reassuring. She collected herself and stiffened her lips, willing them not to tremble.

The hearing did not last long.

For the first time Iza heard about the ambulance and the police medical report, which sadly confirmed the evidence of the two last competent officials to examine her. Internal injuries, fracture of the skull. Death occurred two hours after the ambulance was alerted. The injured party did not speak, apart from a few inarticulate sounds.

The story of the old woman's last day was being assembled.

Gica's testimony, which was characterised by occasional sobbing, was colourful, dramatic and wide-ranging. Those present could clearly visualise Mrs Szőcs arriving with a highly elegant pigskin suitcase and a black string bag, the way she drew close to the fire, carefully trying to fit the unfinished cloak – intended for the preacher at Árcs – around her shoulders. They saw her at the stonemason's being thrilled by the magnificent headstone, a headstone 'she liked so much she went quite pale when she saw it'. They saw her cutting up the chicken, eating a couple of spoonfuls of soup, then, because the events of the morning had been exhausting, squatting in the chair next to the stove, lost in her thoughts, and, lastly, making her way over to her old house when Antal suggested it.

'She just stood up and went,' Gica lamented. 'If she had stayed with me she'd still be alive.'

That was true, of course, and Antal bent his head. Iza simply gawped at him when it came to his turn to speak. That her mother gave in to this man so easily and followed him without a word, volunteering to spend the night in *that* house, was in itself odd even though Iza knew better than anyone how fond the old woman had been of Antal; but that she ate a hearty meal there then washed up, that astounded her. She went to take a bath. By herself? She never dared turn on the boiler in Pest! Everything she heard sounded as incredible as the fact that her mother was no longer alive.

From here on they could only guess at what happened.

Antal said that it never occurred to him that the old woman would go out when he left the house. It was so foggy and so late, and in any case he had locked the gate. But she had a bunch of keys that no one knew about, that had been found on her when the medics undressed her. It was in her coat pocket attached to a piece of blue velvet. 'She had keys?' thought Iza bitterly. 'She never said she had any keys. She tricked me. Why did she keep them? What was she hoping for? Why would anyone hide an old set of keys?'

The police officer wasn't interested in where Antal went in the evening and why he returned with Lidia. Whatever he was thinking was far from the truth, which was that Antal had wanted to introduce his fiancée to the old woman. Antal explained what he had had in mind and what he wanted to offer her. Domokos sat and stared as he heard it. Iza stared too, then immediately lowered her eyes and looked at the pattern on her handbag instead. Gica coughed, half amused, half annoyed by what she heard. What an idiot Antal must be! He had warned her that once he got married he'd no longer need her. That was just talk. What a stupid idea inviting the old woman to look after the house when she lived such a cushy life up in Pest. Oh, yes, she'd come running all right. He wanted everything, this cheapskate: the house, the garden and now Ettie too. Well, let him try to fetch her now.

Iza felt she could stand this no longer.

She put her head in her gloved hands and the tears started. This was the point at which Antal – the man who used to be Antal and from whom she was now divorced, the man who left the house with two suitcases and didn't look back, who went away whistling as if to show that everything would be all right and maybe even for the best, Antal the husband-to-be of Lidia, the owner of their old house – disappeared from her life, disappeared with such finality, so certainly as if he had gone up in smoke or sunk under the ground. Not even memory tied her to this man. Antal's plan offended everyone: her father who used to trundle through the snow with his small change so that Antal might have some money for books at school; her mother whom Antal wanted to turn into some kind of housekeeper in her old age; but most of all herself because he had the nerve to create a new home under the roof where they once lived together and that – as a special treat for his new wife – he would entice her mother, *her* mother, to live with them.

But something else was happening at this terrible naked moment, just as she was sobbing and trembling, and the whole fabric of her body was falling apart. The old woman, despite being cold and dead, had been very much alive and very close. After all, it was less than two days ago that she had boarded the train, dragging her baggage along, waving her hankie from the window. And now, just when life was full of personal memories all busily chattering away like birds, the old woman finally folded her arms and, however restless, incomprehensible and troubled she had been before, was silent and calm, terminally lifeless. At that moment Iza recognised, not only intellectually but instinctively, that her mother no longer existed and, having at last absorbed the knowledge, the loss seemed less painful. Immediately, without realising it, she started forgetting and healing. She snatched her hands away from her face and was able to look up again. The officer couldn't quite understand the situation. What he saw was a rather complicated family scene: an ex-wife and two new couples yet to be established. Iza's expression was a particular puzzle to him because, despite her copious tears and genuine sorrow, what she chiefly radiated was a sense of outrage.

Iza knew the old woman would have left her if Antal called. She had always been very close to Antal and would leave immediately on any excuse, such as that Captain had developed asthma and that he needed proper feeding, or that she had to put her old things – the stuff that Antal kept in the attic – in order. Mama would have come, if only to take possession of some clumsy old cups and to potter around in the old woodshed again. 'She was ungrateful,' thought Iza. 'How ungrateful she was, the poor creature. She'd have swapped me for a cherry-wood walking stick and a tobacco filter. I have always done everything I could for her and strained every nerve to do still more. I shared my life with her, something I could never do fully with a man, but she loved that clutter more than she did me.'

For one last time in Iza's life the old woman forgot her dignified stillness and turned her two enormous questioning blue eyes on her. She stood there for a moment, then vanished in a puff of smoke and became exactly like every other dead person. Iza leaned back, looked for a cigarette and wiped her face. So Antal, Lidia and the old woman were to live in the family house from which only Vince would be missing – and that was just because he'd been carried off by the disease – a house that used to be a personal citadel but which now seemed to be becoming a town. But of course the scheme had collapsed now the old woman was dead and Antal, clever as he was, couldn't now exclude her from everything in which she had a share. 'So you are dead, mother,' thought Iza with the same impersonal pity someone might show twenty years after the death of a loved one while leaning on the railings of the cemetery – 'dead because Balzsamárok, Antal and a few stupid objects proved to be stronger than the love I felt for you. You are dead, poor darling. I tried to do everything I could for you but you didn't know what to do with that love. Well, it's not my fault.'

The ugly yellow chair on which Domokos was sitting gave a creak as he turned towards Antal and Lidia. He could only see Antal in profile. The nurse, whose role in the family was a mystery, sat facing him. 'She is the precise opposite of Iza,' thought Domokos. 'She has an expressive, sensitive, constantly changing face, all feeling and passion. She's not the kind to let a man get on with his work, not if she felt there was something really important to say. Oh, no! She'll gesticulate and shout until he listens.'

Gica was quietly chuckling throughout Antal's testimony, hoping to draw attention back to herself. It was impossible not to notice her, she just had to speak. Iza leaned back, breathing deeply as she listened to Gica's dramatic and sarcastic performance. The cloak-maker was gesticulating and raising her voice, talking about Kolman whom she hated, about the newsagent, about the teacher lady, indeed about anyone in the street and the people at the clinic too who knew Iza, including, if you please, the Kossuth Prize-winning Professor Dekker. Anyone could tell you that Antal's idea was ridiculous. After all, everyone knew what a wonderful life the dear lady – bless her – enjoyed with her daughter who kept her constantly supplied with money, enough for seven such lives as hers, poor thing.

She could never repay Izzy for all she did for her. No parent ever had a child like Izzy. As soon as her father died she took her mother with her to Pest to live in style, in a nice modern flat, and hired a servant for her, and even now when the poor woman — bless her — had just come to visit, she was wearing such a beautiful new coat and a mohair scarf and a new hat. There can't have been a happier mother. No, she didn't say much when she was with her but that was because she was tired and people aren't what they were after seventy after all, but she had nothing to complain about. Her daughter looked after her and was so good to her, was so loving and self-sacrificing. It was Eden on earth in Pest. Why would she leave Iza and return to a living hell?

The drunk was horribly nervous and kept blowing his nose. The nightwatchman coughed. Antal blushed at the ridiculous performance. For the first time since arriving, Lidia looked up at Gica as though she wanted to say something, but then thought better of it. Iza was breathing more evenly now; she felt she was growing to like Gica.

Domokos, whose trade was words, who lived by words, who was a master of precise articulation, began to suspect what had happened to the old woman. It was like standing Gica's fulsome speech on its head and revealing the reality. He gave a great gulp.

The policeman said he was glad at least one issue was clear since today's procedure was to settle any possibility that Mrs Szőcs did not die as the result of an accident but had taken her own life. The drunk and the nightwatchman were watching anxiously as he spoke, the old man's skin stretched tight across his face in suspense and hope. Domokos gazed at them; he had never seen such transparent desire in human faces. 'Please God, let her have committed suicide,' prayed the drunk. 'Let them decide that she killed herself,' prayed the nightwatchman.

Now it was their turn, and as they spoke yesterday's fog lifted and cleared. With Gica's and Antal's help they described the route the old woman would have taken and how she might have arrived in Balzsamárok on foot or by tram. It was almost certainly by tram as she was coming from the Rákoczi Street direction. The nightwatchman mumbled on. Now they could see the well as she tottered along beside it and hear the trickling of water. The drunk kept sniffling and feeling ashamed of himself, saying he remembered nothing, not even the old woman, in fact, only the nightwatchman. He had made a kind of confession in the bar about a matter that weighed on his heart, but once he left the bar his head was full of nonsense. He remembered setting off home by way of Balzsamárok and not much else, except that the mud was unusually deep and the fog was brown and sticky. There was something magical, almost hypnotic, about the way the nightwatchman kept mumbling to himself, 'Let it not be an accident. Let it not be an accident!' Balzsamárok wasn't a pretty country walk, he muttered angrily. 'The only people who go that way are those who have some business there and that's always by day, never by night.'

The sentence was left dangling like some weightless object. People looked at each other. It was Iza's turn now. Her voice was low but sharp and Domokos shuddered to hear the secrets of two dead people turning into data, mere items in an official report. The girl at the desk was even noting down the fact that once in this town there lived a young man and a young woman who would kiss among the trees, and that, for the old woman if no one else, Balzsamárok might have been a rational place to take a walk, particularly the night after her husband's headstone had been installed. All the statements had been taken and every small detail had found its place, but the writer felt sick. Here, according to the account, was a happy, well-looked-after, satisfied, sweet old woman in a fur-lined coat, walking along, her sorrow still fresh in her mind, her thoughts – apart from those about the dear departed – chiefly focused on how lucky she was to have such a good child and what a blessed, happy, peaceful old age awaited her. But because she was timid and easily frightened, as most people of her age were, and because she was short-sighted, poor thing, and too vain to put on her glasses even on a foggy evening, she was so confused by the argument between the nightwatchman and the other person that she got lost in the fog and fell to her death, the fall robbing her of a future that promised her such happiness and security.

Domokos wanted to scream.

'Thank you for your recollections,' said the officer. 'She was old, the poor creature. Everything seems much clearer now.'

'They weren't modern people,' said Iza quietly, moved by a genuine regret. 'Neither my father nor my mother, poor thing, was a modern person.'

'That is all, I think,' said the officer. 'Please accept my condolences.'

He shook hands with Iza. The drunk just had to look at his hand to burst into loud, bitter sobs. For the first time he realised that he had inadvertently killed someone. The nightwatchman mumbled as if he were talking to his dog. The doctor vanished,

Gica smoothed down her coat, sniggering and shrugging, then realised she was being looked at, felt ashamed and pulled a more appropriate face. Iza was simply tired and sad. She had tried to build a life and had just seen it fall apart, brick by brick.

Domokos looked on as, crestfallen, faced with the wreck of her good intentions, she turned to him with a half-smile and thanked him for his support at this difficult time. He saw Gica's broad and scrubbed face, behind whose silly words about a new coat, a mohair scarf and a lot of five-hundred-forint notes there glimmered a truth, a truth to which he had been an unconscious witness in Pest, the flickers of which, much against his own will, he was even now reconstructing into a truth as solemn and blinding as the sun. 'So that's decided,' thought Domokos. 'Settled once and for all.'

Antal and Lidia found themselves next to each other, their shoulders almost touching. Antal's pagan-god face looked grief-stricken. Lidia was standing with her back to the windowsill, the flowerpots, the flowering cacti and house plants framing her like some ungainly autumnal bridal costume. You might as well have stuck a feather or a sprig of myrrh in her hair, it was that inappropriate. The only accessories that would have suited her at that moment would have been a set of scales in her fine, strong left hand and a bright sword in the more tremulous right one.

They registered their particulars, the place names, the dates, everything necessary. Domokos could feel Iza tug at his arm when she heard the nurse's details: Lidia Takács, born 5 October 1932 in Karikásgyüd.

4

It was the first time, in all the time she knew her, that Lidia saw Iza for what she was.

When she first saw her she had been only a few months at the clinic. She felt in awe of her each time she appeared down the corridor. At that time, of course, she felt in awe of every doctor because doctors could tell her what needed to be done and how to save people's lives, but Iza was more than that. People still talked of this remarkable woman who had moved to Pest, the older nurses often mentioning her. One day when Iza dropped in looking for Professor Dekker as usual, someone introduced her to Lidia. Lidia, this is Dr Szőcs who used to work here in the rheumatology department. So this was Professor Dekker's favourite, Iza, the ex-wife of Antal Antal.

Every month she came. Lidia was wild about her and imagined her at the spa with thick glass walls behind her next to a hot bubbling spring. How brave she had been in the war, helping to sabotage the clinic. How she worked alongside the men when it was rebuilt. Everyone she worked with was full of praise for her hard work, quick intelligence and decisiveness. Beyond that, they stressed what a really good person she was, and what a good child she was to her mother and father.

Iza was Lidia's role model.

The porter would tremble with joy whenever she arrived from Pest. 'Dr Szőcs is here,' he'd announce as he rang the upper floor and Lidia would hang around the lift so she could be the first to welcome her. Simply being close to her would improve Lidia in some way, even if it was no more than Iza remarking, 'What do you do with your plants to make them grow so beautifully?'

Then she fell in love with Antal and her feelings towards Iza became more complex.

Everyone at the clinic knew who had divorced whom: those who worked there knew a great deal, not only about colleagues but about patients and even members of their families, nor had Iza made any secret of what had happened. It clearly hadn't occurred to her that the truth could be unflattering to herself. Her friends who, at one or other moment of confidence on the night shift, had asked her about it always received the same answer: 'It's the way Antal wanted it.' Dekker swore, people wagged their heads and for a while Antal was subject to a certain level of hostility, his colleagues giving him a frosty reception. Somebody put it like this, that if Szőcs wasn't good enough for Antal how, for heaven's sake, were simple mortals to relate to him?

When Iza went away to Pest, somehow everything had returned to normal. Antal hadn't remarried and people at the clinic understood that increasingly he preferred to be alone, that he was becoming some kind of lone wolf figure. 'The problem,' his friends said with some sympathy now and the older ones nodded, 'is that an awful lot can happen in a marriage that makes living together difficult. No one knows what Szőcs is like as a woman, none of us has any experience of her in a relationship and she's been with Antal since her fresher year. God knows really – it doesn't matter.'

They forgave Antal, even Dekker did.

Lidia was in despair because she had fallen in love with the kind of man that could have married Iza.

Iza talked to everyone sincerely and without reserve, while Lidia could only talk to the patients, best of all to seriously ill patients; her own reserve tended to break down with those who most required her, she was not really a chatty person otherwise. Nothing exciting had happened in her life, her diploma results were good but not outstanding, she was just a child during the war so couldn't run around bearing arms or delivering illegal leaflets the way Iza did. One summer she had some voluntary work helping to regulate the river but every young person in the village helped in that, as did others from round about Dorozs. Out of uniform she disliked her blonde hair and grey eyes: Iza was dark, with blue eyes.

She knew that, if she very much wanted to, she could become part of the group that occasionally went around with Antal but somehow she didn't want to do that. Antal's relationships with women tended to be brief even by the standards of the clinic and they always aroused the unpleasant suspicion that their nature was essentially biological. Lidia wanted more than that: she was interested in Antal's cares and problems; she'd have like to see him bad-tempered and depressed, then to cheer and comfort him, to feed him when he was hungry and help him in his work if she could. She would have liked to talk to Antal, to get closer to him in more than the physical sense, to talk to him about flowers, about the way some patient suddenly got better, even about what clothes she should wear and what she should read apart from textbooks. Lidia was vulnerably and innocently in love with Antal, and once she became aware of that she looked at Dr Szőcs with different eyes.

She gazed at Iza with longing now and adored her even more. Iza's all round personal excellence was now rendered even more excellent by the secret power that had bound Antal to her and possessed him body and soul. Under normal circumstances the thought of inheriting another woman's husband would not have bothered her so much, but it would be impossible even to think that she should follow Iza in Antal's bed. Once someone had lived with Iza they could never forget her, thought Lidia, and even if they pretended to, she, Lidia, would always be compared to the other woman. Who could possibly compete with the memory of Iza? And if Antal could be dissatisfied with Iza, why should he even notice her?

She tried to rid herself of this plainly hopeless infatuation the way one might cure some childhood ailment, the kind treated through minimal medical intervention and a little physiotherapy. Her long hard hours of duty didn't rule out opportunities for meeting other young people. There was a lively group of young people working at the clinic. Lidia laughed and danced with young men, went to movies with them, ran along the beach in the summer and went tobogganing with them on the pine hills in the winter. She pelted them with snowballs and kissed a few by the bust of the local poet the way all young people did. But then Csere from the finance office made overtures to her, at which point she stopped for a while, frightened to do anything. She feared she had led on Csere without meaning to.

It was not easy weaning herself off Antal because she saw him regularly and talked to him all the time, but that was only about impersonal things, about things that mattered deeply to patients but not to the two of them. Lidia would see him in the buffet or in front of the clinic with whatever woman he had in tow at the time, and that upset her and she felt faintly angry, thinking, 'What does he see in her? In what way is she different from me?' The only time she was truly jealous – and even then the jealousy was mixed with pride and love – was when Iza appeared in the corridor and knocked at the door of some room looking for Antal while he was down in the cafeteria leaning a little too close to some woman or running hand in hand with another through the boxwood meadow. When he did meet Iza he would discuss matters as he would with a man and the professor was always there with them.

Lidia almost wept for shame when she realised for the first time that she was jealous of someone who had not lived with her husband for years. It was a comic but heartbreakingly childish state of mind. She suffered every time she saw Iza with Antal, but was at the same time happy because she could at least be in the same building as Dr Szőcs. Lidia's years of faithful infatuation took on an extra dimension because of this strange new feeling.

There was a time when she completely forgot she loved her but saw that her attraction – because of Antal – was not unambiguous. It was when Iza brought her father to the clinic and Antal asked her and Eszter Gál to look after him. Lidia watched Dr Szőcs teasing the patient, saw how she helped feed him, what patience she showed and how she'd cover the bed with silly gifts, hoping to amuse him, but she also saw how, sometimes after a visit, she'd step out into the corridor and rest her head against the window and look down over the wood as if the trees could respond, as if the wood could tell her why those we love have to die. But whenever the old woman appeared, tapping awkwardly across the stone floor, Iza's handkerchief disappeared and she smiled at her mother, saying, 'He seems to be a little better today, my dear, so don't go weeping at his bedside.' It was what she always said. Every time.

Tending Vince Szőcs had a calming effect on her. By concentrating on him she could forget Antal. A person can forget everything when her mind is on something else, even such things as never were. Her devotion to Antal was ridiculous, ridiculous and superfluous. Iza was once again what she had been before: an adolescent crush. 'She's such a good person' were the first words she heard about her before she got to know her. And she really was, and it was odd now to think that at one time she regarded Iza as an invincible rival. Lidia felt ashamed of herself.

Then one night she got into conversation with the judge.

She thought he was in pain or needed something, but she saw she was mistaken. Vince gave a smile, tried to stretch a little and in a voice that was fully awake said, 'It has been years since I last dreamt, Lidia, and now, half asleep, I have been dreaming again. Just imagine it, I was at home. At home!'

A nurse must be willing to listen at times like this.

She adjusted Vince's pillow and blanket. She was happy to touch him, pleased to do what was necessary. The judge was a clean, quiet, refined little old man, gentle in manner and courageous. 'You'll be out dancing soon,' Dekker used to say when he looked in. 'My father-in-law is already much better,' grunted Antal, who was a hopeless liar. When the old man was expecting his wife he'd ask for a double dose of painkillers so she shouldn't worry about him. When she asked how he was he might perhaps complain that he didn't feel quite *fresh* enough. 'Give me some painkiller, Lidia,' he would say. His small eyes were intelligent and wise. Lidia would turn away at such moments and fuss about on the table so he shouldn't see her face. It's not easy when a patient suspects that he is not likely to live long.

Lidia loved Vince, not because of Antal or Iza, but entirely for himself, for undertaking his heroic role in the usual comedy enacted around those who are incurable. He understood that Iza thought he knew nothing and was wanting to amuse him, so he played cards with her while his strength lasted. He knew what the old woman was hoping to see, so he kept smiling and waving at her with his thin hands that were worn to a shadow. When left alone his body stiffened and he tried to look stronger than his medication allowed. He asked for a radio and for newspapers as long as he could hold them. He joked with visitors. He slept better when Lidia was on the night shift near him and he would pay her compliments when he woke: your complexion is like wild roses, he would say.

He would usually have to be half asleep before he spoke directly of his feelings, only once the painkillers they stuffed him with started working and his snow-white fingers could move across the blanket. He whispered, but not in a flat voice, rather dreamily: like someone preparing to go to sleep, his words articulated into syllables, like a child with a secret who finally gets around to talking about it.

Lidia listened to him.

Sometimes he spoke about Iza as a child, about her lisping, her pinafore, her pigtails and bunches, about the old woman's younger body, about her first evening dress which was pale blue, and the crown of forget-me-nots she wore in her blonde hair when it was pinned up. There were times she found him crying, wanting to talk about his feelings of shame on being drummed out of his post like some common criminal. She even heard him whispering about how the old woman once cursed him because he lost his job. However often she asked him to forgive her for it Vince could not forget it to this day.

She discovered a great deal about Antal too.

The cardboard figure of Antal became a firmly rounded man in the old man's conversation. It shook Lidia to discover how good he was to live with. 'Why did he leave her?' he fretted. 'Such a decent boy and she loved him so. Why did he leave her, Ettie, have you any idea?'

Lidia had plenty of opportunity to think why Antal might have left Iza. No one at the clinic had a clue. Nurses who had worked with him for years said no one had ever caught Antal being unfaithful while he was married and he always got on well with his wife. Everyone knew Iza had only ever been interested in Antal. They knew how they fought together to establish Dorozs, they knew Iza's extraordinary capacity for work and the shy smile she saved for Antal alone.

But now the truth was out. Vince knew no more than anyone what had happened between them.

That night, when the judge started speaking unexpectedly, Lidia leaned close to him. The old woman had stayed longer than usual that day and it was hard for him to sleep after such a visit. The world pressing in from outside and the world within, the world he was well accustomed to, did not quite match: his spirit resented the health surrounding him and undermined the interests of his body.

'Where were you born, Mr Szőcs?' the nurse asked.

The judge smiled and his weak wrist shook a little as if he wanted to make some kind of gesture. For a few days now he had been incapable of completing a movement without help. 'Far away,' he said. 'Out in the country.'

'In a village?' asked Lidia.

'Rural' in rural speech means anything that is neither the capital nor the speaker's home. Kázna, Dorozs, Okolács, Kusu . . .

'Sort of,' said the judge. 'A place called Karikásgyüd.'

Lidia stared at him. She too was born in Karikásgyüd.

The naming of the place established an intimate connection between them, drawing them closer together. 'It's nice there,' said the judge. 'The shore is red before spring and sulphur-yellow after. In my dream I was standing on the dike, not afraid of the river. The water was gurgling under the mill wheel.'

'The old dike is gone,' said Lidia, shaking her head. 'We have a concrete dike now. The river has been regulated.'

This conversation marked the beginning of a strange period when the judge seemed to be getting better. It was a mystery from a medical point of view, an inexplicable three days during which Antal couldn't be certain of his patient's condition. Dekker shrugged and Antal rang Iza in the middle of the night. Lidia was passing his office and heard what he was saying: 'Papa is suddenly well, he feels no pain, I have no idea why.' Lidia hurried on, her feet silent down the corridor.

They carried on talking eagerly to each other.

Lidia had seen the flood memorial in the square at Villánytelep, inscribed: *To those who died in the Gyüd flood*, and had learned in school about the disaster that hit the village in 1887. She knew the row of willows and the old dike that the judge's father was guarding, the one at the bend of the river that she later helped break up one summer when a concrete dike was erected in its place. Everything the judge remembered had vanished: the mill, the old dike and the small thatched houses, all gone. They discussed each street, lane, passage and meadow. Vince told Lidia about the Gyüd that was still a part of his inner life; the nurse told him about Gyüd as it was now with its enormous cooperative farms, its health centre, the machine stores, and the peasants roaring up and down side roads on their motorbikes. There were times they found it hard to understand each other because Lidia called streets and alleys by their new names whereas the judge used the old names. Parts of Gyüd had entirely changed and the nurse would have to draw maps of the village so they eventually realised that either they were talking about the same place with two different names or that these were parts of the village that had not existed at all the last time the judge visited home. Vince tried to prop himself on his elbows and his constantly pale face glowed a little. They talked about the mill where Lidia used to play, which was demolished and replaced by an electric one. Lidia said she was born near the old wooden building and the first thing she would hear on waking was the fresh sound of water as it bubbled through the lock. The judge knew nothing about later developments. The papers had written about the channelling of the river and the building works in the summer of 1953 but it was the only period in Vince's life when he neither listened to the radio nor bothered with the papers: it was the time the divorce was going through.

They talked about each other's private lives too.

The judge had lived a long time and Lidia listened how, as he spoke, the village where she lived just a few years ago came to life again. She met the judge's father, the biological one, and the other, real father: the River Karikás, teeming with fish and crab, that actually supported them financially, who got into a temper one day, rose and killed one-third of the village population. She got to know his terrors, how the child Vince listened through his two blue windows at dawn trying to gauge the mood of the river, imagining how things were at the dike. She heard about Dávid, the teacher at the *gimnázium*, about law school, about Aunt Emma, about Darabont Street and even about Captain.

Lidia's brief life amounted to practically nothing in comparison with the judge's. It was enough for her to act as a kind of living gauge by which to register the changes the judge was so desperately keen to hear about. But her story was only typical to herself; the judge listened to it as he might to a fairy tale. Her father had been a pastor, who didn't survive the war. He disappeared from the sheep meadows of Gyüd the way Máté Szőcs disappeared from the dike. Once she had finished primary school she was put on a train to a boarding school where she matriculated and went on nurse training while her widowed mother supported herself by working in a cooperative retail shop. Lidia didn't get her diploma through a public grant, by receiving a school bursary or because a teacher insisted she should. No one offered her their pittance so that she might buy books; she saved her own money and bought them for herself.

She grew up with as much security as if both parents were alive and maybe more. People took greater care of her because she was half an orphan.

They travelled a long way together those three nights before he died. Lidia had a clearer idea of the village as it used to be than she ever had from her mother's simple memories or her schoolteachers' poor lessons; the judge could follow Lidia down new streets that he could not have remembered or ever have walked, roads down which he would have liked to walk with Iza. 'The mill' – he laughed – 'well of course it wouldn't be there, it's just the way I see it. There's an electric mill instead . . .' He stopped and contemplated what the shore might be like now; he had taken so many photographs of it when he was a lawyer.

If over those three days he responded to everything as if he were healthy, it was because he was, at last, talking about Gyüd.

The old woman's life, he explained, started roughly when they met. As for Iza, she hated sad stories as a child. There was one particular ballad, a beautiful ballad from his student days, that he could never sing to her because she would burst into tears and plead for the dead character to be brought to life again. She never heard the end of the song. Mrs Szőcs wasn't interested in seeing the village and Iza loathed both Gyüd and the Karikás because it brought her father so much suffering. The fact was she couldn't bear him to talk about the past at all, and each time he did she would turn her serious eyes on him over the steaming plates at supper and insist that the future should turn out differently. He had to promise her. 'I can't tell you how good Iza was to me,' said the sick man and his surprisingly healthy face lit up with the joy of the memory. 'Nobody has ever been nicer to me.'

As he spoke Lidia could see the schoolgirl Iza discussing the future with her father. She saw her as her father described her, as a pint-sized redeemer spreading out her school atlas and examining the map of Budapest because she wanted to see a major city, a really big city, and trying to work out where in City Park the statue of the historian Anonymous might stand. Iza loved the look of that hooded faceless figure. She saw it once when she was a young woman visiting Budapest with their petition for the sanatorium, then again as an adult when she was no longer alone but had Antal and other young people at her side. The idea of 'the village' became more attractive to her, not Gyüd of course, but the general idea of villages as a problem or concept: how to solve the issue of rural health care. Listening to her father Lidia saw how carefully Iza examined a newspaper, pointed out a line, faultlessly pronouncing some politician's name, leaning her pretty head against the judge's shoulder. 'She became more sophisticated than anyone I have ever known,' he boasted. 'So clever! Isn't that so, Lidia? How clever! It's just that she never explains things, but when would she have the time to do so? It is like not knowing how the sputnik works. I read about it in the general science magazine but I still don't know. What is that miraculous field at Gyüd called?'

'The electric field,' answered Lidia. 'There's a memorial statue on it, a lawn, some benches and a children's playground.'

'Good heavens,' she thought as he was speaking. 'That girl has done everything for him. She could have done no more than if the situation were reversed, if he were the daughter and she the father. She has kept him alive beyond his eightieth year and though she knows his constitution is weak, the poor little man, as soon as she leaves his room she is close to tears. She barely has the strength to stumble over to the window. She loves him. She has spent her life surrounding him like a living defensive wall. But why did she never go to Gyüd with him? Is it possible that she didn't let him *relate* to things, that she never explained anything.'

The judge's face was as ruddy as if he had been healthy.

'Listen, Mr Szőcs,' said Lidia, unaware that she was shouting. 'There's a memorial statue in the square to the victims of the flood, it's of a young man. He is shading his brow and is looking towards the river as if watching to see which way the foam is running.'

The door of the room, the walls and even the house plants were expanding. The plants were whispering like willows and the hot tap that they had tried vainly to repair that morning started running again, reminding them of water, of rivers and the unusually low March stars that swung above the waters of the Karikás.

For three days the lowland village held the forces of decay at bay.

Propped on pillows, half dead already, the judge took his last imagined walk through the village where he was born. His legs felt sturdy. At one point he started singing. Antal came in astonished, the old man's voice drifting into the corridor like the humming of an innocent, half-conscious, happy child. The judge was sitting up and Lidia was leaning forward listening to the strange song. Antal knew what he was singing, because he too had sung it on the headmaster's name day, strange as it was that Cato should have chosen it instead of a happier song. He had never known that his father-in-law remembered it.

Vince would often sing at home but Antal had never heard him sing this before; it was an old tune with words by József Bajza:

> Up in the castle chamber
> torches blaze and glow
> laments resound and echo
> through the house below.
>
> In the middle of the chamber
> raised high up on her bier
> a lovely virgin bride
> lies dead and cannot hear.
>
> Her cheeks and breasts are pale
> like hills in a white shroud
> her beautiful eyes closed
> like stars behind a cloud.

Lidia was singing along with the sick man, evidently having learned the song, and didn't notice him as he opened the door. The nurse's voice was quiet but clear.

> Ah would it were that I
> lay on that bier instead,
> not you, my lovely flower,
> bright virgin of my bed.

The girl glanced up at Antal — was there ever such a meaningful look? Then she quickly turned her back and shook her head as if to say she had no need for help, the patient was quiet and, however strange it might sound, he actually felt well. Deep inside him Antal heard that strange, unexpectedly happy and innocent voice, half sighing, half out of breath, aware that it was impossible to get to the source of that gentle crooning.

Her cheeks and breasts are pale
like hills in a white shroud . . .

For the first time Lidia knew that if Antal ever asked her to take the place of Iza she could do so and would not, as she had always thought, continually have to be compared with her. The joy this brought was quickly succeeded by a vague sense of regret as if it had suddenly transpired that Dr Szőcs had been born with one leg but somehow nobody had noticed. The lovely virgin whose sad history Iza never wanted to hear was palely glowing on her bier as far as Lidia was concerned, but had also become an idea, a curious symbol. 'Good Lord,' thought Lidia, 'how exhausted she must be with that constant self-discipline, that need to save not only her family but the whole world. How hard to live with the hardness of heart that dares not indulge itself by grieving over dead virgins! The poor woman believes that old people's pasts are the enemy. She has failed to notice how those pasts are explanations and values, the key to the present.'

While Vince was dying and imagined his daughter was sitting beside him, Lidia talked to him as if she were Iza. But when he died and Iza tried to give her money, she felt Iza had been lying to her in some way, that she had cheated on her feelings and that she hadn't deserved such adulation.

Now that Lidia had taken her place at her father's deathbed, Iza's offer of money was positively insulting to her. Here at the police station, looking at Iza's tired face, she felt, for the first time, indifferent to her. She was over both adulation and loathing: there was no more jealousy or pity. She was so indifferent to her now that she could wish her well without any personal ill feeling; all she hoped was that, just once in her life, she might be obliged to listen to the ballad of the virgin the way that everyone heard it or would hear it in this or that form, that, like the knight, she might tread the hall in torchlight, look into the dead bride's face and gaze at her white breast.

Iza's mother, whom they wanted to adopt because Antal said she had become a shadow of herself, someone frightened of everything and quite without resources in Budapest, had not called on Iza in her last moments. Lidia knelt beside her the way she had knelt by Vince in March. The old woman suffered and was thirsty, and kept saying, 'Water.' What had Iza done to her, Lidia wondered as she gazed impassively at Iza's tortured face. What could Iza have done to make the old woman forget her name down the narrow path that lead to her death?

5

The drunk and the nightwatchman had to stay behind, the rest could go. The nightwatchman was waving his hands about trying to explain something, the drunk paid no attention to him. His eyes were searching for Iza. He made his awkward way over to her and put his hand on her shoulder. Iza started back. It wasn't because there was alcohol on his breath; in fact, he had an unnaturally clean smell as though he had spent the morning scrubbing himself in readiness for the police. His eyes were full of tears as he stroked Iza's back and muttered something. Iza retreated from him in disgust. She hated unwanted physical closeness and loathed it when people offered excuses. Cheap emotions were there to be controlled.

Domokos stood between them and gazed at the drunk's silly frightened face. Here was the unwitting clumsy instrument of death. The nightwatchman was still explaining things to the policeman. Domokos took the drunk's hand and shook it. Iza was astounded when she saw him sympathising with the man, saying comforting words. Why was he spending his time with that good-for-nothing sniveller who stank of shaving lotion? 'There was nothing you could do,' Domokos was saying, 'and it's too late now anyway. Don't blame yourself.' Domokos's words hurt her but she didn't want to show it. Why console a stranger, the very man whose fault it all was?

When the group split up it was like breaking the links of a chain.

Lidia was first to leave, saying a brief goodbye as she got into the car. Antal shook everyone's hand and said he too had to go and that they could meet in the afternoon. Iza could arrange where they were to dine, whether at home or elsewhere. Gica could put on the heating and arrange everything. Gica gave him an evil look as he sat in the car next to Lidia and the vehicle started towards the clinic. 'How easily he has learned to sit in big cars and have things on tap,' Gica raged. 'His father used to run about wearing trousers tucked up to his knees and never shaved.' She remembered him – he had brought hot water to their yard also.

Then she too was sitting in a car next to Domokos and she really enjoyed it. She'd have liked to prepare a first-class dinner to impress 'the visitors from Pest', but both Domokos and Iza turned down her offer, saying she should go to no trouble at all and that she should cook only for Antal as usual. They would eat at the tavern. The last thing they wanted was to waste her time.

Their rejection both delighted and offended Gica. At least they knew not to order her about, not like this tankardman's son. They'd not order dinner from her as though she were a cook in a canteen, but at the same time she was jealous and nervous because she felt left out of something and guessed that she might increasingly be left out of things as characters from her early life gradually disappeared. Vince was gone and Ettie too. Iza would be a very rare visitor now, that is if she visited at all, and the nurse didn't look particularly friendly. As for Antal, she never did like him. She realised that sheer penury would eventually force her to revive her friendship with Kolman, though she had sworn never to deal with him again, not since he had obliged her to put her hand-picked potatoes back into the bag seven years ago. At least Kolman remembered what the town was like in their youth and was chatty with everyone who used his shop. Gica suddenly felt like crying though she couldn't have explained why. She took in Domokos's dog-like eyes and ginger mane and thought, 'He's not an ugly man.' They took her home and she stepped proudly from the car, glancing round to see if anyone was watching.

*

Domokos was lost in his own thoughts.

It was a new experience for him to examine himself rather than others and it felt strange. Ever since childhood Domokos had loved looking at things and he could make his way among people. Being neither vain nor lyrical, he wasn't greatly interested in himself. Before, he would have committed the hall of The Lamb to visual memory, noting those fittings so tasteful yet tasteless at the same time, those glass cabinets with local items such as the clay pipe, the glazed honey cake and the fancy needlework. He would have noted the agronomists with their briefcases and hotel bills, as they slapped down their enormous room keys on the reception counter. He would have mentally photographed the dining room. Not this time. Though the menu offered some dishes he had never heard of, specialities of the town, he didn't linger over it but ordered a simple wiener schnitzel.

'This is a life-changing moment,' thought Domokos. 'I must make a decision the way I did at the outbreak of war. It is exactly as when I am writing. I must not only decide what to write, but know why I am writing it. It's like being at the edge of a cliff. One wrong step and I fall. I must take the right step. I'm pretty sure I want to live. I don't know it for certain but I think so.'

Iza ate slowly, without appetite, then pulled herself together and the colour returned to her cheeks though she still looked tired and sad. From time to time she glanced up from her plate. Their chairs were close together. They were more intimate now, she thought, than at any time in Budapest, however passionate. She resolved to cut all contact with the town and to bring the matter of Antal to a close too.

Domokos didn't know how the morning had affected her but felt there was a space behind that stiff, all-comprehending façade, a void he might fill if he wanted to. Iza looked gentle, quiet and graceful. 'Help me,' said the arc of her neck, said her silence, said all her calm tired movements. 'I trust you. Heal me! I am in great pain! I dearly loved my mama.'

They walked home slowly, Domokos leaving his car in front of The Lamb. He didn't look at the shop displays but took the odd glance at the leaden autumn sky and at the dignified yellow mass of the church. Iza occasionally nodded to someone and Domokos too bent his head as they went by. He was pale, tense and unhappy. They were already at the gate when the writer said he wouldn't go in because he had to lie down quietly by himself for a while. The day had not been easy for him either.

'Stay,' said Iza. 'Why go back to Dekker's just because you're tired? There's room enough here.'

Domokos said he'd sooner rest at the clinic.

Iza looked away quickly. She was rarely wrong in her diagnoses and could read symptoms, even hidden ones, because she was insistent, careful and patient. But she was mistaken this time, though she didn't know it, in thinking about why Domokos didn't want to rest precisely *here* in her old family home. 'Shall I come with you?' she asked uncertainly. She was afraid he'd say yes. She would have hated to have been anywhere near her mother's poor broken body.

Domokos shook his head. Iza had to relax too, he shouldn't deprive her of her rest. He'd ring tomorrow, and they'd arrange a time and place to meet. There were crowds of people at the clinic and she must have had enough talking for tonight; they should both get some sleep. Iza agreed, though she would have preferred not to be left alone and feared letting him go too far out of her sight. She couldn't have said why it frightened her that he wasn't going to stay, it just did.

Domokos knew that she was begging him to stay though she hadn't actually said anything; she simply stood at the gate, her hands clutched together, pleading with her eyes. 'One wrong step and I fall,' thought Domokos. 'I'll fall the way the old woman fell. When I was in my teens I had a statue of justice on the shelf above my bed and twice a day I prayed to it. I pray to it now. God help her, the poor thing!'

He kissed her: a long, thirsty, compassionate kiss. Iza felt how hot his face was and how his kiss was different, sadder, somehow despairing. It was not the way he used to kiss her. His expression was unusual, so flushed, so unhappy. The guardian angel that had flitted from the old woman's side when she chased her away at Balzsamárok appeared for a moment, hovered behind Iza and whispered in her ear that she shouldn't let Domokos go, that she should run after him, weep, plead, clutch at him. But Iza stood silently and watched as the man vanished down Budenz Alley, passing through the narrow, almost touching walls, and she did not hear what the angel said because only the old woman had ever been able to hear it after all.

She locked the gate with her key. If Gica came now she would not let her in. If anyone rang the doorbell she'd look through the front curtains and admit only those she wished to.

It was warm and dark inside. Gica had lit the fire while they were dining and had gone home. It was quiet, the sort of unreal quiet when you can hear the ticking of a clock you never normally notice. It was the old clock, the one that made a lot of noise, the wicked thing. She went into the inner room and closed the door behind her.

She knew this would be the last time she was in this house and that the brief time until the funeral would really be the last ordeal she'd have to undergo. The town would sink and vanish along with other memories, and she knew that there would be no more intercity calls to disturb her peace of mind, and that she was alone, entirely alone, answerable only to herself. When she had received her medical diploma it was an ambivalent feeling: something had vanished for ever and something was just beginning, something more grown up, something more demanding . . . The walls that observed her as a child, that watched her infant legs stumbling along and heard her laugh and cry, were now dutifully and solemnly offering her tired mind shelter for the last time. Iza was exhausted with all the tension and fear, and the previous sleepless night was taking its toll. She fell asleep by the stove in Antal's low, wide-armed chair.

It was how Antal found her, asleep.

He thought she had gone and lit the lamp, but when he saw her he stopped beside her. The room was untidy – as if the constitutionally tidy Iza had escaped from something and had no time to cover her tracks. Her coat, her hat and her handbag were strewn over bits of furniture as if she hadn't the energy to cross the room one last time to get to the wardrobe.

He watched her. The sleeping face was that of the girlhood Iza, pale, overstudious Iza. It was gentle, sad and full of suffering. She had Vince's fine brow, the curve of his eyelashes and the same sharp eyes, but the old woman's snub nose, child-like lips and soft chin – all these features combined in a single face. 'I loved you once,' thought Antal, 'I loved you so much, in a way I never can and do not even want ever to love again. But it was always I who was yours: you were never mine, you were distant from me even when you were in my arms. Sometimes at night I wanted to wake you from your sleep and shout, say the word, the word that would allow you to be yourself, the word that would save you and tell me where to start looking for you so I might find you. I wept when I first realised that you were simply selfish, that you allocated bits of yourself to this or that person so as not to be distracted from your work. You never heard me weep but even if you had done you'd have thought it was a dream. You respected and loved me; men don't cry, you thought. If I did I would no longer be a man.

'I knew I had to leave you before the terrible discipline you imposed on your own life to save you from distractions took me over too; before I grew so much a part of you that I could only see through your eyes and think of Dorozs as a sanatorium made of concrete and glass, rather than as an ancient spring and an intense desire to put right something that time should put right.

'I couldn't live with you.

'When I first saw you, you were like a child conscript before a battle. You were standing next to your father who was the most generous pauper who ever walked the earth. I thought you would be like him and, like the two simple souls either side of you, offer your generosity to anyone who needed it. But I have never met anyone as emotionally tight-fisted as you, so grudging in your generosity, nor anyone more cowardly, not even when you carried grenades in your briefcase and said to the policeman who stopped you, "What's the matter, have you never seen a student before?"'

Captain was panting and gave a great human sigh. He had followed Antal through the partly open door. Antal took a cigarette but tipped over the ashtray while reaching for a match. Iza gave a shudder and opened her eyes, immediately wide awake, immediately conscious of where she was. Captain hid under the table. It was dark outside and she checked her watch. It was gone six.

She sat up, straightened her skirt and stretched out her hand for the cigarette. Antal offered it to her.

'Why did Domokos leave?' asked Antal.

He got no answer.

'I looked for him outside, but saw neither him nor the car.

Dekker told me he had called on him to thank him for the hospitality, then he said goodbye. At half past two he set out for Pest. Will he come back down for the funeral?'

He didn't know what effect his words were having until she turned to him and he could see her tense face and note the sudden dampness at her lips. What he saw was one of the damned to whom one is not supposed to offer shelter or even a drop of water. The clock juddered and gave a mighty slam. *Slam-slam-slam* they both heard as if some fearsome beast were locked into the mechanism. *Slam!*

Iza carried on sitting for a while, gazing at the smoke and taking big deep breaths, like someone who had long been aware of the precarious state of her health. 'She doesn't understand,' thought Antal with infinite pity. 'She really doesn't understand.'

He leaned over to her the way Iza had only yesterday desired and drew her close. It was years since he had touched her, not once since he told her he was leaving. Iza tore herself away, stood up, looked into his face as if about to tell him something but changed her mind and hastily started grabbing her belongings. She ran into the bathroom where the carefully folded yellow bath towel still hung. She gathered up the necessary things and threw in her nightdress. Her hat and coat were beside her. She hadn't said a word.

'Thank you for your hospitality,' said Iza. 'Now that the conference is over there should be room at The Lamb.'

She didn't wait for an answer but went straight out. She didn't look back, she didn't glance round. It was dark in the house but she didn't knock anything over, she just left as if something were leading her. It was how they had left eight years ago, Iza leading even then with Antal following, both with suitcases in their hands. Antal knew then it would be for the last time. There wouldn't be a third time.

Captain set off after her but Iza swept past him not even touching him. The evening above the garden was starless, without a moon, somehow locked down. The light in the arch over the gate was still on. Iza stopped and turned round.

'Hold on a minute, I'll get my coat and see you up there,' said Antal.

'No.'

They didn't shake hands. The gate did not creak, nor did the inside door that turned smoothly on its hinges, softly swinging back into position. Antal waited until the familiar steps faded away, then bolted the door.

She could only see the upper half of Kolman – it was as if he'd been cut in two. He was pouring milk into a blue plastic can, his loaves like a set of smiling faces behind him. The shop window displayed tins, glazed jars filled with strawflower on top of them, and, under the tins, a small open sack and a pile of walnuts. She crossed over and waited heartbroken for the grocery door to open. Kolman must sense that she was there. She longed for the touch of Kolman's old onion-smelling hands and for his friendly grumbling voice. Surely he would rush out, embrace her, stroke her hair and say, 'Izzy! You're the best little girl in the whole world.' The top half of Kolman's body was bending down behind the counter. He was talking to some unknown women. His moustache was glossy. Now he was slicing bread and playing with the scales.

She walked on past the shop.

The news-stand on the corner was empty. Iza stopped. She

never used to look back having gone this far. It always made her nervous to feel that she was being watched all the way to Budenz Alley. In any case she was worried for the two old people watching her. What if they caught a chill or got too excited watching her go? Not that she could ever dissuade them from standing outside, however it might snow, waving their handkerchiefs, or gazing after her until she disappeared inside a taxi. Vince would stand without a coat or an umbrella, holding the drainpipe under the dragon-shaped spout even when the spout was drenching him with water, peering at her however dark it was, however dense the veil of water, and the old woman would be there too, always without a headscarf, never worrying about the wind or snow, just so she should be able to see the back of her daughter's head or the shape of the glistening car. There was nobody standing there now. Even the street was mysteriously quiet. The light had just gone on in Antal's street-facing windows. Seeing this, she grabbed her suitcase and set off as if the lights were a reminder not to hang about near a stranger's home.

The garden in front of the church had been dug up and she stepped carefully round the ridges. Yesterday she hardly noticed how many more neon signs there were along the high street; neon letters flowed along the rooftops. A neon coffee pot was flashing on and off, neon coffee pouring from its nozzle into a round neon mug. On top of The Lamb, a neon sulphur-yellow lamb looked down on the central square, one front leg raised like a dog's when it is fully focused on something.

The swing doors were heavy, heavier than they had been in the morning. It was warm inside, the dry warmth of central heating. A young man was at the reception desk just putting down the receiver. She set down her case on the ugly mosaic floor and asked for a room.

'Single?' asked the young man.

Of course. She thought of Domokos and ground her teeth. Her ballpoint pen wouldn't work so the receptionist gave her another one to complete the necessary form. She wrote in a slow, large hand. She felt cold.

'Were you born here?' asked the young man with a show of hospitality reserved for visitors from Budapest who had once had something to do with the place. 'The lift isn't working, I'm afraid. Room one-one-six.'

The room was on the third floor and the stairs took time, so she was a little puffed out by the time she got there. The hotel was quiet, unusually empty. She didn't meet anyone in the corridor. She had been given a corner room with a balcony. She closed the door and looked around. The room was just what you'd expect: impersonal, a floral still life on the wall, a radio on the bedside table.

She opened the door to the balcony and stepped out. A gust was rustling the boughs. It messed up her hair. It was a northerly wind from the plains. She gazed down over the town, looked at the sky and ran her eyes along the roofs.

'Mama,' said Iza to herself, addressing them for the first time. 'Mama! Papa!'

The wind blew, the badly propped door behind her slammed. The neon coffee poured from the neon coffee pot, scarlet now, like fire.

The dead did not answer.